About the author

Dan Meakin was born in Clacton-on-Sea in the mid '60s where he spent his childhood and young adult life. He worked in the construction industry for over thirty years before deciding to become a full-time author. He read Literature at Essex University as a mature student and currently lives on a narrow boat with his wife enjoying the British canals, not weeding the garden and perhaps the occasional beer.

THANKS, EVE, FOR THE APPLE THING

Dan Meakin

THANKS, EVE, FOR THE APPLE THING

Vanguard Press

VANGUARD PAPERBACK

© Copyright 2017
Dan Meakin

The right of Dan Meakin to be identified as author of
this work has been asserted by him in accordance with the
Copyright, Designs and Patents Act 1988.

All Rights Reserved

No reproduction, copy or transmission of this publication
may be made without written permission.
No paragraph of this publication may be reproduced,
copied or transmitted save with the written permission of the
publisher, or in accordance with the provisions
of the Copyright Act 1956 (as amended).

Any person who commits any unauthorised act in relation to
this publication may be liable to criminal
prosecution and civil claims for damages.

A CIP catalogue record for this title is
available from the British Library.

ISBN 978 1 784652 28 9

*Vanguard Press is an imprint of
Pegasus Elliot MacKenzie Publishers Ltd.*
www.pegasuspublishers.com

First Published in 2017

**Vanguard Press
Sheraton House Castle Park
Cambridge England**

Printed & Bound in Great Britain

To George and Sylvia, my parents, who taught me the truth about life and what it means to love.

Acknowledgements

My thanks go to Crispin Cockman who started and encouraged me on my journey into writing and to Jane Meakin who bought me my first book.
My eternal gratitude goes to my family who have provided me with unfettered love and support in all my endeavours.
To Angelique Teychene for her help with the design of the book's cover.
And to my wife, Claire, my muse, my love and my life.

Chapter 1

Most of the time we live life switching between past memories, present moments and future hopes and we are usually content with that arrangement; it takes something dramatic or extreme to shift the focus of our attention. For me it was something dreadful and horrifying.

Chapter 2

Although I was using the same coffee, filtering through the same machine that stood on the same black stone worktop in the same kitchen, it was just not the same – nothing was any more. Looking out to the garden as the coffee percolated, I could see that the grass desperately needed cutting and the beds weeding. The slatted fence towards the shed required a new head rail and the whole lot could do with a fresh coat of stain. The cherry tree had only a few white blossoms left, the rest were lying around the trunk like a thin cotton sheet. The cloudless sky held the promise of a warm late spring day; my favourite time of year – full of hope and new beginnings. It was mocking me now, crow-like and gothic. I felt something tug my shirt and looked down to see Charlie looking up at me.

"Daddy, what time is Nanna and Gramps coming?" I lifted her little five-year-old body and sat her on the worktop.

"They should be here any time now," I said smiling. She looked so damn perfect in her little blue dress with her long black curly hair framing her delicate face and porcelain skin. She grinned at me, wrinkled up her little button nose and held my attention with her big hazel eyes and lashes like butterfly wings. She was so like her mother it was almost spooky.

"Want some breakfast?" She shook her head.

"I'll have some at Nanna's."

"Coco Pops?"

"And juice."

"Have you got Uncle Toby?"

"He's sitting on the stairs with Jenny holding hands. They are waiting for Nanna and Gramps too. Uncle Toby and Jenny will have toast because they don't like Coco Pops but they can have some of my juice."

"That's very good of you. It's always nice to share, isn't it?" She nodded slowly and began to play with the button of my shirt.

"Will Mummy wake up today?" It was the question I had answered every day for the last six weeks.

"I don't know, Charlie, I hope so." I put my arms around her and fought back the tears as I had done many times and kissed the top of her head.

"Don't forget to give her my present?"

"I won't." The knock at the door made me jump slightly.

"It's Nanna and Gramps!" Charlie wriggled and so I lifted her down and she ran out of the kitchen. I poured myself a coffee. Muffled greetings came from the hall and then Julie entered followed by Tom.

"Hi, Don," she said. She wore a long pink pleated dress with large splashes of pastel blue and yellow flowers. Her brown hair was tied back into a small hair band and I could see a small line of grey showing at the roots. For someone in their early sixties she had hardly a wrinkle and usually her face was flushed with health – today, however, her skin looked dull and although she smiled, there seemed to be a shared darkness hidden just under the surface. "Going to be a hot one today I think."

"I think you're right," I said and kissed her on the cheek. "Tom?" I shook his strong hand. He offered me a broad smile but again I could see a strain underneath – I wondered what I looked like. It had taken Tom a while to accept me. When I had first met Beth I was working as a project manager for a construction company with a background in carpentry. Tom had worked all his life as a joiner/cabinetmaker and so had initially nodded his approval but eventually I gave up my job when my first novel was published. "He should stick to what he knows," he had said to Beth. After my third novel he reluctantly admitted that maybe I could make a career out of writing.

"Just finished that table," said Tom.

"Oh, well done," I said. "Were they happy?"

"I guess so, they couldn't see the repair." Although Tom had retired he still took the odd commission, mainly beer and holiday money.

"That reminds me," I said picking up a business card from the oak table he had built. "You remember I told you about Peter Lines?" He nodded. "That's his card. He wants a display case made for his soldiers."

"Oh, right then, I'll give him a call. Bit odd though that a grown man still plays with toy soldiers don't you think?"

"Each to their own, Tom," said Julie slightly reproachfully. Charlie came into the kitchen carrying a small teddy bear and a doll.

"Can Uncle Toby and Jenny come?" she asked looking up at Julie.

"Of course they can," said Julie giving her a big hug.

"We're going to the zoo today and it's a long drive so we'd better get going." Charlie looked at me with her eyes wide.

"It's a very big place, Charlie," I said. "You know that programme you like with the animals?" A slight frown appeared. "You remember the one that has that huge house owned by that man with the big beard?" The frown continued. "We saw it the other day. They had that giraffe that had a baby giraffe that wobbled when it tried to stand up?" The penny dropped and her eyes flashed with excitement.

"Are we going there?" she said jumping up and down.

"Yes, we are," said Julie, "and we had better get going."

"Her case is by the hall," I said. "She hasn't had breakfast yet."

"We'll stop on the motorway."

"Come on," said Tom. "Let's put your case in the car." We all moved out to the hall. Tom picked up the little case and walked out onto the drive and flipped the boot. Charlie opened the back door and slid into the child seat with Uncle Toby and Jenny on her lap.

"What time will you be at the hospital?" asked Julie.

"About six," I said.

"Call us?"

"Of course I will." We moved to the car and I buckled Charlie into her chair and gave her a big kiss. "You have a really good day and don't let the lions and tigers eat up Uncle Toby and Jenny."

"They won't eat them, Daddy. They only eat meat and chips and mice and ice cream."

"Well, that's all right then." I closed her door and stood back. Julie opened her door as the engine kicked into life.

"Don," she said, her eyes watery.

"I know," I said and offered her the best smile I could. She nodded and then slipped into her seat and closed the door. I blew Charlie a kiss and waved until the car turned out of sight and went back to the kitchen and my coffee.

I had a meeting with the publisher at ten to sign off the front cover of my fourth novel and then I would take the drive down to the seaside town where I grew up. Writing from home made it easy to look after Charlie. I would take her to school and then write for a few hours and then pick her up again in the afternoon. I needed some time to myself, to get to grips with a decision I might have to make soon: a decision that nobody should have to make. I let Charlie have the day off school; Tom and Julie were going to spoil her rotten and let her stay with them overnight. I guess I had been a bit selfish in not letting them help as much as I should but the thought of her not being at home, a part of Beth not being at home, was hard to deal with – I guess the true value of anything is realised in its absence. I finished my coffee, grabbed the keys from the table and locked the house.

The sea air was warm with only a slight on-shore breeze. I dropped the hood of the Jeep, pushed a Dido CD into the player and headed off along the coast road. Twenty minutes later I entered the village of Tuddle and parked directly outside the office of George Gilbert Publishing. It was a terraced cottage that sat in between a post office and a florist. The ground floor had been converted into a reception area while the top two bedrooms were offices. George Gilbert and his wife Doris mainly published local historical and factual books but a few years ago had elected to take a chance with fiction. Having been rejected by all of the big players, I had decided to try some of the smaller provincial publishers. Doris was the history buff but George was the one who was keen to branch out into fiction. He took a chance with mine and it paid off for the both of us. My first book was well received and since then my readership had been growing steadily. Now I was their biggest client.

"Hello, Sue," I said to the receptionist. The short tiny figure looked up from the laptop and offered a smile which conveyed both sympathy and understanding.

"Hi, Mr England," she said with a slight Norfolk twang. "How are you?" Her face was sweet and bright and her blue eyes showed a sharp intelligence.

"I'm OK, George in?"

"Go straight up." I climbed the narrow stairs to the landing and gave a gentle knock on the door to the right.

"Come?" said the rasping voice of a forty-a-day man. The walls of the room were stacked with manuscripts and framed first-edition covers. The large desk had two piles of manuscripts either side and through them I could see the plump ruddy face of George Gilbert. He stood as I entered and offered his hand.

"Fuck, you look tired," he said.

"I am tired, George," I replied as we shook. I sat in a leather high back chair that Tom had repaired for him last year. "So, found any new authors?"

"Fucking pile of fucking dog's shit!" Doris must be out.

"So, that's a no then?"

"You get all excited, ask for a few more chapters and then realise that they can't write a fucking shopping list." He ruffled a thick but greying mop of brown hair and let out a cross between a yawn and a sigh.

"How's Doris?"

"Yes, she's OK, just gone down to the printers. She said to say hi." He reached down to the left of the desk and handed me an A2 folder. Inside was a copy of the proposed front cover for my new novel. The background looked like parchment and my name, Don England, was written at the top. A third of the way down was the title "Plantagenet" in gold gothic script. My books had centred on a character, an archer, called Toby Kent, set at the end of the War of the Roses. They were loose historical fiction about the life and tribulations of a boy growing up in medieval England.

"I am waiting for some reviews to come back before choosing the quotes. What do you think?"

"I like it, very *Sansom-esque*."

"Good, I'll tell the printers." He grabbed a cigarette from the packet on the desk and pushed the window fully open. Outside on the sill was a large ashtray almost overflowing with butts. He lit the cigarette and took a deep drag and blew the smoke out of the window. The slight breeze blew it back.

"You are breaking the law by doing that, you know that?"

"They can all go and fuck themselves," he said taking another draw. "Listen, Don, you might want to really consider getting an agent."

"No way, George, I've…"

"No, listen to me for a second. Have you heard of Ambritt Productions?"

"No."

"I've just had a call from them. They are a US-British production company, mainly American money with British actors and directors. They are interested in making your books into films?"

"Really?" I was shocked. Although I had always loved the idea that a film would be made from one of my books, I never thought for one moment they would be.

"Yes, really, you could be talking a lot of money here, Don. You need to be represented."

"I told you, George, *you* are my representative."

"Don, I am a publisher, that's what I do. This is going to involve transatlantic   marketing and film and publishing rights. You need someone with more experience."

"No way am I going to get myself another body involved. You took the risk and you have stuck by me. You know enough, George – end of."

He carried on for a while trying to persuade me otherwise but I would not back down. Part of the banter was that he knew he could do both roles but genuinely wanted me to make the right choice. In the end he threw up his hands and surrendered.

"I'll write to them and express an interest and maybe a meeting, how's that?"

"I won't get my hopes up but…" As soon as I had said that I felt my heart thump. How many times had I heard the consultant at the hospital say that? George must have noticed.

"Well, none of these things are rushed," he said waving a hand about. "Has there been any change with Beth?" His voice had softened.

"No, there's nothing new to report." There was news, but I didn't want to get into it. "I'm going up tonight. Got some things to do – Julia and Tom have got Charlie for today and tonight."

"Well, give that stunning kid of yours a big kiss from Uncle George and now you can fuck off cos I've got a whole load of shit to read."

I laughed.

"OK, George, give me a ring when you've heard back from Armpit or whatever they're called." I shook his hand. "…And give Doris a kiss from me?"

"Sod off, you do it."

"See you, George."

Back in the Jeep I realised that the potential of turning my books into films should have had me jumping the walls. It's strange how priorities can change in a blink of an eye, or in this case, a slip on the ice. I drove out of the village and then onto the coast road again. I could have joined the main road but decided to take the coast road because the next village was where I met Beth.

Chapter 3

There were six of us in total who had decided to hire a cottage on the coast for a long weekend. Kath I had known nearly all my life and Bret, Des, Simon and Sue were Kath's London friends but I had known them all for at least ten years through Kath and her extraordinary parties. We were all in our early thirties and all single. We arrived at the four-bed cottage at about midday. The neighbour gave us the key and said she would be round shortly to show us where everything was. It was typical of the area. Rendered walls on the outside were painted a Norfolk pink and the small sash windows were newly glossed white. The white picket fence enclosed a paved area with an assortment of terracotta pots containing flowers and shrubs. The front door opened into a large hall with natural wooden flooring and a set of carpeted stairs led to four bedrooms and one large bathroom. The lounge contained an inglenook fireplace and to the left a modern TV and video recorder. Two three-seater drop-down sofas were arranged around a pine coffee table. A few paintings by local artists depicting various seaside scenes adorned the walls and to the far right a large arch opened into the dining area with a long old pine table that could comfortably seat eight. Through a door to the right of the dining room we found the expansive kitchen. It too contained a large table that was set aside from the old pine kitchen cupboards, five-ring gas cooker and copper hood. Large French doors set in the rear wall looked out into a small but well-maintained garden complete with paved patio area and a portable barbeque. Kath and Sue decided to share the double master bedroom, Simon and Des took the twin bedroom, Bret took the smaller double bed and I had the last single bedroom. The neighbour, a plump and fresh-faced woman called Mrs Hewitt, showed us how to use the shower, where the fuse board was, what to do if we lost the key and a host of other things we had forgotten by the time she had left us. Before hitting the pubs, we stocked up on beer, wine and stuff for a barbeque from a large Tesco just outside the village – the weather was cloudy but the forecast promised a sunny weekend so the barbeque would be on the Saturday. Any other cooking was down to Des – to take that duty away from him would be like trying to remove gravity.

We shared the small cobbled lane with three other cottages that seemed to be in competition for the "chocolate box cover" award, and by the looks of them, it would be a photo finish. The High Street contained the usual array of shops: an assortment of clothes shops, a post office, two banks, a café/tea room, several antique stores, a charity shop, a hotel, two pubs, one Chinese takeaway, an Indian restaurant, an art gallery/book store and those naff gift shops which are essential to the make-up of a small seaside English town. It ended at the sandy beach where several typical shops lined the walkway and one large pub, The Ship. Our first drink, however, was in the Red Lion. The flashing jukebox and gaming machines seemed out of place next to the oak beams and panelling of the 15th-century thatched public house. The guest ales included Nun's Wimple, Dog's Arse and Fanny's Brew but I stuck to my usual Guinness. We moved on to The Chessman's Hotel and Bar, had a couple of pints, and then finally ended up at The Ship. The front of The Ship had a large raised patio area that sported several wooden benches with sun shades set in the middle. Inside, the main bar had a sweeping front with a small seated section off to the side that was separated from the main bar by a small arch. The whole place was decorated with a mass of ships' items: bell ropes, lines, knots, bits of old canvas, barometers, compasses, ships' wheels, rudders and anything else maritime. A blackboard displayed the menu and another stated that a local folk band, "The Balding Barnets", were playing tonight and Saturday night would be host to "The Kebabs". We decided that The Ship would be the place to be in the evenings. Des said he was going to go back to the cottage to cook up a pot of spaghetti bolognaise – we had another couple of drinks and then followed him.

Our stomachs lined properly for an evening of drinking, we made our way back to The Ship. A few people were seated outside even though it was not particularly warm. I could see the "The Balding Barnets" had already set up and were getting ready to play. The band consisted of two acoustic guitar players who were short, chubby and with completely bald heads. Although the bar was reasonably busy we managed to find a table near the band. We had a whip-round and I said I would get the drinks. There were three people serving behind the bar. A tall young man with a quaff of stylish blond hair was serving a group of men in the small alcove while a slim woman in her fifties, who I guessed was the landlady, was serving a young couple to the left of me. A door was open to the rear of the bar which I assumed led down to the cellar and could just make out someone behind it. The door closed and a woman about my age appeared. She was about five foot eight with long shaggy black hair that tumbled around her shoulders. Her skin had an even tan that was augmented by a white lace, buttoned short-sleeved shirt over a tight pair of faded jeans. Her eyes were deep hazel under thick long lashes. Her full, hourglass figure approached me and she offered a warm smile showing small even white teeth.

"Hi, what can I get you?" she asked. Her voice was soft with a very slight Norfolk accent. She was stunning. She had that sort of gypsy-type look to her appearance. I was so taken aback I had forgotten what the order was. I eventually blurted it out and then carried the drinks over to our seats.

"Christ, that's some woman!" I said to the lads. Bret, Des and Simon looked up and eagerly agreed. Bret was one of life's smooth operators when it came to women. He was about five foot ten, trim frame and had a thick head of cropped brown hair. His handsome sharp features were enhanced by blue eyes and a winning smile. He wore designer everything and always had his jumpers draped around his shoulders. He never took off his sunglasses; when the sun was out they were in front of his eyes but at all other times, including at night, they were perched on top of his head – the latter always infuriated Sue. The band burst into life with "Mrs Robinson" but I found my attention kept straying back to the bar.

I was impressed with the band. They were competent musicians and, with the aid of a backing track, had a full sound that filled the large pub without it being too loud. I noticed the drinks were getting low so decided I would head to the bar again.

"Same again?" said the barmaid with the long black hair and deep hazel eyes.

"Yes, please."

"You on holiday?" she asked as she slowly poured my Guinness.

"We've hired a cottage round the corner. We've just come up for a long weekend, going back on Monday." She let the Guinness settle and then started to pour out two lagers.

"Who's the odd one out?" she said nodding over to my friends.

"How do you mean?"

"I can see possibly two couples and an odd one out." I smiled.

"We are all single." I gave her a very brief history of how we knew each other.

"I wasn't trying to be nosy," she said slightly guardedly.

"No, it's fine. We often all go away together and you're not the first to ask. I guess it's odd that none of us has settled down." I paid for the drinks and carried them over to the table and went back for mine.

"Your friend over there with the jumper round his shoulders?" she asked.

"Bret," I said, slightly down-hearted but not surprised by her interest; Bret always attracted the attention of women.

"Why is he wearing sunglasses at night?" I laughed.

"They are screwed into the side of his head. The doctors say if they attempted to remove them, his arse would fall off." She laughed out loud and then put her hand over her mouth as if she was surprised at her sudden outburst. It was a deeply honest laugh and then she gave me a gentle slap on the arm.

"I would like to apologise for Bret in advance."

"Why?" Her eyes seemed to show a kind of anticipation.

"At some point tonight he will chat you up. It won't be obvious. He will say something like…" I leaned closer to her as if I was going to whisper; she leaned slightly towards me in response. "He will say something like… *I bet you get chatted up on a regular basis? No I mean it; it must get really irritating sometimes. After all you're a good-looking woman…*"

"And you think that's not obvious?" she said.

"Well, I don't know. It will be something like that."

"No, I don't think he will."

"I bet you a pint he will."

"He's coming over!" I glanced back and sure enough Bret and Des were making their way to the bar.

"So are you going to introduce us?" said Bret. I realised I did not know her name. She came to the rescue.

"I'm Beth," she said.

"I'm Bret and this is Des." He shook her hand and gave her a slightly longer than comfortable look. "Over there," he said indicating our table, "is Kath, Simon and Sue, and this is Don." I stood aside as a bloke in a checked shirt and white stubble wanted to get to the bar. Beth took his order and walked to the back to open a bottle of wine.

"I'm going to sit down," I said to Bret and went over to join the others.

"Those two are unbelievable!" said Kath. "It was obvious you were getting on with that barmaid but they couldn't stand it."

"I was just chatting to her that's all."

"I know and those two could leave you to it but, no, they have to go over." I felt awkward. I never have been one of those blokes who could chat up women in bars and clubs. Most of the women I had dated I had known for quite a time – but now I felt under pressure to perform and so would have to try to pull the barmaid because someone had observed I had been "getting on" with her. I have never been able to do "cool" like other people can. Every time I think I'm being a bit "cool", it all hits the floor with an almighty crash – no, not for me. Perhaps "un-cool" is the next "cool", and if so, I will be there, front row and centre.

The band finished another song and the customers clapped enthusiastically. One of the players, the singer, changed from an acoustic to an electric guitar and then went straight into a blues riff.

Chapter 4

I parked the car outside The Ship and switched off the engine. A few people sat outside on the benches looking out to sea with their lagers, bitters and glasses of wine. The clock on the dashboard showed it to be half-past eleven; Charlie would not be at the zoo yet, especially if they had stopped for breakfast along the way. My heart ached to be there but I realised it was good for her to spend some time away from me. Although she was too young to fully understand what was happening, she was old enough to pick up on the tense vibes that must have leaked from my pores over the last few weeks. The zoo, with the animals and the rides, would be a good distraction for her and for Beth's parents who were feeling the strain as well. Roger, Beth's older brother, was due to fly in from Australia on Sunday night. He was in his mid-forties and had emigrated three years before I had met Beth. I had only met him the once, at our wedding, and he seemed very much like her Dad: a man with an old-fashioned outlook and one of few words. A man and a woman walked alongside the Jeep swinging a little girl between them as they headed for the beach. The small blonde-haired girl was shrieking with delight with each swing and her laughter seemed to infect her parents. My thoughts drifted back.

Chapter 5

Bret and Des had returned to the table as the pub was filling up and Beth had little time to chat.

"That's one fine woman," said Bret.

"Yes, she seems nice," I said not trying to sound too interested.

"Unfortunately she has a boyfriend."

"Never mind, Don," said Kath patting my leg sarcastically.

"What? All I was doing was talking to her."

"Look at that!" said Sue nodding towards the band. A few people had got up to dance and a couple in their fifties were jiving to a rock 'n' roll number. They were no amateurs and the rest of the dancers had moved away, giving them room. When they had finished we all applauded, cheered and whistled. They took a bow and headed back to their seats with that smile that said "that's what dancing is really all about". Beth suddenly turned up at our table and placed a full pint of Guinness in front of me, picked up the empty glasses and headed back to the bar after offering me a slight wink.

"What was that all about?" asked Bret. I suddenly remembered the bet I had with Beth and smiled.

"Oh, just a little private bet I had with the barmaid," I said giving Bret a wink.

"What was the bet?" Sue asked leaning across the table towards me. I shook my head.

"Come on, what was it?" Kath and Simon joined in the interrogation.

"Mystery is the key to the door of exciting possibilities," I said.

"You are so fucking full of shit, England, it's untrue," said Bret. "I bet you said to her to bring over a pint then wink at you just so you would get a reaction out of us." He was using his "I'm totally offended" pretence.

"Not at all, old boy," I said enjoying the moment. "Let me just say that the bet was one purely based on observation and that, my dear friends, is all I am permitted to say."

"Go on," Sue persisted.

"No."

"You're right," said Sue to Bret. "He is full of shit." I smiled and held my drink up.

"Cheers, everyone."

"Bollocks," said Bret. The band announced that they were going to play one more and then take a short break; I took my pint outside for a bit of fresh air. The clouds were thinning and I could see a few stars peeking through the thin white veil. Sitting on one of the paved steps, I took out a packet of cigarettes and removed a small joint, one of several small-skins made earlier. I had only taken a couple of draws when suddenly someone sat next to me. It was Beth.

"Is that what I think it is?" she said with a smile.

"Yes, I hope it's not obvious – I'll put it out if it's a problem?" She glanced briefly over her shoulder.

"Give us a quick puff." I handed her the joint and she took a couple of drags.

"So I won the bet then?" She nodded, held her breath for a few seconds and then let out the smoke.

"He said I had nice eyes and that I would be a rich woman if I had a pound for everyone who had said that to me." I laughed. "Then he said that he hoped my boyfriend realised how lucky he was."

"And what did you say?"

"I said that my boyfriend told me every day how much he loves me." She handed me back the joint. I took a couple of puffs and handed it back to her but she shook her head. "Best not get too stoned as I'm working."

"Is your boyfriend here tonight?"

"I don't have a boyfriend."

"Oh," I said trying to sound indifferent.

"My stock answer to being chatted up." She pulled her hair away from her face and over her ear which held a small silver pendant.

"So you have not fallen under the Bret charm then?"

"Not my type."

"What is your type?"

"I like short fat bald men with huge wallets."

"I'll let the band know." She laughed in that genuine way she had earlier.

"I had better get back," she said getting to her feet. "Thanks for the smoke."

"Thanks for the pint."

"A bet's a bet."

"Where did you go?" asked Des, when I was back inside.

"I went outside for a smoke."

"What, a joint?"

"Yes."

"Well, thanks for telling me!"

"You've got some haven't you?"

"Yes, but that's not the point."

"If you do light up one of yours, go round the corner. That crap you smoke smells like a plastic bonfire."

"I think I'll do that right now," he said. Simon, Bret and Kath said they would join him.

The band started up again and the rest of the evening we spent dancing, drinking and stepping outside for herb help. Beth was busy serving, collecting glasses and apart from the occasional smile, I saw nothing of her for the rest of the night. On the way back to the cottage Simon snapped the strap on one of his sandals and went into some ridiculous tirade about how the quality of goods in this country had gone to pot – we just let him get it out of his system. Sue flashed her bra at Des who was so stoned all he could say was "nice" and then promptly fell over a low wall into a garden hitting his head against a small wooden dingy. Bret quipped that "loose tits sank ships" and then we all got a fit of the giggles. Back at the cottage, Kath opened a bottle of wine, Des said he was off to bed and Bret and I started a brief conversation about the impracticalities of nihilistic proposed societies and we were eventually told to "shut up you boring wankers". Kath put on some REM, I rolled another joint and before long we were all dancing. Gradually Kath retired and then Bret and Simon. I shared the last of the wine with Sue although we had drunk far too much already. I sat on the edge of the sofa and she lay with her head on my lap looking up at the ceiling. The music had turned to Dave Gilmour. She hitched up her top and looked down at her lace-covered breasts.

"Do you think I need a breast reduction?" she said slurring her words.

I looked down and studied them with blurry eyes.

"No, I think they're fine," I said equalling her dribbled eloquence.

"I think they are too big."

"They would be if each breast required two hands but yours are definitely single-handed." She took my arm that was lying across her stomach and opened my hand and placed it on her right breast.

"They are much bigger than your hands."

"It depends how you measure them. If you take into account my fingers as well then they are definitely single-handed breasts but if you take the palm only then I would agree they are two, maybe, three handed." Even though I was completely out of it I could feel myself getting slightly aroused and wondered where all this was headed. I remembered having a drunken sloppy snog with her at one of Kath's Christmas parties about three years before and we had both laughed about it the next day but nothing had ever happened since. She had short brown hair that sported some streaked highlights and the type of skin that required plenty of protection from the sun.

"Maybe they're not too big after all," she said letting out a sigh.

"It's not the size but the overall appearance," I said trying to stay focused.

"What do you mean?"

"Well, from a bloke's point of view they have to be balanced with the nipples."

"What, big tits big nipples, small tits small nipples?"

"Not exactly, it depends on the bloke. Some men like small pert tits with pilot thumb nipples while other men like…" She fumbled her arm out of her sleeve and slid off her bra strap and pulled down her cup to fully reveal her right breast. Her dark button nipple sat erect like it had just been asked an interesting question.

"OK," she said, "what about my nipples?"

"I think they are in perfect harmony with the breasts." I could now sense myself getting fully aroused. I gently took her nipple between my finger and thumb and gave it a gentle squeeze. "They are not too soft and not too hard." I traced my finger around her dark island and then back to the nipple, cupped the whole breast in my hand again and began to gently stroke her soft skin. "I conclude, taking in all aspects of breast size and nipple orientation, I think you have very nice breasts." Dave Gilmore was reaching a crescendo of haunting guitar as I continued to stroke her breast. The room began to spin slightly as the alcohol and hash was taking its toll. I wondered what my next response should be. Should I make a play to expose the other breast and offer a full comprehensive evaluation using both hands? That strategy would require me to shift my position. Maybe I could put the ball, so to speak, in her court and ask her opinion on penis preferences. Dave Gilmore was now thrashing out the finale to his track. Drums rolled and cymbals crashed, guitar screeched and then, in a final power chord, the song abruptly ended. Sue was snoring.

I folded her breast back into its housing and got up, laying her head gently down onto the cushion. I removed a throw from over the other sofa and covered her, switched off the light and stumbled upstairs to bed.

The smell of bacon and eggs greeted me when I opened my eyes. Des was busy in the kitchen and Kath poured me a black coffee as I entered. Sue looked a little worse for last night but made no indication that anything had happened. I thought I would just let the matter rest. Simon had been out earlier to purchase a pair of flip-flops to replace his broken sandals and was waxing lyrical about how nice the weather was and that we should eat breakfast and get down to the beach.

Chapter 6

I locked the Jeep and walked down to the beach and then sat outside a small café with a coffee looking at the steady flow of sun worshippers picking out their spot. The couple who had passed me earlier, swinging their daughter, had erected a small sun-shade and set out towels and a large hamper. The little girl wore a white floppy hat and a pink swimsuit and was already busy trying to dig up the beach with a small plastic spade. Although it was seven years ago, it only seemed like a week since we were all piled onto the beach nursing a hangover from the night before. Some memories are opaque and lack continuity while others I have are fixed and dilated. An old couple shuffled along the promenade. The man wore a straw trilby and had green-coloured plastic shades fitted to his prescription glasses. His short-sleeved tailored shirt was tucked neatly into his equally tailored shorts but the quintessential English quality was due to his grey socks and brown leather sandals. His wife, adorned in a calf-length floral dress and wide-brimmed hat, walked with difficulty next to him with her hand gently clasping around his pinkish forearm. Hip replacement, or at least due one, I thought. He was just finishing an ice cream. She pulled him up short and took a tissue from a pocket in her dress and carefully wiped away the excess from the side of his mouth. She replaced the tissue and then kissed him with such tenderness and duration that it implied a lifetime of love and equal devotion. I was suddenly stabbed with a sense of jealousy for their history; whatever time they had left with each other sat upon a mountain of shared memories. A shout from the beach made me look as two men charged into the water and were whooping at the sudden ball-clenching temperature of Norfolk's sea.

Chapter 7

We had arranged our towels and wind breaks and Simon, Bret and Des were already kicking a white plastic ball to each other. I sat on the towel next to Kath and rubbed plenty of sun cream on the parts I could reach.

"Which lucky girl gets to do my back," I said offering up the bottle. Kath took it from me and emptied some into her hands.

"Sit up straight," she said and then started to smear the lotion over my shoulders. "If you get a hard-on, I'm going to pour this over your head."

"You wouldn't see it anyway," said Sue on the other side. Kath laughed.

"You girls are so hypocritical. You say that size does not matter and then go and suggest us chaps don't have enough meat in our sausages." I flicked sand over Sue's newly lotioned legs.

"You rotten sod!" she said.

"A rotten sod with a very small penis," said Kath and then the two girls did a high-five.

We spent the next few hours dipping in and out of the cool box, exchanging clever insults and swapping the football for a Frisbee and then back again. I announced that I was going to take a walk up to the general store to pick up a packet of fags, and as nobody expressed a desire to come with me, I quickly donned my T-shirt and headed back up the beach to the High Street. It was an unseasonably hot day and by the time I reached the store I was sweating. In contrast, the store had air-conditioning blasting out and within seconds my arms were covered in goose bumps. I paid for the cigarettes and was just leaving when I noticed a revolving metal unit that was displaying a number of paperbacks. I picked up a thriller and read the blurb:

Paul Parks returned from a business trip in Europe to discover his home had been demolished and his wife and three kids missing.

Sheriff Chip Henderson thinks Parks is suffering from some kind of breakdown because there is no record of his family, or his trip abroad – in fact Paul Parks does not exist.

It's only when someone tries to kill Parks using a CIA experimental weapon that Henderson begins to suspect Parks is real.

"I think you'll find the bloke with one eye did it." I looked up and saw Beth standing just behind me.

"Hello," I said. "Have you read it?"

"No, but it's always the bloke with one eye isn't it?" She was wearing a pleated thigh-length skirt that showed her shapely tanned legs and a low-cut tight top, her jet-black hair spilling over her shoulders.

"Yes, and it's normally the first person you meet. Let's have a look." I picked up the book, opened it on the front page and pretended to read. "Paul Parks entered the plane and he found himself sitting next to a small man with a patch over his eye." She laughed that laugh again and gave me another friendly slap on the arm.

"What you doing today?"

"We're slumming on the beach. You?"

"Just picking up something for lunch. Are you down the pub again tonight to watch 'The Kebabs'?"

"Are they any good?"

"Yes," she said. "They play mostly covers but some of their own stuff as well."

"Are you working there tonight?"

"No, I only work Friday night and Sunday lunch but I'll be there tonight with a few of my girlfriends."

"Christ, tell them to wear anti-Bret spray."

"Oh, he's not that bad." She hit me again.

"So what pays the bills?"

"What?"

"What do you do for work?"

"Oh, mostly dull stuff for an insurance broker – and you?"

"I'm a moth gynaecologist on Friday night and Sunday lunchtime but during the week I'm a dull project manager for a construction company." That laugh again.

"So what time will you head for the pub?"

"We've got a barbeque first but I guess we will be there for about eight. What time does the band start?"

"They're on about nine but the pub is open until late so there will be a disco as well."

"Sounds good, I'll see you there then, Beth?"

"Yes, see you later, Don." She turned and walked to the end of the store and I walked back to the beach and reported back about the band that night. The rest of that day all we did was enjoy the sun and watch the world go by.

Beth and two blonde friends arrived about eight-thirty. Bret was twitching within five seconds of seeing them arrive. He walked straight over; sunglasses perched on his head, and then invited them to our table. They ordered their drinks and came over. Bret managed to engineer it so that Beth had to sit next to him with her friends on the opposite side. Beth gave me a knowing smile as Bret launched into his offensive. Her friends, Victoria and Louise, were good company and were definitely not blonde bimbos. Victoria taught mathematics at a technical college and Louise worked in IT support for a bank. After a while the seating arrangement changed as Kath got talking to Victoria and Des and Simon were vying for Louise's attention with Sue giving Louise moral support. The dynamics appeared to work well and before long it seemed we had all known each other for ages. Only Bret seemed to claim sole rights on Beth. After a while the band thundered into action and Beth was right, they were very good. I decided to go to the bar for drinks. I took the order and Beth said she would give me a hand.

"I'll help," said Bret. I did not show my irritation. As Bret ferried the last of the drinks to the table, Beth held back and grabbed my arm just as I was about to follow.

"Have you got any funny tobacco on you?"

"Yes, you want some?"

"Why don't you nip outside and I will follow you out shortly."

"OK," I said. Bret got up to let Beth sit inside again but she ushered him forwards so she could sit at the end. Without saying anything, I left my pint on the table, headed outside and took up my seat as on the previous night. A few minutes later Beth sat next to me and I lit up the mini joint and handed it to her.

"Is Bret giving you a hard time?" She smiled and let out a stream of smoke.

"He's fine, a bit full-on but OK. He kept asking about my boyfriend but in the end I had to tell him the truth – I hate lying."

"Christ, I bet he's gone up a gear now."

"Full throttle." She took another draw and handed the joint to me. "So how come you are single?"

"I was seeing someone about a year ago but it just didn't work out."

"You finished it or did she?"

"She did. Well, she got a job offer working abroad so she took it. We were never going anywhere with it so I guess it was the right decision. What about you?"

"Local bloke. Lasted about six months until I caught him down there." She pointed to a large pile of rocks on the beach on the far left of the bay. "He was doing the horizontal dance with some woman. He thought I'd gone into town with the girls but we decided to keep it local. I guess he did too."

"Shit, that's nasty."

"Oh, he tried to tell me the usual crap, you know? 'It didn't mean anything' and 'I've only realised how much I really love you' yadda, yadda, yadda."

"So were you very upset?"

"I was upset because he made a fool out of me. I don't think I cared for him that much but there you go." I gave her the spliff. "So Don, have you ever really fallen for someone. You know the full works, thinking of marriage?" I looked out to sea for a moment before answering.

"There was someone once. About six years ago. We had been seeing each other for about three months. She had an accident on her motorbike and had to have her legs amputated."

"Oh, shit, Don, I'm sorry."

"No, it's OK. It turned out she was a bit of a drag." Her hand went straight up over her mouth to stifle a laugh.

"That's terrible! No, that's an awful joke!"

"I'm sorry, you're right that was *not* funny."

"No, it wasn't." She hit me hard on the arm.

"Ouch!"

"You deserved that," she said trying not to smile. The music suddenly got louder as the doors opened. I looked back to notice Bret and Des walking towards us.

"So there you are," said Des. "You've not been smoking again without inviting us?" I took another joint from my packet and handed it to him.

"Nice one, Don." Beth and I stood at the same time.

"I'm going back in, see you in a while," I said. I could see Bret was indecisive. He couldn't just turn around and go back inside; that would be far too obvious considering he and Des had just come out for a smoke. Back inside Beth sat next to me and this time Bret would have to sit opposite. We talked about likes and dislikes. I found out she loved mussels in white wine with chips and mayonnaise. (A big thumbs-up considering my father was from Belgium.) She hated celery and loved cheese on toast; she didn't mind Pink Floyd but loved The Manics.

She felt that God was man-made and she adored Walnut Whips. She loved the idea that I wanted to write for a living and was really interested in my story about a young boy named Toby Kent who eventually went to fight at the Battle of Bosworth field. Ultimately our conversation was interrupted by everyone getting up to dance. The band played "Losing my Religion" by REM and then "Love Shack" by the B-52's. I noticed Bret was doing moves around Victoria and Sue while Kath seemed to have attracted the attention of two tall dark strangers. Simon and Louise were sitting at the table deep in conversation and the pub seemed to gel with a happy vibe. Des had cornered a woman with the biggest breasts I had ever seen – last night's image of Sue filled my thoughts for a split second and then the band started up with "Desperado" from the Eagles and I wasted no time at all in grabbing Beth for the slow dance before Bret had chance to recognise the fact that it was indeed a smooch. She accepted my invitation to dance as if it was ordained. When we put our arms around each other I would like to say that electricity sparked between us, or that I felt that we were the only ones on the dance floor and we were surrounded by a blue light that filled our minds with the sound of the wings of a million doves in flight – bollocks. It just felt warm and comfortable, easy and familiar. We slowly moved around in that slow clockwise circle that a billion other couples had done since the dawn of the handbag.

"Oh shit!" said Beth.
"What?"
"Joe just walked in."
"Who?"

"My ex, the local lad with the wandering dick? Don't look now! Wait till we turn around."

"What does he look like?"

"A prick."

"Perhaps a little more definition would help."

"A prick in a pink T-shirt with ripped jeans. Oh shit, he's just seen me." She buried her face in my neck. As we turned I could see a tall blond-haired man in a pink T-shirt with ripped jeans looking at me as though he was about to shoot laser beams from his eyes and cause writhing agonising death – he was bigger than me as well.

"When did you last see him?"

"About a month ago and he still wants to get back with me."

"I have to tell you that if you are relying on me to take him outside and bloody his nose then you've backed the wrong horse. I'm no fighter." I wasn't lying. The last punch I threw in anger was at the tender age of twelve years old – and I missed. I'm not a weakling. I'm six foot two and played blindside flanker for my local rugby team for about seven years but I absolutely abhor violence. I have always found that I can talk my way out of most situations resorting to bluffing if necessary. This guy looked like fighting was something that he could order from behind the bar along with a packet of pork scratchings. His jaw looked like it had been cast from pure granite.

"I don't think he'll cause any trouble."

"You don't *think* he'll cause any trouble?"

"No. He knows I have no intention of getting back with him." Coming back round again I could see he was with three other men who, although not as tall, looked equally at home with DIY dentistry.

"How do you want to handle this?"

"If he starts I'll just tell him to fuck off." I was hoping for a little more lateral thinking.

"I've got an idea."

"What?" She looked up at me with those deep hazel eyes and lashes that would keep you dry in a thunderstorm.

"Why don't you go over and say hello?"

"Why should I?"

"Because it's the last thing he would expect." She shook her head.

"Last time we spoke, we got into an argument. He said I was a hard bitch and can't anyone make a mistake?" The slow music finished. I have no idea why I did what I did, but I did it nevertheless.

"I'm going to get a drink," I said. "You want one?" She nodded but looked nervous. She walked back to the table and I went to the bar. Joe was leaning on the counter and looking at me as I approached.

"What can I get you?" said the older barmaid.

"Can I have a Guinness and a bottle of Becks please?" She started to pour the Guinness. Joe turned to me.

"I notice you know Beth?"

"Yes," I said turning to face him. Up close I noticed he was neither as tall nor as big as I thought. He was perhaps six foot and slim, not as bulky as me but I still did not fancy my chances. "My name's Don," I said and offered my hand.

"I'm Joe," he said but did not take my hand. I ignored the childish gesture.

"I know." A frown appeared on his face.

"How do you know?"

"Beth told me when you walked in."

"She what?" He puffed up his muscles.

"She said you were an item at one point."

"How do you know her then?" He put his drink on the bar.

"I'm a prosecution barrister on a case at Norwich Crown court – GBH. I've been staying locally. Jury came back in today. I got the bloke sent down for five years. He was a gay basher. It felt especially good considering I'm gay as well. Anyway, I met Beth and we got on like a house on fire. She told me all about you."

"What... what did she say?"

"She said she caught you fucking some bird on the beach." His face was a picture. "Anyway, she said that she ended it and you have been giving her a bit of a hard time."

"I just wanted to tell her that..."

"Yes, you are sorry and it won't happen again. Look, Joe, you are a good-looking bloke – don't worry; you're not my type – time to move on I think. And don't give her a hard time, her cat died two days ago, got run over – she's very upset."

"She hasn't got a cat."

I shook my head.

"How long did you date her?"

"About six months."

"And you didn't know she had a cat? Christ, Joe, and you wonder why she won't go out with you again. Move on, buddy." I paid for the drinks. "Why don't you go over and say hello and tell her you are sorry her cat died. Show some heart."

"OK, I will."

I got back to the table.

"What were you talking about?" said Beth looking extremely anxious.

"You."

"What?" I noticed he was making his way over.

"Whatever he says just go with the flow, cos if not, I am a dead man."

"Hi, Beth," said Joe

"Hi, Joe," said Beth smiling her best.

"Listen, Beth, I'm sorry your cat died." I kicked her foot under the table.

"Oh, right, thanks. You OK?"

"Yes fine."

"Good."

"I just wanted to say sorry, you know, about the cat?"

"He had a name," she said. Christ, she was quick.

"Yes, erm…"

"Fudge."

"Yes that was it, Fudge. Sorry about Fudge." She nodded. "If there is anything…"

"Yes, thanks, Joe." He nodded.

"Catch you later?"

"Yes, catch you later." He walked back to his mates.

"I think you and I need a chat," she said, "outside, now." We sat on the step again and I sparked up another joint and told her what I had said. I thought she was going to wet herself laughing.

"So, he now thinks you are gay?"

"Yes."

"Fucking hell, Don!"

"And a barrister?"

"Yep."

"Fucking hell!"

Chapter 8

The phone rang. I looked at the number. It was Julie.

"Hello?"

"Daddy! Daddy!" It was Charlie. "A big monkey with a pink bottom has broken Gramps... Gramps..."

"Aerial," I heard Julie whisper.

"His hair rail," said Charlie, "and the monkey did a poo as well and..." she shrieked. "He's done another poo!"

"Let me speak to Daddy," I heard Julie say.

"Bye, Daddy."

"Have a good day, sweetheart." I heard the rustle of the mobile being handed over.

"Hi, Don."

"Hi, Julie, sounds like she's having a blast."

"Oh, yes."

"Tom's not happy about the hair rail?"

"No." I laughed – it felt good.

"At least you won't be able to listen to Classic FM on the way back."

"Thank God for small mercies."

"Indeed."

"I'll get her to ring you when we get back."

"OK, Julie, and thanks for this."

"Our pleasure."

"Sorry I haven't been..."

"Don, it's OK."

"Thanks."

"Speak soon." The line went dead. I ordered another coffee from the waitress. The little blonde girl was holding her Dad's hand as he walked her along the water's edge while Mum, it seemed, was taking a few minutes of peace with her magazine. The old couple had taken a bench a few yards away and were taking in the view, as I was doing but for different reasons no doubt. I wondered whether going back through my memories was going to help me make the decision – Off/On; Yes/No; Death/Un-death. It was a simple binary choice turning off her life-support but it had huge implications. I wanted to make sure that the decision I made was based on a long and considered thought process. This was no doubt an emotional choice intertwined with a practical rationale that rarely shook hands with each other. Maybe what I was doing was indulging my emotions, wrapping me in a blanket of comfortable melancholy until time caught up and forced my hand – Off/On. I am, of course, a product of my mother's and father's DNA and a life of experiences that helped to shape the person sitting here now, drinking coffee. But do I not know *who* I am? Have I simply just let those life experiences settle on the shelving of my mind, collecting dust, until a neural forklift comes along and picks them off the shelf and places them back in my consciousness for a quick examination? Heidegger once said "we must pay great heed to the journey". How many of us actually take any real notice of the journey we make. It seems we spend most of our lives being washed down the river trying so much to avoid getting smashed onto rocks that we forget to look up and take in the scenery. Maybe the answers to the difficult questions lie in the re-examination of the experiences that make us who we are.

Chapter 9

The disco span its last record and we were left, slightly sweaty, finishing the last of our drinks.

"Taxi for Harris?" the driver said from the doors at the front.

"That's me," said Beth waving her hand and then draining her bottle of Becks.

"Your name is Harris?" I asked.

"Yep." Victoria and Louise were already standing and saying goodbye to us. Beth got to her feet, grabbed her handbag from the seat, bent down and offered me a very light, brief peck on the cheek. "If you are around tomorrow at lunch, I'll see you then."

"Yes, OK," I said and was beginning to rise but she was already making her way to the exit. I noticed Joe was watching her leave. When she had gone I felt a little strange about the way she said goodbye. Considering how well we had got on, I expected a bit more intimacy from her. I don't mean a full-on, tongue-wrestling snog, but something more in keeping with the overall feeling of closeness I was sure we both felt. Maybe she could have whispered something to me or she could have squeezed my hand as she left but she didn't and that left me feeling a little… empty, low, an anti-climax to an otherwise superb evening. I was quite silent on the way back to the cottage and went straight to bed when I got in.

The next morning I decided to go down to the pub before the others and see if there was something wrong. We spent the morning on the beach again as the day's forecast was identical to yesterday's cloudless sky and high temperatures. Fortunately the others were not interested in a pub lunch so I excused myself and headed for The Ship half an hour after the doors opened. The tables outside were full but inside there were only a few individuals propping up the bar. I could not see Beth; only the tall, older woman was serving. I ordered a Guinness and then felt a little self-conscious just standing at the bar with nobody to talk to and nothing to read. I had just one mouthful left in my glass and was preparing to leave when the rear door behind the bar opened and Beth walked out – my heart gave a little thump. She was wearing a plain white, lace-trimmed summer dress and white leather flip-flops. She gave me a broad smile and came right over.

"Hello," she said. "How's the head today?"

"Fine," I said. "Yours?"

"Not bad. Where are the others?"

"Still on the beach, they didn't fancy the pub."

"So you're the alcoholic then – same again?"

"Please." She took a fresh glass and began to pour.

"I wanted to come and see if you were all right. You left very quickly last night."

"Oh, I know, I'm sorry," she said, the tone of her voice and the frown helped frame the apology. "It was Joe. He would have wanted a lift back. He only lives three streets down from me and he would have just started going on about him and me again."

"I thought maybe it was something I had done," I said with relief.

"No, don't be silly. I had a great time." She patted the back of my hand.

"Joe might have wanted to come back to yours to pay respects to your dead cat?" She laughed.

"I can't believe you did that last night!"

"Neither can I," I said wrinkling up my nose. "I must have been drunk."

"Were you?" There was a slight accusation in her voice.

"No, not really, I was a bit squiffy but not drunk." She put the full pint before me and I offered her a drink but she refused.

"When are you heading back to London?"

"Tomorrow, late morning probably," I said regretfully. "Are you out again tonight?" She shook her head.

"No, I'm going to Mum and Dad's for tea. I haven't seen them in over a week." We grabbed snatches of conversation between her serving people but as the day wore on, the pub began to get so busy that conversation was almost impossible. When there was a slight lull, I took the opportunity.

"Any chance of getting your address and maybe email, I would like to keep in touch if that's OK?"

"Yes of course, I would like that." She walked the back of the bar and started to scribble something down on a piece of paper which she handed to me. It contained her address, mobile number and email. I pulled out my business card which had my mobile number on it and I scribbled my address on the back and handed it to her.

"You are really busy so I shall say goodbye now and drop you a line soon," I said feeling a sense of sadness at having to leave her company even though it was becoming increasingly ephemeral. She leaned over the bar and she gave me a kiss on the lips that was short enough to show proper deference for having only just met me, and long enough to indicate that she was serious about keeping in touch. She offered me a little wave as I turned at the door and I headed back to the beach feeling bloody good about life.

That night we stayed at the cottage and had another barbeque, drank a few beers, had a few smokes and listened to music before retiring to bed reasonably early.

I got back to my one-bedroom flat just after three o'clock on the Monday afternoon. I put a load in the washing machine, jumped in the shower and then was going to head for my local and catch up with any gossip I had missed in my absence. I was searching for a book I needed to return to a friend when I came across an empty rosewood box that had contained cutlery I'd been given as a moving-in present two years ago. Suddenly I was struck with an idea. It took four shops to fulfil what I needed. I got back to the flat, switched on my laptop, plugged in the printer and began to write a covering letter to Beth.

Dear Beth,

I would like to sincerely thank you for your kind and pleasant attendance over my short vacation at your delightful seaside resort. My slight melancholic mood on my arrival, no doubt as a result of a touch of the vapours and ill-balanced humours, was lifted beyond recognition, due, in no small part to your light and cheerful disposition. The evening of musical entertainment was equally joyous and I hope my behaviour was not too unbecoming of a Gentleman of my standing through an overindulgence in your fine ales. I do regret, however, bearing false witness towards your former close acquaintance, Master Joe, in reference to my proclivity towards those of the same sex and informing him of the untimely demise of a cat that you have never owned nor even existed. Please pass on my sincerest apologies for my dishonest deeds. My actions were based purely on the protection of your honour, misguided as they were. I would like you to accept this small token of my thanks, and if I may be so bold, my affection. I hope that we may meet again soon, and when we do, that I may find you in good health and spirit.

*Your humble servant
Master Don England.*

I placed the items I had bought in the rosewood box, wrapped it in silver paper, included my letter and then set it aside for the post on my way to work the next day. I then went to my local and told all my mates about a woman called Beth.

I posted the package the next day and then was on tenterhooks for the rest of the week hoping for a reply. It arrived Saturday.

Dear Don,

I would like to thank you Sir for your kind, generous words, and the wonderful gift. I must admit to being devilishly curious at receiving such a splendid rosewood box and most amused and touched by its contents. How wonderful it was to lift the delicate lid to find thirty-five Walnut Whips standing, soldier-like, to attention. I have never received such confectionery displayed thus. As for Master Joe, I have yet to pass on your apology as I have not had the displeasure of his company, and hope to never have again. I would like to extend to you a formal invitation to the Norfolk fair at the end of this month. It is such a gay affair that I feel it would lift the deepest melancholic humours in attendance. I will only be able to offer you my modest but comfortable sofa for accommodation if you so choose to accept. As you must be aware, it would be unseemly for a Lady of my standing to extend alternative sleeping arrangements since we have only just met. I do hope you are free to attend as I greatly enjoyed your company and handsome countenance.

I look forward to your next correspondence.

Your humble admirer,
Mistress Beth Harris
Ps. You, Sir, are barking fucking mad.

That was it, I was hooked.

Chapter 10

I returned to the Jeep, changed the CD to *The Dark Side of the Moon* by Pink Floyd and headed out of the high street to pick up the motorway to the seaside town of my youth.

Chapter 11

The gritters had been caught out by the sudden cold snap. It had rained for most of the previous day but when the clouds had parted the temperature had plummeted and by morning a sheet of ice covered most of the east coast; in contrast, the kitchen was comfortable and warm as we ate breakfast. Uncle Toby and Jenny were sitting next to Charlie and she was helping them eat their toast. Beth sat opposite me reading the newspaper, picking at a bowl of muesli and I was enjoying a bacon sandwich and strong coffee.

"There's been another stabbing," said Beth shaking her head.

"Another kid?"

"Fourteen years old."

"I'm so pleased I moved out of London." She turned the page.

"Oh, look, another premiership footballer has been caught with his pants down."

"But can they still score goals?"

"Bloody stupid rich…"

"Daddy, Mummy said a naughty word!" said Charlie.

"Sorry, Charlie," Beth said. "You're quite right I should not say that word."

"Naughty Mummy," I said and winked at Charlie. She gave me a wide jam-faced smile and concentrated on her toast.

"Mummy was certainly naughty last night," I said quietly. Beth looked up and wrinkled her nose at me with a sly smile.

"Don't think you're getting the same tonight," she said. "I've got a management report to do when I get in."

"Oh, and I was hoping to play Twister."

"Dream on."

"You are so harsh!" She got up and placed her bowl in the sink and then put her arms around me and gave me a kiss on the cheek.

"My poor baby, so hard done by," she said

"You know it."

"Right, I've got to get ready." She went upstairs while I took a wet flannel to Charlie's face, then to Uncle Toby's and Jenny's as well.

"Come on, young lady, let's get you dressed; we have to take Mummy to work." Fifteen minutes later Charlie and I were by the front door, coats on waiting for Beth to find her keys, phone, note book and many other small but essential items for a manageress of an insurance brokers. Ten minutes later we were set to go. I opened the door and the sudden cold blast hit us hard.

"Christ, the temperature's dropped!" I said. "Looks like Jack Frost has put in for overtime and is up for a bonus." I stepped aside and let Beth out first. She took two steps and suddenly her feet flew out from under her and she fell flat on her back, cracking the back of her head on the step. "Shit, love, you OK!" I bent down and slowly helped her to sit up. She was rubbing the back of her head and I could see tears well up in her eyes.

"That really, really hurt," she said.

"Let me have a look." I eased the mane of black hair aside but could see no blood. "It's not bleeding but I think you're going to have a fairly large bump there. Are you OK?"

"Yes, I think so. I saw stars then." Charlie was in the doorway looking frightened, her bottom lip quivering.

"It's all right sweetheart. Mummy's OK, she just bumped her head." I gave Charlie a quick hug and a kiss and then helped Beth to her feet. She gave Charlie a heartfelt but painful smile.

"That was silly of Mummy wasn't it?" she said and then reached out for Charlie's hand.

"That's a naughty step," said Charlie angrily and then gave the step three sharp smacks.

"That's right, Charlie, you tell that step off," said Beth and then rubbed the back of her head again. "Come on, I must get to work." I buckled Charlie in the kid's seat and then fired up the Jeep. It took a while before the heater had cleared the ice. I selected four-wheel drive and edged out onto the road. I had to take it really slowly because the back roads were like an ice rink. Eventually I pulled up outside Beth's office in town. She opened Charlie's door and gave her a kiss.

"See you later, sweetheart."

"You have got to kiss Uncle Toby and Jenny." Beth kissed the teddy and dolly. I wound my window down.

"What time shall I pick you up?"

"I'll give you a call. It's Rachel's birthday and we were going to go out for lunch but it depends on the day. Might have to have a quick drink after work, is that all right?"

"No problem. Just call me."

"If it is after work it won't be late. See you later." She gave me three quick kisses on the lips and then headed into the office.

Charlie's school was just at the edge of the village and I took her into the large adapted detached house. Claire Newport, head of the pre-school, took Charlie's coat and hung it on the hook. I said goodbye to Charlie and said I would be back to pick her up.

Back home I put the coffee on, flipped open my laptop and opened the new document of my recent work. My last novel was already with my publisher for proofing; I had decided that it would be my last of that particular tale. In my second book, one of my characters, Kathy Woodman, I had made disappear without a trace. She was an early would-be wife for the main protagonist and so I thought it might be worthwhile to write a trilogy about her life. I was in the early stages of plotting and had several off-shoots to try and tie up. I had based her character on Beth: strong, kind, determined and with a deep love of life. I typed away merrily for about two hours when my mobile sprang to life: the caller name showed it was Beth.

"Hello, you at lunch already?"

"Hi," she said. "I'm not feeling too good can you come and pick me up?" She sounded sleepy.

"Yes, what's up?"

"I just feel really nauseous and a bit dizzy."

"OK, I'll be there in ten minutes." I grabbed my coat and keys, left the laptop running and headed out the door. The sun, weak as it was, had managed to lift the temperature up enough so the roads were not too bad. I had to be careful where the roads fell into shade but still, I made decent time. Beth was already waiting at the office door as I pulled up. She slid into the passenger seat; she did not look good. Her face was white and pasty. I took her face in my hands and looked into her eyes. Her skin felt clammy and I could see her left pupil was fixed and dilated.

"I'm taking you straight to A&E," I said, selecting drive on the automatic shift.

"I'll be OK, I just need to go to bed for a few hours."

"No, love, you've had a bang on the head and I don't like the look of your eyes. Best get it checked out. More than likely you're coming down with a bug but better be on the safe side." She did not argue. She relaxed the back of the seat and closed her eyes. Ten minutes later I pulled up at the hospital. We went to the triage assessor and he took one look at her pupil and took us straight through. Beth, coat still on, sat on the bed and the nurse pulled the screen around. About thirty seconds later the Doctor appeared and I gave him a brief description of what had happened earlier and then I went back to reception to fill in some forms with the nurse. Beth's private medical insurance with her company was a good one and I always carry a copy of her details and the company's details with me. I also had private family cover as well, but in this case, as she was taken ill at work, I used the card. After about fifteen minutes I made my way back to Beth. As I turned the corner I could see several nurses and two doctors rushing around the cubicle where Beth had been taken. As I approached, Beth was rushed out on the bed along with a monitor on wheels hooked to her somewhere. I sprinted after them.

"What the hell's going on!" One of the doctors stopped.

"Are you Mr England?"

"Yes, Beth's my wife."

"OK. Your wife lost consciousness when my colleague was assessing her. We are taking her to IC to stabilise her and so we can run some tests. It might be that the trauma to her head has caused some swelling of her brain which may have caused her to lose consciousness but I'm reluctant to speculate too much at this time. Please have a seat in reception and I will find you as soon as we know anything for definite, OK?" I just nodded and he followed the bed towards the lift at the end of the corridor. I was stunned. I found the coffee machine and then took a seat in the corner by the table loaded with magazines. Waiting for news, good or bad, is not an experience I enjoy. My mind ran through a thousand scenarios from relief to despair and a whole range in between. I got another coffee and flicked through *Country Life*, *Which Car*, *Woman's Own*, *Reveal*, *GQ*, *FHM* and *Reader's Digest's* "Laughter is the Best Medicine". I looked at my watch and saw it had just turned one o'clock and still no news. I put on my coat and stepped outside to use the mobile.

"Julie? It's Don."

"Hi, Don, how's things?"

"Erm... not good actually."

"Why, what's happened?"

"Beth fell over on the ice this morning. She seemed OK but called me later to say she was feeling sick. We are at the hospital and when she was being examined she lost consciousness."

"Oh, dear God no!"

"She's been taken up to IC so they can stabilise her and run some tests. I have no more news yet."

"We are on our way."

"Julie, could you pick up Charlie from school?"

"Oh, right, yes of course. Tom can drop me at the hospital first and then he can bring Charlie back here."

"Thanks, Julie, I will call you as soon as I know anything."

"See you soon." I walked back inside and started to pace the corridor and reception area. About twenty minutes later a tall silver-haired Doctor walked to reception and the nurse behind the desk pointed at me. He came over.

"Mr England?"

"Yes." He offered his hand.

"I'm Doctor Joyce, I specialise in head trauma, will you follow me please?" We walked down the corridor, turned right and then up one flight of stairs, then took the third door on the left. The office was filled with shelves full of files and a PC sat on the desk. He indicated for me to sit in the leather chair while he sat behind the desk. "OK. Your wife has suffered a trauma to the rear right-hand side of her head just slightly above the line of the ear." He animated this with his hand showing the exact place on his own head. "This caused a small, local internal bleed to the area and as a result there has been some swelling which caused your wife to lose consciousness. Her blood pressure is stable but we have had to put her on a respirator because she was having difficulty breathing. Nothing as yet gives us too much cause for alarm. However, she will have to undergo a small surgical procedure to drain off the fluid and relieve the pressure. Scan results are positive and they suggest no permanent damage but as yet it is still far too early to tell."

"When do you want to operate?"

"We are preparing her now but I will require you to sign a consent form."

"Yes, of course, whatever you think best. How long will the operation take?"

"About thirty minutes. She should be out of surgery about half-past two and you can see her about three." He pulled out a form and asked me a few mundane questions. I signed the form and he told me to wait back in reception.

"I know it's difficult but try not to worry, Mr England." He showed me the door and I made my way back to reception. Try not to worry? Is he fucking kidding or what? Julie was at the front desk as I arrived.

"What's happening?" Her face was twisted with worry. I took her over to the seats by the magazines and told her all that Dr Joyce had said.

"All we can do is wait," I said and gave her the best reassuring hug I was capable of. Julie stepped outside to call Tom and tell him the news.

"Charlie's fine," she said on her return. "Tom said she's watching the TV. He won't tell her anything yet. Let's just wait and see." I nodded.

To kill a bit of time we went to the small cafeteria and although we were not hungry we purchased a couple of scones, jam and two large mugs of tea. We avoided talking about the situation simply because we had no knowledge. Julie asked about my new novel and she told me that Tom had a couple of pieces of furniture to repair. I have always liked Julie: she's strong both emotionally and physically. Tom, at first, took some getting used to. His silent ways seemed somewhat distant and unapproachable but in the end I realised he was mostly shy and had a heart as big and as generous as anyone I have ever known. I love them both. My father had died ages ago and my mother three years back so I genuinely looked on them as surrogate parents and, according to Beth, they thought the world of me too.

"We've booked Portugal again this year, end of August," said Julie picking a crumb off her plate.

"Algarve?"

"Of course. Why don't you come out with us this year?"

"Sounds good, we haven't thought about it yet but I'm sure we could get the time. Beth got an extra week's holiday with her promotion so as far as I'm concerned, it's a deal." Last year we had taken two weeks at the beginning of June and flown to the Canaries. We had a fantastic time with Charlie in the play pool and the beach but that left only two weeks for the rest of the year so we couldn't go to Portugal. We ended using up the rest of Beth's holiday time taking long weekends. We did sneak off for a dirty weekend in Barcelona. Julie and Tom were more than happy to spend some quality time with their granddaughter and we enjoyed our quality time alone. I won't go into details, some things are private, but it was the Barcelona weekend that we invented our own version of Twister. When Julie got the actual game out at Christmas, Beth and I had to use Herculean strength of discipline not to collapse in fits of hysterical laughter; that would take some explaining.

We walked back to reception and five minutes later Dr Joyce returned and said we could go and see Beth. He explained on the way that the operation was without complications but she was still on a respirator and unconscious. Time, apparently, will tell. We were led to a wash basin just before the IC ward where we had to clean our hands with some strong-smelling pink liquid and don a gown and cap over our hair and clothes. The private room was tastefully decorated with two comfortable seats either side of the bed. Beth was lying slightly on her side with an array of tubes and wires fixed at various areas of her body and connected to machines and drips. The only sound was from the respirator – it sounded like Darth Vader had popped in for a visit. I took the seat facing her and held her hand. She looked pale and vulnerable and her long, black, curly hair lay flat against her face. The doctor told us we could have a few minutes and then come back tomorrow. Julie and I exchanged a few words about the machines in the room and that she was in the best hands possible and maybe a few more well-worn clichés and then the nurse popped her head around the door and told us it was time to leave. I bent down and kissed her forehead and stroked her hair away from her face.

"I love you so much, my sweetheart, see you tomorrow," I said and looked at Julie. Her eyes were brimmed with tears. She gave me a hug, she kissed her daughter and then we walked back in silence to the Jeep.

As I tucked Charlie up in bed I explained that Mummy was in hospital because she banged her head this morning and she was asleep and having a good rest and she would see her soon. In my own bed I stared at the empty space next to me and then I sobbed. The last time that happened was when I held Charlie for the first time. Her little wrinkled face, contorting and twisting into a host of expressions, forced the floodgates open as I gently rocked her in my arms. She was the most beautiful, perfect miracle of life that I have ever experienced and in that moment, my life was as rich and complete as any man who had walked this earth from the very beginning of creation. Now my tears fell from fear, helplessness and anger. I reached over and pulled Beth's pillow towards me and offered a prayer to the heartless, cruel and vindictive fucking non-existent God to save my wife, otherwise, when I stood before him, I would kick the living shit out of him, Allah, Jehovah, Buddha and any other fucking deity or prophet he cares to bring on. Sleep was not forthcoming until Charlie woke from a dream. I brought her in our bed and folded my arms around her and let the gentle rhythm of her breathing send me into the blissful darkness of my own sleep.

Chapter 12

I drove into the seaside town of my youth and eventually found my road and the house where I spent the first twenty-one years of my life. Coming back here for me was a kind of therapy and perhaps a way to make sense of all that had happened; to put the 'now' into some perspective or maybe to immerse myself in more innocent and carefree times. I parked up on the quiet road of a small estate directly opposite; I grabbed my cigarettes and phone, locked the Jeep, crossed the road and stood outside my old house. It had hardly changed over the years. It had a new roof and fencing down the side separating it from the meadow we used to own. I would have dearly liked to knock on the door and ask for a quick look around but I thought better of it. It was a bungalow which my father had designed when he had returned from living in Canada for two years with my mother, two older brothers and older sister. I was born about two years after the bungalow had been built. However, this was not my first port of call. I walked past the entrance to the meadow, over the road bridge and turned right and followed the tarmac path that ran parallel to a stream known as "the ditch" until I reached a small footbridge where my memories of childhood began.

Chapter 13

Before I leave the bungalow I want to impart a particular event that always makes me smile and one I would like to share. Over the years my parents were members of different clubs. At one time it was badminton, bridge, golf (mainly my father) and table tennis. The latter they continued with for many years. Every now and then my dad and mum opened our home up to committee meetings and they would sit around the large round table to discuss the business in hand. Antony Roundtree, bank manager, Chairman of the league, and his wife Sheila, Vice Chairman, were always present and worked very hard year on year to keep the table tennis alive and kicking. I was about five years old, maybe six and on this occasion I was watching television as the meeting was being held. We had a large lounge/dining room and so I had to have the TV on low so as not to disturb the meeting. It was very early evening and I was in my pyjamas ready for bed and was waiting for the meeting to finish so Mum could read me my bedtime story. What I liked about them having the meetings at ours was the fact that if I kept quiet, they would inevitably forget about me and so I would end up staying up much later than normal. I would get to see TV that I would not be able to watch under usual circumstances. I can't remember what the show was that I was watching but it involved women taking off their tops thus exposing their bra-clad breasts. I guess the meeting had reached the "any other business" stage and was winding to a close when I needed to speak with my Mum. I sidled up to her and tugged at her arm. The meeting went politely silent as I spoke.

"Mum?"

"Yes, darling?"

"Why does my willy get all stiff when I see those ladies take their tops off?" There was absolute silence. Then one of the committee members spoke.

"I think over to you, Mr Chairman?" The room erupted with laughter and I joined in of course not knowing what I was laughing at. I can't even remember if Mum actually answered my question but the story lived on and was told many times whenever I brought a girlfriend home.

Chapter 14

8 YEARS OLD

THE DITCH
CHIP & BESS

MISS MILLINGTON

The ditch was separated into three parts and each part had its own unique identity. These three personalities were created by thousands of years of natural forces and us, or me to be more precise. I make this claim because my father owned a long meadow that ran alongside the middle section, however, by my eighth year, the ownership had reverted to the local council, who, incidentally, did nothing with it for ten years. There were no fancy names for the three parts just: Top, Mine and the Tunnels. The Top part started at the large concrete sluice gate with rusted bars that prevented would-be explorers from entering the land drains and ended at the footbridge and a second, smaller, concrete sluice but with similar metal bars. This section followed a wire fence that formed the boundary of both my infant and junior schools' playing fields. The Mine section ran from the footbridge to the road bridge, and as I have said, followed alongside the meadow. The Tunnels section ran from the road bridge to the railway tunnels. Beyond the tunnels the ditch continued through a caravan park and then I have no idea where. In fact, I have never traced its source nor ending. The distance from the tunnels to the large concrete sluice was no more than about two-thirds of a mile but that was our world and it was plenty big enough.

Heavy rain forced the normally gentle stream into a raging torrent and one year I can remember it flooding across the road bridge. But whatever the state of the river, it was a constant source of sticklebacks, frogs, water rats, wasp nests, newts, eels, mosquitoes and above all, wonders and adventure. The ditch, in its normal state, was no deeper than about two feet, its shallowest part being only a few inches and we knew exactly which parts would pour over our wellingtons and therefore send us home, a wellington boot in each hand, a ring of mud around our calves and our socks flapping at the ends. Falling in completely was a yearly occurrence and my mother was used to dishing out towels, cheese on toast and cups of tea to me and my friends while waiting for our clothes to dry; sitting under our veranda in our pants seemed as natural as breathing.

I must explain briefly the complexities of fishing in the ditch. There were many easy accessible parts of the bank to the water's edge but there were some which were defended by tall nettles and blackberry bushes so long trousers were definitely required. Inevitably, when long trousers were not available, the brave and the fool- hardy would tentatively tread a path to the water only to end up spending an hour in search of dock leaves to relieve the bubbling nettle stings and thereafter sport white legs containing red rashes and green stains for the rest of the day. The standard fishing net was universal. Nylon netting was woven around a loop of wire which was then inserted into the end of a bamboo cane which would always come adrift within half an hour's use. The nets were usually available in four colours: green, red and yellow, and blue could be had but that was quite rare. When the net detached itself from the cane, there would follow a disgruntled walk back to my house to either the shed for electrical tape, or the lounge and the writing bureau for sticky tape. This distraction was at best an irritating inconvenience but by the age of eight I had worked out that it was better to apply the tape to the new nets *before* we ventured out. My mother's sieve was a splendid alternative when pocket money became an issue although it did require string, a stick and a fair supply of patience in order to obtain the same reach as the conventional shop-bought item. It also required an equally large effort of stealth and inventiveness in order to remove my mother's sieve from its home, next to the oven, and replace it without any evidence of slime still attached without getting caught. The last essential item required was of course the jam jar and as my mother seemed to make marmalade and jams of all description at all times of the day, week and year, it was down to me to provide the glassware.

Before we continue with the ditch I want to talk to you about Chip and Bess.

Bess was my age, a school friend and bit of a tomboy which I guess was inevitable due to being the sister to three older, tough, rough brothers from a tough, rough estate in town. Her hair was strawberry blonde and reached down to the top of her jeans. Her deep blue eyes were the focus within a frame of peach-rose cheeks, a small button nose and full red lips. She had a slight permanent huskiness to her voice as though she was in the last throws of laryngitis and a laugh that made you want to join in. She was the best gymnast in the school and her body was strong and slim. Yet, despite her tomboyishness, she retained a grace and femininity that some of the more elegant girls could only hope for. Next to her, I looked like a plump, awkward bumbling oaf – which I was. I also had ginger hair and skin that went bright red when the sun showed itself for more than three minutes. I wanted to be her boyfriend so much that it felt like I was permanently carrying fluttering rocks in my stomach. We used to hang about together at play times and gather a few more friends to play British Bulldog or football. She always got picked first. Sometimes we would sit in the corner of the playing field at lunchtime when the sun was shining and throw stones at a lolly stick. Often she would make daisy chains and put them in her hair which was such a contrast to her throwing some boy to the ground in a crunching bulldog tackle that made me wonder whether she was two people in one body. Other times we would play on the climbing frames. I was always amazed at how agile she was at jumping from bar to bar; to her it was as natural as walking.

Chip arrived at my school in the spring of my eighth year and looked like a male version of Bess. He was perhaps an inch or so taller and his blond straight hair was just shy of shoulder-length. His blue eyes matched hers, his cheeks were just as rosy and he was as fit and athletic as she was; however, there was nothing girly or feminine about him. They looked so much like brother and sister that some of the teachers had to check the register just to make sure they were not related.

Within a few weeks the three of us were inseparable at school. At the weekends Chip would either come down to me and we would explore the meadow or the ditch, or I would walk up to his and go and play on waste ground at an industrial park at the top of my road. Chip could scale fences and climb trees without any sense of danger or fear of failure and never made me feel as though I was crap at it – which I was. Then the first day of our summer holidays started and the prospect of six weeks of play and excitement stretched in front of me like the Pacific Ocean.

The first week Chip was away with his parents so I did very little except call on a couple of mates and get in trouble for being home late. On Sunday afternoon Chip rang me to say he had returned and that we should meet up the next day about ten.

"Give Bess a ring," he said as if it was the most natural thing for me to do.

"OK," I said as if it was. The phone was shaking in my hand when I called, the ringing sounded like the anticipating drum roll to a tightrope act.

"Yeah?" It was one of her brothers.

"Is Bess there, please?" I was trying to sound cool and unaffected but I was sure my voice didn't make the grade.

"Who's that?"

"Don."

"Who?"

"Don."

"Don who?"

"Don from school, I'm Bess's mate."

"Oh." There was a pause and then a clunk as the phone was put down on a table or desk. The silence seemed to go on for ever.

"Hello?" The familiar husky voice was slightly cautious as though she did not receive many calls.

"Bess, it's Don."

"Oh, hiya," she said, caution giving way to instant recognition. "What's up?"

"Chip is back. Thought we might do something tomorrow. You want to come over?" The fluttering rocks in my stomach and heartbeat fought for dominance.

"What are you doing?"

"Don't know, maybe go down the ditch."

"What time?"

"Ten?"

"OK, I'll come over to you. See you tomorrow."

"OK." I called Chip back and then could not wipe the smile off my face.

We ate tea in front of the box and watched *Alias Smith & Jones* with Pete Duel and Ben Murphy, my favourite programme ... "and in all the trains and banks they robbed, they never shot anyone." Life could not get better than this. I hardly closed my eyes that night.

By nine-thirty I was dressed in a blue T-shirt chosen because Bess had once said the colour suited me, a pair of running shoes of which she said she liked the logo and a pair of jeans that she had never offered an opinion on. I had gathered three fishing nets and secured the heads with tape. I put the better one aside for Bess along with the bigger jam jar and waited in front of the TV not quite paying attention to the plot in *Scooby Doo*. The day promised to be cloudless and hot and I wondered if I could get out of the house without my mother swamping me in suncream. At nine forty-one the doorbell announced the first guest. I hadn't seen Chip come past the window. It was Bess.

"Hiya," she said with a wide smile and shining eyes.

"Hi, come in." As she moved into the hall her bare arm touched mine and it took me two attempts to shut the door.

"Want a drink?"

"Got any coke?" She sat on the sofa as I went into the blue laminated and glass kitchen. I had just taken the bottle out of the refrigerator when Bess shouted.

"Chip is here." She jumped up and answered the door. I felt a mixture of conflicting emotional messages. I was disappointed that Chip had arrived early but glad that he had so I would feel not so... so, on the spot I guess. I was excited at spending a few minutes with Bess on my own as she had never been in my house before and that made it somewhat more intimate. I was also scared shitless at the prospect. I bought out the cokes and we sat discussing what to do with the day. I mentioned the fishing nets and got a favourable response from both. Ten minutes later we were carrying our nets and jars through the meadow to the footbridge, Chip and I with Bess in the middle.

I don't know too much about sticklebacks, their spawning habits, their genetic heritage or the result of a university study on them in that actual ditch, but what I do know is that to catch a pregnant red-throater is extremely rare indeed. The sticklebacks are small, usually no bigger than about a centimetre in length. A red-throater can grow to about five centimetres. There was always the even more rare opportunity of catching a newt or an eel but that was just fantasy land. The other side of the bridge connected to a long dog-leg field that continued to follow the ditch. The bank opposite the meadow formed a sort of beach area where the water trickled over rocks and shale at about three to four inches deep. Towards the small sluice the water was deeper at about a foot to a foot and a half – wellington boot limit. We filled the jars with water and then separated along the bank. Bess announced the first catch with a husky "whoop" of delight. Chip and I came over immediately to inspect. She laid her net on the bank and Chip picked out the two small minnows and dropped them into her jar. Their tops were green and their side shimmered silver as the sun bounced around the glass. Another half an hour of thrusting nets into dark places produced another five for Bess, three for Chip and a big fat zilch for me.

"You're really crap, Don," said Bess with an easy smile.

"I'm going for the red-throater."

"What's that?" I explained what it was and how difficult they were to catch.

"You won't catch one yet, too early," said Chip like he knew what the hell he was talking about.

"I will, just takes time."

"Yeah right." After a while I suggested we move back downstream towards my house where there were overhanging trees and slightly deeper water. There is a locally famous old oak tree that grows on the meadow side of the ditch. In its branches there were odd planks of wood, remnants of a tree house that had been constructed by my brother and his mates years before. A rope hung down from one of the bigger limbs and so one could swing from bank to bank. We put our nets down and so began the Tarzan and Jane routines. Soon the fun turned into a semi-serious competition to see who could land on the bank the farthest away. Being taller I could get a better height and leverage and made my mark that the others found difficult to beat. While they tried, I picked up my net and began fishing about ten feet away from the Swinging Blondinies in my quest for the red-throater. About five minutes later a shout went up from Chip: he had apparently beaten my jump by about six inches. I looked around, slightly annoyed to see two beaming red faces grinning back. I was in two minds whether to go back and attempt to better the mark or ignore it as if it wasn't such a big deal – of which it was of course. I took my anger out on the fishing and began to thrust my net in as if I was spearing blue whales. My net went deep into some mud and I pulled it out with considerable effort. I drew the rod in and examined the pungent mess. Something stirred under the surface of the mud.

"I think I've got something!" I padded back up the bank and onto the meadow and lay the net down. Chip and Bess joined me. I put my hand in the mud and immediately jumped back as an eel about nine inches long struggled to the surface.

"Shit!" I said and fell back.

"It's a bloody eel!" said Chip.

"Look at the size of that!" said Bess jumping up and down. Chip tried to grab it but the thing proved more than a match. Bess took a couple of steps back.

"Don't hurt it," she said as Chip tried harder to pin it down.

"I can't get hold of it." Suddenly he lifted the eel but only momentarily and then it slipped out into the grass and slithered down the bank into the water.

"Shit! Sorry, Don," said Chip.

"It's OK; I was going to put it back anyway."

"You caught an eel!" said Bess and she put her arms around me and gave me a quick hug .

The next hour we were all frantically trying for another eel except I was concentrating on something else. I can feel her arms around me now as I write this, such was the imprint on my being.

About fifty yards from the oak tree on the field side was a small roundabout, a set of swings and a couple of see-saws. I suggested that I would go and make some sandwiches and meet them there. Peanut butter was the consensus and so I left them to take the nets and jars over to the play area. Having made the sandwiches and took the remainder of coke from the fridge, I headed for the fields and saw them swinging in the distance. Before we ate, Chip had invented another competition. The idea was to swing as high as you could and then throw yourself off and see who could get the farthest. Chip won.

We ate the sandwiches and shared the coke from the bottle on the grass to the side of the swings. Afterwards I lay back and to my utter amazement, Bess did the same at ninety degrees to me, resting her head on my stomach with her legs stretched out. Her hair flowed all over my arm. Chip, on the other hand, was sitting cross-legged facing me. His right knee was resting just on hers. I was confused to know which of us had the better spot. Although her head was resting on me I could not see her face but Chip could. He began to exploit the situation by flicking bits of daisies at her and then she would pick one and try to flick it into Chip's open mouth. My left arm was behind my head and my right arm felt sort of awkward. The natural thing to do would be to lay it across her stomach but that would be too obvious wouldn't it? I was tortured by indecision. If I left it too long the moment would pass and the opportunity lost. However, if I made the move and she moved my hand away I would be mortally wounded, crushed by embarrassment. I wasn't sure if Chip felt the same way I did about Bess; he never indicated anything of that nature to me – he was certainly playing it cool if he was. If I was going to do it then it would have to look natural, not forced or contrived. The moment came. Chip had flicked a daisy which landed in Bess's hair towards the front of her fringe and she was searching for it.

"Hang on," I said and picked the daisy off and flicked it at Chip who ducked his head in response. I then let my arm go swiftly across her stomach and held my breath. She didn't move it off and tell me to get stuffed. She didn't suddenly get up awkwardly embarrassed. What she did do was to start to gently pick the hairs on my forearm. My neck hurt from straining to watch. My other arm was beginning to get pins and needles and her head was resting on my half-full bladder but God and his mighty war angels pelting me with wasp nests could not have moved me from that spot. Chip sat on his side and for five minutes the only sound was that of a single blackbird trilling in the silence and the gentle plucking of my arm hairs.

Chip broke the moment by farting.

"Oh, you smelly shit!" said Bess struggling to her feet laughing. I took a little longer getting up as I could feel practically nothing in my limbs. She chased Chip around for a few moments trying to hit him but then gave up. We walked towards the top end of the ditch, but not as far as the large sluice, trying to look for a good spot for eels. My whole being was fixed on all the small nuances and actions emanating from Bess. Every word, every sound she made I was totally in tune with, focused and augmented in every way. Much to my frustration and slight annoyance, it was Chip who was closest to offer a hand to her as we stepped across stones to get to the other bank and then back again. No matter how I tried to contrive the moment where *I* might hold out my hand, the moment was always lost to Chip. If I did not know any better it was as if Chip was doing it deliberately but there were no signs to indicate he was bothered in any way. We tried a few places but no luck. We gradually headed back towards the footbridge as the late afternoon sun began to stir the tiny midges that hung together in small dancing clouds. Bess and Chip walked back over the bridge and sat with their legs dangling over the concrete wall to the small sluice and began to flick small stones at a large flat stone on the opposite bank. I moved gingerly across some of the stones in the shallow area in order to reach a deep part to the far left side of the sluice gate. I plunged my net in a few times but came up empty. To the left of me and to the centre of the stream, I could see a large flat stone which would give me a choice of two areas of deeper water. I determined that it was too far to step; I would have to jump. The stone looked green and slippery and so the jump would have to be perfect otherwise I was going in, big time.

My mind weighed up benefits and disadvantages to the risk involved. If I tried and fell that would be the end of my day and be the subject for absolute ridicule. If, on the other hand, I made the jump, it would give me a chance to get at a bit of the ditch that wasn't normally accessible without wellingtons. I decided to take the risk. I edged around on the two stones I was standing on, judged the distance and which foot I was going to land on. I favoured my left. I jumped. As my foot made contact with the stone it slipped slightly forward then gripped. I lost balance momentarily, arms waving madly and then managed to bring my body under control. I shimmied my feet to get a proper purchase and then began to probe the water with my net. The first few attempts were fruitless, however, on my fourth strike, I pulled the net in to discover, not once, but two red-throaters and about ten small sticklebacks. I made the jump to the bank but my foot slipped on take-off and the tip of my trailing foot hit the water. I felt ice cold water bleed into my shoe and my sock. It wasn't disastrous and certainly not something that would induce me to curtail my day. I got to my jam jar and dropped the fish in. I held it up in triumph for Chip and Bess but they were gone. Their nets and jars were still resting on the concrete wall so they hadn't gone far. I took my jar and net, climbed the bank and walked across the bridge. The meadow's path was obscured by several trees and bushes so I put my equipment down and went in search for my two missing friends. After about twenty paces the path forked. The right-hand path led straight down the meadow while the left cut into the bushes and trees and followed the bank all the way through to the old oak with the rope swing. I could see they weren't ahead of me so I guessed they had taken the other path through the trees. I started walking and then saw them in a clearing about fifteen yards ahead. I stopped dead – they were kissing. They were bloody kissing! My numbed brain was trying to take in what I was seeing. They were definitely kissing but it looked awkward. They held each other's arms like two warriors greeting each other after surviving a bloody and desperate battle. Their lips were together and they were moving their heads in a fast circular pattern as though they were doing it in time to disco music. Aware that I might be spotted, I backtracked and sat down on the concrete wall. How could this be happening? It's not right! I gave her the best net and the biggest jam jar; she rested her head on my stomach; she was plucking the hairs off my arm for God's sake! There was silence except for the sound of running water and the trill of a blackbird, its complex song held within it a sudden sense of sadness and fallen hope and my sock was wet. I heard them approaching from behind but I did not look round.

"Hiya," said Bess sitting next to me and Chip on the other side.

"I caught two red-throaters," I said trying not to sound as though my world had collapsed in an apocalyptic earthquake, which it had. She bent down at my jam jar and tucked her hair behind one ear. Five minutes ago that ear had been the cutest ear I had ever seen. Even cuter than Samantha's had been until I discovered she smelled of turkey soup. But now I did not know how to feel about that ear now.

"Where did you get them?" she asked.

"Down there." I pointed to the large rock in the centre of the stream. "You have to find the deeper spots to have any chance."

"Look, Chip!" She held up the jar.

"Cool," said Chip with obvious false interest. It was clear where his thoughts were.

"It's getting late," she said. "I had better get home." After a quick discussion we decided to walk Bess back. We put the fish back into the ditch and I hid the nets and jars ready to be picked up on the way back, then the three of us began the walk back, Chip and I with Bess in the middle. I was painfully aware of my foot squelching every second step but if they noticed, they didn't say. Conversation was limited to an exchange of ideas for things to do for the rest of the holiday. Bess was going with her family down to Devon for two weeks and then she was having two of her cousins staying so she doubted whether she would be about much. Maybe towards the end of the week she would be free. We arranged to meet up on Thursday and that she would give me a ring. The whole journey for me was agonising. Were her and Chip boyfriend and girlfriend now? Did he kiss her or did she kiss him? When she was free would that mean that Chip would spend time with her alone or would I be invited along? I doubted whether I would be able to take it seeing them walk hand in hand or kiss again. We walked through a small estate and then into the village. Chip announced he wanted some sweets and so disappeared into the shop while Bess and I sat on a bench around the corner.

"It was really good fun today," she said in her slightly husky voice that now seemed to have more resonance about it.

"Yes, it was great," I said.

"You OK?" I forced myself to look at her. The twinkling blue of her eyes seemed to reach deep inside me.

"Yep, I'm fine." Then she kissed me. She laid her hand gently on mine and leaned forward. Her lips touched mine and she began to open and close her mouth and move her head in the same kind of circular way I had seen her do with Chip although it felt slower somehow. I had never kissed a girl before and it grabbed me completely by surprise. It took me a second to get into her rhythm and then the world span away into the stratosphere. I had no idea how long we kissed but it seemed as though every microsecond was like a whole summer. Eventually we stopped – just as well as I doubted I could have held my breath for much longer. I smiled and she smiled back, her nose wrinkled up – the cutest nose I had ever seen. Chip returned.

"Chewy nuts?" he said, offering the bag.

We waved our goodbyes and the walk home began. I didn't want to ask Chip about his kiss, I was just happy and contented to keep mine for myself. I knew that Bess was not my girlfriend and I knew she was not Chip's either. There was equality between us that did not need examining and I was just content to let things be. I liked to believe, however, that my kiss had been more real, more personable and more correct. My world was repaired, my sock was drying and by the time we retrieved the nets and jars the blackbird's song was trilling with a lighter voice that hadn't been present before.

We took the path through the bush and wooded area and walked past where Chip had received his kiss. The image snapped into my mind and was gone almost as quickly. We reached the oak tree with the rope swing and then continued on. Something caught Chip's eye and he suddenly forced his way through the undergrowth and pulled out a small bag. Inside there was a magazine with the front cover missing.

"Shit, look at this!" Chip opened the magazine that showed a naked woman sitting on a chair with her legs open. We dropped the nets and the jars as if we had just been stung and sat down in the long grass and began to carefully thumb our way through page after page of naughtiness. One page grabbed my attention more than the others. It was a picture of a woman holding her boobs up against a man's floppy penis. I could not understand how that was possible. I had never seen pictures like this before but Chip said he had found some similar hidden at the top of his Dad's wardrobe. On the odd occasion I had glimpsed a woman on the TV in skimpy underwear my penis would go all stiff. I had no idea why, it just did. So how was it possible that this man's willy was not all stiff when he had it resting on a woman's boobs? On the adjoining page it said "Mary Millington invites you into her fantasies". The next few pages were with Mary in various states of undress with the man with his hand on various bits still with a floppy willy. Mine, incidentally, wasn't. Tea time beckoned and so we decided that we would take turns with the magazine. I took Mary home but not to meet Mum and Dad.

I folded the pages up and put them down the back of my jeans. Mum was in the kitchen making supper and Dad was in the shed making something out of wood. I deposited the forbidden pages at the top and to the back of my wardrobe behind half-made Airfix kits and various forgotten toys. I washed my hands and Mum called me in to eat. We sat around the big table and Dad asked what I had been doing all day. I told him about the eel and the red-throaters and he gave a nod of approval when I told him I had put them back. After apple crumble we sat in front of the TV and *Tomorrow's World* with Raymond Baxter. After, I jumped into the bath, got into my pyjamas and had a cup of tea and a piece of cake. I said my goodnights and went to bed after retrieving Mary from her hiding place. I spent about fifteen minutes scrutinising every detail of Mary's fantasies and was excited and confused by most of them. I put her back and switched off the sidelight but it was not Miss Millington that I took to my dreams, it was Bess.

Chapter 15

I watched as a small leaf bounced and bubbled under the bridge and then drifted down the stream until it disappeared from sight and wondered where its journey would end. How many thousands of leaves, twigs and other flotsam had passed this way over hundreds of years and how many people had sat where I sat and watched them float by? How many thought back through their lives, as I am doing, trying to make sense of it all, get a handle on the moment or simply just appreciate the continuing motion of time. I remembered on many occasions as a boy just sitting here or somewhere like here, trying to figure out my feelings about people like Bess, Chip and Mary Millington. I think the difference now, compared to then, is a sense of history and the consequence of one's actions based on that history. As a child, there is very little history and a whole lot of future possibilities. When I discovered that magazine with Miss Millington, although at the time I would have never known it, I lost the first edge of innocence. The excitement that Bess had evoked within me was hidden from my knowledge; it existed, it happened, but without any history, it became a discovery. I was the pioneer of the horizons of my future history and I simply stumbled towards them with wide eyes and the safety net of childish innocence beneath me.

I slapped the dust from my jeans and decided to walk to the first main sluice gate. The tarmac path that ran along the perimeter of my school's playing field had been renewed and the chain link fencing had been replaced by galvanised slatted fence panels with twisted sharp spikes on the end. The trees were taller and the bushes thicker. The sluice gate itself was barely visible through a mass of brambles and bushes. It seemed smaller, less imposing and the green slime hadn't changed nor had the rust on the metal gate. The one thing I noticed that was markedly different was the noise from the children at play – when I was playing here as a child there was only silence because I, like every other child, was on holiday. It seemed really strange to hear the screams and shouts wafting through the trees and across the fields; it didn't feel right – it was though I shouldn't be there – I should be in school with the rest of them – I was a truant. I walked back along the ditch and passed the bridge and stopped briefly at the old oak and to my surprise I could see a rope hanging from the massive branch. I scrambled down the bank, hopped over the ditch and brought the rope up the other bank. I assessed the strength of the rope and the branch and guessed it would take my weight. I reached up the rope as high as I could and then swung over the ditch and back again. I moved farther back this time and then gave it another try. When I reached the other side I let go and landed with a grace best suited to a walrus in ballet shoes. I marked the spot where I landed with a twig. "Beat that, Chip!" I said with a smile. I climbed back up the bank and made my way to the small play area. The swings and roundabout were in the same position but both were brand new. There were now three see-saws instead of one and a climbing frame that was never part of the original design. I could just about squeeze my arse onto the swing's seat. I began slowly and then took courage and went higher. The thought of throwing myself off at the top of the swing appalled me now; I would probably break every bone in my body. I let the swing naturally come to a halt instead of using the toes of my shoes as I would have done as a kid – much to the annoyance of my parents – "Do you know how much shoes cost?" – "If I catch you doing that again you won't sit down for a week!"

I remember Beth taking me around some of her old haunts. We looked around a rotten barge once that had been stuck on a sand bank for as long as she could remember. It was a place where she had experienced some of those events where *her* innocent corners had lost their sharp edges. As she recounted some of the stories I tried to picture it happening as though I was part of that history but of course it was impossible. I could only relate to them in a way that my own experiences shared similar emotions and situations; I could not be her as much as she could not be me. We cannot share grief; we can only share in the common experience of it. We own grief in the same way as we own our history and we can't remove it from ourselves and hand it to someone else; it is there, fixed and dilated.

From the swing, I could see the housing estate opposite my old house and could remember it being built. The entrance off the main road was once occupied by a small bungalow with land that stretched behind all the neighbouring properties. The bungalow was eventually demolished for the developer to come in and begin to create one of the best playgrounds any young boy could hope for.

Chapter 16

8 YEARS OLD

THE BATTLE OF THE FLASHING ROAD LIGHT
THE BAD MAN

Directly opposite where I lived was a vacant bungalow. It used to be owned by the Blacks who kept two pigs, some chickens and a few other animals. I used to be friends with their son when I was much younger but then they simply moved away. Their home was the last before the field close to the old cemetery and the land extended up behind the other bungalows. I guess the Blacks sold to a developer because the bungalow was knocked down and the diggers moved in. Now it's a small estate of about fifty houses or so. Something must have happened to halt the project for a while because after the diggers made mounds and trenches everything seemed to stop. This was great for us because it opened up a whole new place for adventure. Some of the Blacks' old sheds were still intact and there were a few water troughs scattered about. A number of us got together that summer to play the odd game of war or simply to mess about generally.

It was Saturday. I know this because my brother, who was already married, would pop in for a cup of tea and then normally go to the shops for something or other. I had already made arrangements for Chip, Fluff, Stomp, Piggy and Bongo to meet up after lunch for a game of war. We were usually armed with the standard Western-type cap gun and a few rolls of caps – you know the ones I mean. They were made from red paper and were studded with raised brown dots which exploded when the hammer from the gun hit them. There were about two hundred caps to a roll and very often you had to break the gun and free the jammed paper; a tricky operation when you were under fire. There was a newer type of cap available which required a completely different gun. The caps were small cylinders set in a plastic ring which turned round once every time you pulled the trigger. There were ten caps per round and the advantage to these was that they very rarely misfired, plus the guns seemed to be more substantial, more real perhaps. The gun I owned was an old type silver Colt 45 with a red plastic handle which was slightly loose and a dodgy trigger that seemed only to fire every second shot but on the good side, the paper never seemed to jam.

My brother arrived as usual and declared that he was going to the shop to get some cigarettes and would I like to go with him. I nodded eagerly. I loved spending time with my older brother because he was like a big kid and because he was an adult he got away with doing some outrageous stuff. He also had a convertible Spitfire and unless it was raining he would always have the top down. The weather was overcast, warm and humid so I knew the top would already be down. The car also had a map reading light that was pen-shaped and attached to a curly black lead; it was great fun pretending it was some sort of James Bond device. We jumped in the car and sped up the road accompanied by the sound from the distinctive throaty exhaust.

The village shop was split into two parts. One side contained the confectionery items, newspapers, magazines, pens, paper, envelopes and other such useful things, the other side contained nothing but toys. My brother went down one side while I went and looked at the toys. Within a few moments I had spotted something that I could barely take my eyes off. It was a pump action shot gun with back holster that took the new type of caps. The pump part was imitation wood that matched the stock, the under and over barrels were jet-black and the trigger section was chrome. The whole thing was encased in a long cardboard box with a clear plastic front. My brother saw me dribbling and came over following my gaze. He removed the box and studied it carefully.

"It only comes with five caps," he said. "That's nowhere near enough." He walked straight up to the counter and spoke to the woman shopkeeper. "How many caps in a box?" The woman rummaged under the counter and came up with a brown cardboard box.

"There are ten shots per cap and there are one hundred caps in a box."

"I'll take a box then please." She put the gun and a box of caps in a large bag, gave my brother his change and then he handed me the package on our way out. My mouth was working but nothing was coming out. My brother had a huge grin on his face and eventually, when my initial shock subsided, I said,

"Oh my God, thanks so much, this is fantastic!"

"You're welcome, little brother," he said and fired up the Spitfire. Incidentally, he still calls me "little brother" to this day. Even with the top down I barely looked up from the bag on my lap. My mind was racing forward to the game of war that afternoon. Everyone will want a go of the gun. It will be: "bagsey me first, bagsey me second, bagsey me third" and so on. The only other boy who had the new type of cap and gun was Chip. His was a Smith and Wesson similar to the ones that the TV American cops use but it was merely a little pea-shooter compared to the one now sitting on my lap. When we got back I raced into the lounge and gently unpacked the box and laid all the contents out on the carpet. To my surprise, the back holster also came with five tubes that clipped to your own belt that held a capacity of ten caps each. They had small springs in the bottom so as you removed one cap another would automatically jump up to take its place. I broke the gun and inserted one of the caps and took it outside for a test fire. I pumped the action and pulled the trigger. I was convinced the gun had a louder, deeper sound than the other guns but in reality it was probably no different. Lunch couldn't come quickly enough.

I watched from my front window as my mates started to arrive at the site and when they were all present I put on my back holster, inserted the gun, made sure I had a full complement of belt clip ammunition and then walked out to meet them. Chip, Fluff and Stomp were sitting on top of a mound of clay while Piggy and Bongo sat on the slope slightly lower.

"Donny!" they shouted as I approached.

"Where's your gun?" said Bongo when I got to them.

"Here," I said. I reached up behind my neck and in one swift, practised motion, pulled out the gun, pumped the action and fired it from the hip. I wish I could have taken a photograph of the faces in front of me. There was a split second of nothing then, all at once, they all came charging around me. "Where did you get that? Let's have a go? How cool are those? Shit look at that!" When they had all held it, fired it and examined it in every detail, we decided to play war. Now I need to explain a bit about war and our particular rules. You probably had your own rules and I dare say some were the same but it's important to know exactly what was involved.

First was choosing sides. As there were only six of us, it wasn't going to be too much of a problem. If there were many more then a captain had to be chosen who would then take it in turns to pick a player. Nobody wanted to get chosen last. On this occasion it didn't really matter as we would probably all switch around after every game. On my side were Chip and Fluff. The next step was to choose and build a camp which we all spent a bit of time on to get them right. We would always swap to each other's camp after each game as well as change the sides around. Our team's camp was set on the north of the site. A big mound of soil had been tipped next to a pile of broken up concrete rocks. We used these rocks to form a sort of castellation along the top rim of the mound with gaps to shoot from. We found two old wooden doors which we used to make a kind of hut or shelter to protect us from the grenades. Grenades were generally lumps of loose clay that disintegrated when they hit the ground but I'll come to that in a minute. We found an empty diesel drum which we lay at the side of the mound for extra cover and then gathered heaps of grenades about the place as ammunition dumps. The other camp was to the south and slightly east of ours and they had a similar mound of earth to use. They placed two of the metal water troughs down in a similar way to our diesel drum and had dragged over an old fence panel and used it in the same way as our doors. Between the two camps were several piles of sand, ballast and clay and to the left was a long trench that I can only presume was to be for a foundation to one of the proposed houses. Two diggers and a dumper truck stood idle about halfway between us and to the far left were three metal storage units so there was plenty of fire cover for both teams. Once the camps had been constructed we all met in the middle to discuss the rules.

The main objective was to kill the opposition. It was generally agreed that a shot from a gun would only count as a kill if it was from about ten to fifteen feet away and a kill was only if you managed to get your shot off first; the gun had to actually fire to count, a misfire or "click" would not do. The person who had been killed was expected to die in a dramatic way and lie there until the battle had been won or lost. However, as there were only a few of us, we agreed that someone could get up from being killed and re-join the war after about thirty seconds. We were all expected to pretend at some point we had been wounded and then limp about clutching a leg or arm. As I have said, the grenades were made from loose lumps of clay and they would disintegrate when they landed. We never threw them directly at each other and we had to shout "grenade" whenever we threw one. A kill from a grenade was only if part of the disintegrated clay hit you anywhere on your body. This rule was the subject of most arguments but generally it worked OK. Because of the "get up after thirty seconds" rule, we would only agree on a winning team by an unwritten kind of democratic declaration which would be which team seemed to have scored the most kills and which team shouted about it longer. After agreeing the rules we went back to our respective camps and began. The game would start when we all shouted "waaarrrr" at the same time and then began shooting or lobbing grenades.

We had a couple of what you might call warm-up battles. It was a way of getting used to the terrain and what each member was capable of so that we could balance up the teams for the final showdown. Fluff was so named because he was short and clumsy with a big mop of fluffy blond hair and blue eyes. He always looked scruffy and in need of a good scrub but ironically he didn't stink. He had an agreeable manner and very rarely lost his cool. Chip you have already met. Stomp was so-called because he used to stamp his leg when he got angry like some villain in a pantomime. He was short, like Fluff, but had straight black hair and large eyebrows that very nearly met in the middle. He had a wiry frame, could never sit still for long and his temper flared several times a day but never amounted to much and was forgotten as quickly as it had started. Piggy or Scoff as he was sometimes known was tall and large-framed, not exactly fat but you could tell he would have trouble keeping the weight off for most of his life. He had short cropped brown hair and large pink cheeks on a kind and happy face. He always laughed at jokes, even if they weren't particularly funny but you never got the impression it was false or exaggerated. Last but not least was Bongo. His full nickname was Beagley-Beagley-Disco-Beagley-Taurus-A-

Bongo and it was said with a little chant and a dance. We soon shortened it to Bongo. I have absolutely no idea how his name came about but rumour had it that Fluff once said it off-the-cuff and it seemed to stick. That doesn't surprise me as Fluff could be quite a surreal kid at times. He owned a Chopper bike which he named "Algebra Tony" so, thinking about it, he was probably responsible for Bongo's nickname. Bongo was as tall as Piggy but a slimmer frame with massive hands and feet. He favoured his hair with the short crop look and his dark hair was in contrast to his pale skin. His broad nose and full lips made him look like a boxer but he never got involved in any fighting, which was just as well because he was ridiculously strong.

We decided that for the final battle Chip would change sides and I would get Bongo. I stayed in my original camp and so we gathered more piles of clay lumps for grenades. It was during this process that Bongo found a brand new flashing workman's road lamp. It was bright yellow and everyone wanted to take it home. It was agreed that the winning team would take the lamp and then decide who would keep the lamp for the first month. The truth was whoever took the item first would usually end up keeping it permanently. And so the battle of the flashing road light began. After a brief plan, the cry rang out.

"Waaarrrr," we shouted. My team launched three grenades from the off screaming "grenades" as we threw them. As soon as we let go, Bongo scrambled to the right, Fluff went left and I jumped over the top and headed for cover shooting as I went. Bongo dived into the mound of sand while Fluff took up position behind one of the digger tyres – I made for the trench. We just got there before the others began shooting.

Chip saw me enter the trench and so threw a few grenades but I ducked from sight and scrambled a few yards forward. The grenades never touched me, honest. I took a peek above the top of the trench and saw Stomp trying to sneak his way around the back of the mounds along a line of bushes in order to surprise Bongo. Piggy did a dramatic dive over his camp's top wall, rolled down the other side and came up shooting at Fluff who had now left the wheel and was pelting towards my trench. I leaped out and tried to make one of the shed's walls but Chip was already shooting his way towards the same shed so I changed my angle and tried to make the pile of ballast but Bongo suddenly turned his fire on me before I got my shot off. I made this outrageous movement as though I had been shot in the chest and crashed to the floor – dead – but only for thirty seconds. I got up after about twenty and made for cover. It was stalemate for a while. We all threw a few grenades and fired some shots but nobody wanted to break cover. I could no longer see Chip at the shed so I kept low and made it behind a pile of blocks about ten feet from the east side of the wooden shack. Suddenly Chip appeared on the roof of the shed and threw a grenade at Fluff. He hadn't seen me. I jumped up and shot him four times before he even pointed his gun at me. He clutched his chest, wavered for a second (we had all stopped to watch) and then fell forward and rolled off the roof and onto a pile of sand about five feet below. It looked fantastic and we all burst out laughing and gave him a small round of applause. He lay still for a while then re-joined the war. And so it continued. At one point I think we were all wounded and were limping everywhere. Stomp went into a bit of a fit because apparently Bongo was not "taking his shots" but was placated when Chip got him with a grenade. Fluff panicked when his paper caps got jammed and Stomp was charging towards him but then Bongo leaped over the sand and shot Stomp from behind. Fluff got his gun working again, took three paces and then fell over just as Stomp recovered from his death and promptly shot Fluff as he lay sprawled out face down in the grass. A brief moment of manic gunfire and grenade throwing and it was all over. The battle of the flashing road light was won. Chip's crew had clearly killed and wounded more than we had so they were declared the winners. Stomp claimed dibs on the light first and then we all made our way back to my house for orange squash and biscuits.

We sat outside under the veranda and talked through the events of the war. We all agreed that Chip did the best death dive and that my gun was the best they had ever seen.

I had some seriously great friends back then who not only made the summers memorable but had helped to shape the person I am now. We never really fell out I guess, we just drifted away from each other as new people entered our lives as we grew older, but I think back to those early days, the boys from the battle of the flashing road light, and my heart swells with pride for being able to call them my friends.

It must have been a week later; Chip came down to see me. We hung about the house for a while and then decided to head back over the road to where the previous battle took place and do a bit of exploring. The site was exactly the same as we left it and so we started exploring at the far end where we hadn't really been. A six-foot chain link fence had been erected to form an open compound. To the right was a series of large concrete drain pipes stacked three high in a kind of flat top pyramid shape. We crawled in and out of these for a while picking up grazed knees and then moved on. Behind the pipes we found a long rusty metal container without a lid. There were several boxes inside and we got quite excited when we thought we had found one full of money. It turned out to be small metal discs, like washers, but without the holes in. We had no idea what they were for but we took a couple each and put them in our pockets. We moved round to the other side of the compound and saw that several trees had been cut down and sawn up for logs then stacked in a way similar to the concrete pipes. Chip kicked at a log and a snake shot out and disappeared into the long grass. I think we both left the ground by about three feet and I refused to go anywhere near the logs again. We started to make our way back past the first camp we had made, over the mounds of sand and ballast until we came to the shed. The shed itself was wedge-shaped with a flat roof made from corrugated metal sheets with walls constructed from slatted timber. The south wall, the lowest side, had a windowless opening and the east side had a rickety wooden slatted door. Inside, the shed had one dividing wall that looked like it was once a pen for a pig or goat. There was a faint smell of urine and dung that became stronger depending on where you stood. The floor was made of rough concrete and covered in various bits of timber, the odd nail or screw and a wrinkled newspaper was stuffed in a gap between the wall and the roof. Chip kicked over a few bits of timber and discovered an old wooden-handled claw hammer. Apart from its age it looked in good order. We examined everywhere more closely after the discovery but found nothing more of interest.

"How did you get up on the roof last week?" I asked Chip.

"I'll show you." He led me out of the shed and across the front where the sand had piled up under the window down past the other side and to the rear. A branch of a large oak hung just over the roof at the back and a fence post was nailed to the trunk. Loose wire draped sadly down from the post and was connected to another post farther back. Chip threw the hammer onto the roof and it made a loud clang as it landed on the corrugated tin. He put his foot on the post and in one swift movement jumped up, grabbed the branch above his head and swung his knee up onto the roof. He made it look so damn simple. I copied his exact movements and, to my surprise, found it much easier than I thought it would be. We sat on the roof and I found the slope was steeper than it looked from below and I had to keep the soles of my running shoes flat against the roof's decking to stop myself from sliding down. We just sat in silence for a while enjoying the view of the battleground and the sun on our faces.

"You know when we went fishing in the ditch at the beginning of the holiday?" said Chip quietly.

"Yes, it was great."

"Well… I kissed Bess." I heard what he said; I understood what he said but the shock of him saying it sent my mind spinning. Had he known all this time that I'd seen him? Had he seen me kiss Bess as well? Why was he telling me? I did not know how to react.

"Did you?" I said trying to get the right mix of slight surprise and nonchalance at the same time.

"Yes. It was when you caught that red-throater, just before we walked her home." Chip looked at me and offered a smile but I sensed a hint of worry behind it; it was also inconclusive, like he wanted to say more.

"What happened?" I asked. What I really meant to ask was "why did it happen?"

"We were having a wrestle and I was pretending to try and throw her down the bank into the water, you know the bit where that open part is in the trees?" I nodded. "Well, we were struggling and then, well, it just kind of happened."

"What, you suddenly kissed her?" I wasn't trying to make the question sound like an accusation but I guess I wanted to know who kissed whom. For me that was important.

"No. I didn't kiss her and she didn't kiss me, we just sort of kissed each other if you know what I mean?" I nodded like I knew exactly what he meant but the trouble was I could remember how Bess and I kissed. She definitely made the move towards me first but maybe, to someone looking in from the outside, it could have looked like we did it at the same time but that didn't mean we *did* do it at the same time. Chip was describing it like that; like someone from the outside looking in. But Chip was on the inside so either he made the first move or she did.

"So are you boyfriend and girlfriend now?"

"Oh shit no, no way!" he said in sudden and overly dramatic way. "I haven't seen her since. Anyway, I don't like her like that?"

"Don't you?" I said with genuine surprise.

"No, no way. No, what I mean is, she's pretty and everything but it's Bess, you know? She's a mate. Not like you're a mate, but we hang about and stuff. I just, oh, I don't know." He began to pull the laces on his monkey boots and we went silent again. I was pleased he didn't think of Bess in the same way as I did but I couldn't understand why he was telling me now. It was nearly five weeks ago, we would be back in school in another week or so. Maybe that was it? Maybe he wanted to tell me now in case it came up in school. Maybe he thought Bess might have said something about kissing Chip and he wanted to give me the story first, get the facts straight or something? I was thinking things through when the next thing he said made me nearly slide off the roof.

"She really likes you, you know?" I span round and had to put my hands down hard on the tin to stop myself from copying Chip's dramatic dying fall.

"What are you talking about? What's she said? Has she said anything to you then?" I suddenly realised I had blown my earlier attempt at feigning nonchalance and it would be too damn obvious to backtrack now. I doubt whether I could have hidden my excitement even if I knew what was coming.

"Well, it's just, you know, her saying that she thinks you're sort of cool?"

"What do you mean?"

"What do you mean, *what do you mean*? She said she thinks you're cool, you know?"

"I know what cool means, Chip. What I mean is, does she mean cool as in, you know, cool, or does she mean *cool*, you know, as in she likes me?" Chip laughed and shook his head.

"Listen, we were just talking about stuff and things and I said what a good mate you were and everything and then she said that she thought you were cool."

"But that doesn't mean she *likes* me. I bet she thinks you're cool as well, like a cool mate."

"No, it wasn't like that. It wasn't like she came out and said 'I really like Don', it was over a whole time when we were talking, bits and pieces."

"When was this? Not the time we went fishing? Or was it when I went to make the sandwiches?"

"No, it was at school."

"When?"

"The day before the day we broke up for the holidays. You had to go home before the lunch break because you had to go to the dentist, remember?"

"Oh yes, I remember." I seemed to have spent my whole childhood at the dentist. Every time I went for a check-up they said I had to go back for a filling.

"So it was at lunch break. She said you were cool and that she really liked you but not in all one go, you know, spread out."

"So you think she likes me then?"

"Yes."

"Cool." Chip started to tap the tin roof with the hammer which I guess signalled the end of that conversation. I sat next to him with all the happy and nervous thoughts about seeing Bess again. I made up my mind to call her when I got home but what happened an hour or so later kind of put that right out of my mind.

Chip had spotted a piece of ply wood about three feet by two. It was slightly cracked and bleached by the sun but he thought it would do fine and of course he would be the first to try it out. He took the ply onto the roof's highest point, sat on it and held onto the branch until he was ready, then he let go. He shot down the roof and landed safely on the heap of sand below the shed's window. Then it was my turn. I copied his pre-flight procedure, let go of the branch and, like Chip, landed safely. We did this half a dozen times each and then Chip began to experiment; first on his knees, then standing up. It was tremendous fun. On a couple of occasions my landing wasn't exactly elegant and I ended up rolling down the other side of the sand heap with arms and legs thrashing about madly in the air. We were both on the roof contemplating the idea of finding another sheet of ply and then trying it side by side when a voice shouted to us from somewhere below.

"What do you think you are doing?" We both looked to the side and saw a man standing just a little distance from the shed's door. He was tall with straight, shoulder-length greasy hair, about the same age as my brother, early twenties. He wore a denim jacket and jeans that looked as though they hadn't seen the inside of a washing machine for a couple of weeks and his feet were clad in brown, eighteen-hole boots.

"We're just messing around," I said cautiously, thinking we were doing something wrong.

"Get down from there right now!" he demanded, pointing to the floor beside him. As we climbed down I wondered whether he was one of the builders or perhaps owned one of the diggers and he had come to kick us off the site. We walked around to where he was standing and he was much taller than I first thought, he was well over six feet. He swung the shed door open and stepped to the side. "Get inside," he said in the same demanding, angry voice. Something immediately didn't feel right but I was too scared to react. We went into the shed and stood with our backs to the window with both our hands clasped together in the same way you stood in front of a teacher when you were about to be told off. He stood about five feet away with his back to the door. At first he said nothing; his eyes were just scanning the floor as if he was looking for something in particular. Then he stopped and stared at us individually for a few seconds as if he was studying us in some way.

"Now, what were you doing on the roof?" His voice held less anger, more even, quieter, but somehow that seemed worse. I took a quick glance a Chip and could see he was as scared as I was.

"We were just sliding down on some wood into the sand." I turned slightly and pointed to the heap outside the opening as if to reinforce the truth.

"Why?" Chip and I looked at each other and shrugged our shoulders.

"Just for fun," I said. He then looked at both of us again the way he did before but this time he seemed to be studying our clothes. There was definitely something about him that was wrong. I couldn't put my finger on it but it seemed as if he was kind of lost.

"What are they doing with all this stuff?" he asked indicating all the machinery and sand.

"I don't know," I said. For some reason I had become the unelected spokesman. He slowly bent down and picked up a piece of timber. It was about three feet long, two inches wide and an inch thick and on the end I could see a rusty bent nail. He pointed the stick at Chip and then asked him the same question.

"I don't know," said Chip and I could hear the tremor in his voice.

"I'm going to ask you again," he said, now pointing the stick at me. "What are they going to do here?"

"I think they might be building some houses but I don't really know, honest," replied Chip.

"Maybe it's a bridge over the railway lines or a tunnel, I heard something like that," I said. The man went silent again as if he was digesting the information. Sweat ran down the sides of the man's face and the smell of urine seemed to increase in the heat of the shed.

"Where do you live?" he asked looking at me.

"Up the road," I said. He turned to look at Chip.

"And you?"

"Up the road," said Chip. My house was less than a hundred yards from the shed and I don't know why I said it was up the road. Looking back, maybe it was because I didn't want him to know exactly where I lived; he may have decided to come to my house. I think by telling him I lived some way away I made a mistake because when I told him, I could see him nod his head ever-so-slightly and the corner of his eyes lifted as though he was smiling to himself.

"We should go home now," I said.

"Shut up!" He lifted the stick towards me and took half a step closer.

"We should have been home ages ago," I said.

"I said shut up!" Then he hit me across the face with the stick. It was not a full swing, more of a hard tap. I put my hand to my stinging cheek and tears began to well up. "When I tell you something, you do it." Anger was back with a vengeance and his eyes were wide but oddly distant; it seemed like he was here but not here. "I want both of you to pull your trousers down and your pants then turn around, spread your legs and lean on the window sill, got it?" I remember thinking what a strange thing to ask us. I could not imagine why he wanted us to do it but something deep inside, a feeling more than knowledge, that this was wrong, out of place and that whatever happens, I should not do as he asked. I shook my head but kept silent. He hit me with the wood again. It was a little harder this time but still well short of a full blow. "You," he said, pointing the stick at Chip. "Do as I say." I looked at Chip and he shook his head as well. Then the man struck Chip with similar force. Tears were rolling down our cheeks but we weren't sobbing. "Take your trousers and your pants down and face me. Open your legs and put your hands behind your back." I thought by saying this, he wanted to hit us between our legs with the stick or kick us. I shook my head again and the stick came up and struck again, same force same cheek. Turning his attention to Chip, the same process followed: order, refusal and then the stick. "Put your hands down by your sides," he ordered. Chip started to move as if he was finally complying. The man's eyes shot to Chip and then looked down at Chip's groin. Chip suddenly brought his hands back together. Hit. He looked at me and I did not move a muscle. Hit. The man was breathing hard as if he had just stopped running and then he lifted his gaze between us and out of the window. He was biting his bottom lip and frowning and then, all of a sudden, his face went completely blank and his eyes kind of glazed over. He stood that way, blank and unmoving for about a minute and then took a few steps back, dropped the timber and went out of the door but he didn't go away.

"Come out of there," he said in a shallow calm voice. We cautiously moved towards the opening, me first, then Chip. We got to the door and he stood aside and we walked slowly out and faced him. The coolness of outside compared to inside the shed was dramatic and my skin tingled with the chill. "Right you two, go home and never come back here again, you understand?"

"Yes," we said together. As if a starter pistol had gone off, we sprang forward and charged towards my house. As I approached I could see my brother's car in the drive next to my Dad's. I think I only half-checked to see if there were any cars coming on the road because we hardly broke stride when we crossed. I fumbled for my front door key and burst through into the lounge. To my surprise, my uncle was there talking with my Dad and brother. Dad took one look at us.

"What the hell happened to you?" he said, concern strewn across his face. The tears were still falling but now, in the safety of my home and family, the sobbing flowed up and over into my words. It took us about two minutes to explain what had just happened between the tears and the sobbing. We pointed to the shed across the road.

"Show us," said my father and then all three shot out of the front door and pelted towards the shed, followed by us. My brother got there first and burst through the shed door but the man had gone. We all stood around looking while I gave them a description. Suddenly Chip shouted and pointed.

"Look! There he is!" Chip was pointing to a paddock behind the shed which was south of the ditch. The man was on the other side and heading to the bushes in the field opposite. Dad said he was going back to call the police and my brother and uncle took up the pursuit. We made it across the field in good time but the ditch took some negotiating to find a clear spot to get across. On the other side we looked about. There were several large patches of bush that were dotted all over the field. My uncle went one way and Chip and I went with my brother. We searched for maybe five minutes and then I spotted him. The man was heading for the railway tunnels at the ditch. We called my uncle and headed off after him again. I had to show my brother the way to get to the tunnels. We had to cross the ditch again, climb up the railway embankment, skirt the sides and then down a small gap between some bushes and then drop to the mouth of the tunnels. They were constructed from brick and the stream was diverted into both tunnels. The water was low enough so that you could sort of take a couple of steps and then jump to the other side and back again in a zigzag fashion until you got to the end. Chip and I were used to doing this but my brother seemed not to care about keeping his feet dry. He thundered down the right-hand tunnel kicking up ditchwater as he went. At the end, the ditch converged again and the stream continued. To the right there was a grass bank that led to a holiday camp. We climbed onto the grass but we could see the man had completely disappeared among the hundreds of caravans.

"Let's go back," said my brother. We headed back down the tunnels. My uncle had stayed on the other side and as we entered he shouted down to us.

"Did you get him?" His echo was bouncing around the damp bricks.

"No," said my brother. "The fucking bastard got away." We climbed up the bank and headed into the paddock. Outside my home I could see two police cars and then two policemen walking towards us. My brother told them where we had chased the man and I gave a brief description again. The policeman spoke into a radio and repeated what we had said then one of the police cars sped off up the road. Back at my house the policeman said that someone from CID would be along in about an hour to question us and then they jumped into their car and followed the other up the road. Chip called his Mum who came down immediately and we waited for CID. Eventually two men arrived in suits – cups of tea were made – they turned down the opportunity for cake – and they then began their questions. The shock of it all had subsided and was replaced with giggling from us and a degree of patience from the two officers. We told them exactly what had happened and I remember having a feeling that we had somehow done something wrong but the two men seemed satisfied that we had given a full account and said they would be in touch if they had any developments to report. I had one more visit the following day, but then we never saw the police again.

Two months later we were having a family meal and I happened to notice about six or seven blokes walk past the house on the opposite side of the road. In the middle was the bad man. I jumped up and pointed him out. My brother flew from the table, closely followed by my Dad and charged straight across the road, grabbed the man around the throat and began to throttle him. Such was the anger emanating from my brother that the other men just stood back, looking at each other in bewilderment. Had my Dad not intervened then I think the man would be dead. My brother dragged him to his feet and promised more of the same if he came anywhere near me or my friends again. The matter was now closed. I guess attitudes were different back then. If the incident had happened in today's climate there would have been a much greater response from the authorities, but times change.

Chapter 17

After receiving Beth's letter of thanks for the Walnut Whips, I wrote back, in the same style, and accepted her invitation to the Norfolk fair. For the next three weeks we corresponded by letter continuing the same theme – no email and no phone calls. It was fun and quirkily romantic. In my last letter to her before the fair I wrote:

... and if all goes well, I shall be arriving in due course within the carriage of the great iron horse on the eve of the fair at a quarter of the clock past the seventh hour. If you are unable to attend my arrival I will be glad to take a carriage to your home.

Your ever humble and devoted servant
Master Don England.

I had a flash of inspiration and decided to surprise her by stepping off the train dressed in an early 19th-century costume. I hired the garb complete with top hat, a silver-tipped black cane and a canvas travel bag. The ticket inspector seemed impressed. I stepped onto the platform at Norwich train station, donned my top hat, passed through the ticket barrier and headed for the main entrance. I stepped outside and then stopped suddenly. Standing on the pavement looking directly at me was Beth dressed in a satin 19th-century wire dress complete with a lace bonnet. We took a second to register each other and then collapsed into laughter.

"Hang on," I said when I eventually took control of myself. "Let's start again." I walked back inside the terminal, waited a few seconds and then walked out.

"Good evening, Mistress Harris," I said doffing my hat, offering a slight bow and trying to keep a straight face.

"Good evening to you Master England," she replied with a slight curtsy and offered her hand which I took and lightly kissed. "I hope your journey was a pleasant one?"

"Indeed, Madam, it was comfortable and without incident."

"Our carriage is this way," she said indicating the short-stay car park. She took my arm as we walked towards the car. "I hope sir has not already eaten as I thought we might venture a curry and a few pints of wife beater?"

"I have not eaten, Madam, and look forward to the exotic fare."

"May I be so bold Sir to say that you look like a right fucking twat in that hat?"

"You may indeed, Madam; I have always admired your honesty. And if I am allowed a small observation of my own, I would say that your arse most definitely looks big in that tent." We could keep it up no longer and collapsed laughing again. I threw my arms around her and we hugged.

"I can't believe we both had the same idea," I said as I slid into the passenger seat.

"Actually, it was Jane who came up with the idea." Jane was Beth's house mate. Beth owned a small two-bed terraced cottage that she had bought two years ago and Jane, whom she had known since school, moved in to help pay the mortgage. At the cottage, we changed into our normal clothes and walked into the village for a pint at The Three Cups and then on to the Indian restaurant. Our conversation was easy and natural – we felt comfortable with each other and talked about anything and everything.

Jane was there when we arrived at the cottage. She was shorter than Beth, slim frame, shoulder-length blonde hair, bright blue eyes and sharp features. We recounted our meeting at the station, Beth popped a bottle of wine and I rolled a joint at her request and then we sat in the lounge listening to music and chatting. The cottage was tastefully decorated; the walls were painted in pastel shades of green and cream. The lounge had an open working fireplace and two armchairs were either side of a three-seater sofa all in cream fabric. The kitchen was modern and was big enough to accommodate a round table and four chairs. The first floor contained two double bedrooms and a bathroom with a chrome shower over the bath.

At about midnight, Jane said goodnight and went upstairs. When she had gone, Beth lay on the sofa with her head on my lap and I had a sudden sense of *Déjà vu* and I remembered the incident with Sue four weeks before. We finished the wine and then Beth patted my arm and sat up.

"I'll bring down your bedding – are you going to be all right on here?" she said apologetically.

"Of course I will." She smiled and kissed me full on the lips. It was a kiss that said we are not yet boyfriend and girlfriend but we are more than just friends and let's see where this goes. It has always amazed me how much information can be communicated through a simple kiss.

I was woken gently with a cup of tea.

"Morning, sleep well?" Beth was wearing a towelling blue dressing gown and big fluffy slippers.

"Christ yes. This is very comfortable."

"I know, I've often fallen asleep in front of the TV and woken up in the early hours of the morning." She bent down and gave me the same kiss as the night before. "What do you want for breakfast?"

"Toast and coffee for me please, slave."

"Right you are." I had a quick shower and then sat down at the kitchen table with a couple of slices of toast and fresh coffee while Beth tucked into a bowl of muesli. After we had finished eating she said she was going to have a quick shower and then we would head off for the fair. I washed up the dishes and then folded away the bedding placing it on one of the armchairs. She came downstairs dressed in faded jeans, a white shirt and carried a lightweight, black leather jacket. After a few moments of checking her bag, looking for her keys, mobile phone and checking her bag again, we went out the door and jumped into her Astra sports car and headed off to the fair.

We were ushered by an attendant in a long white coat and reflective yellow bib to a parking slot on a field already packed with cars. We followed the line of people through a gap in a hedge and into a massive field filled with an array of farm equipment, stalls, burger bars, fairground rides, antique cars, sheep and cows in temporary pens and so much more. Music was piped through a series of trumpet-shaped speakers set in groups of three on top of scaffold tubes. The music had a tinny quality to it and occasionally was interrupted by a man's voice with a heavy Norfolk accent announcing that some event or other was about to start or could someone move their car. We took a slow walk around stopping occasionally at a stall or something of interest. After about twenty minutes I heard an announcement that "It's a Knockout" would shortly start over in the blue field. We both agreed it was a must and started to head over and as we walked we held hands. It somehow felt natural as if we had been doing the same thing for years. The blue field contained a roped-off area filled with an assortment of brightly covered obstacles for the two teams to negotiate. There was a large crowd gathered but we managed to squeeze our way to the front. The announcer said that the two teams competing were The Norfolk Knockers against The Suffolk Stuffers. Each team was made up from the respective police forces and consisted of five women and five men in each team. The idea was for one team to negotiate around the obstacles dressed in huge foam farmer outfits and attempt to fill up a long, clear plastic tube at the end of the run with coloured water collected from various points along the way. The other team's job was to try and put them off by knocking them over using giant swinging balls. The event was to raise money for charity and several people with buckets came round collecting cash. It was genuinely hilarious and before long I had tears in my eyes from laughing and was delighted to see that Beth was in a similar state. It was a close run thing but in the end, much to the embarrassment of the locals, Suffolk Stuffers were declared the victors. We moved away with the crowd and my suggestion of a hot dog was well received. Next to one of the burger vans was a large tent with several stalls selling home-made jewellery. Beth wanted to have a look and I said as there was a queue for food I would get the hotdogs and meet her there. When I got to the front of the line I realised I didn't know whether Beth wanted mustard as well as ketchup or just ketchup; my first real test. In the end I got one of each. As I entered the tent I saw one of the stall owners hand Beth some change and then she placed whatever item she had bought in her handbag.

"Spending your money already?"

"You were not meant to see that," she said.

"I didn't think they sold Rampant Rabbits at these places, did you get the batteries as well?"

"God, you are so rude, now I am offended, sir, and your only way to redeem yourself is to hand over a hot dog immediately."

"OK, I have ketchup and mustard or just ketchup?"

"Which do you prefer?"

"I'm not fussed."

"Neither am I?"

"I think you're fibbing."

"So are you."

"OK," I said. I placed the hotdogs behind my back and pretended to swap them about. "Which hand?"

"Left." I handed her the one with both sauces.

"Oh," she said disappointedly and cast down the corners of her mouth.

"Go on, have the other one."

"No, I was joking."

"OK, but I wanted that one."

"Then you have it."

"No, I was joking." Then a voice to our right intervened.

"Please eat them or I'll have to arrest you." We turned and realised the voice belonged to a policeman. We laughed.

"On what charge, officer?" asked Beth.

"Under the 1990 Banter over Hot Dog Act, section two, paragraph three. It carries a maximum penalty of five years' hard arguing."

"Right, come on, Beth, you heard the policeman," I said and we began to eat.

"Now run along," said the policeman.

"Yes, officer," said Beth. Who said the police do not have a sense of humour?

We took in a few more stalls and then hit the rides. She won a fluffy panda at one of those shooting galleries and she insisted I carry it for the rest of the day as she had won it for me and his name was Gavin. We found the beer tent and sat down for a couple of lagers – Gavin had crisps. A long line of restored vintage cars were on display and I spotted a beautiful Mark 1 Jaguar for sale for twenty-three thousand.

"If you loved me you would buy me that," said Beth.

"If you loved *me* you will never mention it again."

"Touché!"

We decided to go. Beth held my hand on the way back to the car and I held Gavin's.

"Fancy going out for pizza tonight?" I suggested.

"Yes, OK. There's a Pizza Hut in town or there's a small Italian in Bacton."

"Where's that?"

"The next village up from me."

"OK, will we have to book?"

"I guess so; I'll call when we get in."

When we arrived back at the cottage, Jane was in the garden bringing in some washing. We told her of our day.

"What you up to tonight?" said Beth to Jane.

"I was going out with Toni but she cancelled so I am just going to chill."

"We're going for a pizza, why don't you come with us?" I asked.

"Oh no, don't worry about me." I could tell she felt disappointed about Toni, whoever that was.

"No, come along," said Beth.

"Yes," I said. "I've had to put up with Beth all day so come along." Beth hit me.

"No, you two should…"

"That's settled you're coming."

"OK, thanks." Beth booked the table and we all showered and headed off to Bacton. We found a good pub that advertised live music later on that night, had a couple of liveners and then went to eat. Jane was good company and we all exchanged stories and jokes and generally had a very pleasant evening. We had a joint on the way back to the pub and felt pretty giggly when we arrived. The live music back at The Cock & Pheasant had to be seen to be believed. It consisted of a blind pianist who kept knocking his drink over and wore a wig that simply did not fit, and a singer/bass player who constantly forgot the words or simply just made them up. I have not laughed like that in years; Beth was almost choking and Jane had to run to the toilet. We found out later it was all an act and a brilliant one at that. What an evening. We called the cab and got back to the cottage at about two in the morning after a lock-in by the landlord and Jane staggered straight to bed while I made mine up again on the sofa. I was already under the duvet when Beth came down to say goodnight.

"That was very sweet of you asking Jane to come out with us tonight," she said sitting on the side of the sofa.

"She's good company." Beth leaned forward and gave me a kiss and this time it said: I really want to go further and if you grab my arse I might not be able to stop myself so I will pull away before you do.

"Night, sweet prince," she said

"May angels sing you to your rest," I replied.

"Not too fucking loud I hope." She switched off the light on the way out and I heard her soft footsteps climb the stairs, and then her bedroom door closing and I wished I was in there with her.

Jane cooked breakfast the next day as a way of thanking us for the evening.

"So do you think you will get published?" asked Jane.

"Well, I hope so. I've been rejected by four of the main publishers so I just might try some of the smaller, more provincial ones. It's a long process because you can't simply send loads of copies out, they will just get binned. You have to do a bit of research first to see if they have any authors on their books with a similar audience to yourself and then make a list. It's always polite to tell them who you've sent them to previously as well." Jane was at university reading law. She was in her final year and hoped to become a solicitor.

"It's never easy going for the things you want," she said.

"Try we must," said Beth clearing away the dishes. I suddenly became aware that I was falling for Beth in a big way. I know all about the honeymoon period and all that but somehow this felt different from all the other relationships I'd had. There was something earthy and real about Beth, a connection at ground level that seemed to communicate a sense of well-being and mutual understanding. It was with a heavy heart when she dropped me off at the station because I did not want to go home. She walked me to the platform and I could see my train was due to leave in ten minutes.

"I had such a good weekend," I said turning to face those hazel eyes.

"Me too." I put my arms around her.

"It's your turn to come down to London."

"Oh, you want to see me again then?"

"No, but I'm very polite."

"How can I refuse an offer like that?"

"I'll call you."

"OK, but can we still write. I like the letters we send each other."

"OK, I will write and call."

"OK then."

"OK." I held her face in my hands and kissed her long and passionately.

"Just as well you didn't do that last night," she said. "I don't think my virtue would be intact now."

"And what about my virtue?"

"Your virtue is in the fact that you *didn't* kiss me like that last night. A girl likes a bloke who can wait."

"I'd better get the train," I said and we kissed again. She reached into her bag and pulled out an envelope and a small paper bag folded into a small square. "What's this?"

"A present, wait until you get on the train."

"Thank you." I picked up my bag and gave her a wave before getting on the train. Three minutes later it pulled away from the station. I opened the envelope and inside was a letter in familiar prose.

My dear Don,

I would like to say that it is so rare to meet a Gentleman of such fine quality and good virtue that I feel maybe the devil is playing his tricks with my senses. Your company this weekend has been, at the very worst, a delightful and exquisite distraction. You, sir, are the kind of Gentleman that possesses the faculties to affect a Lady of my good standing in such a way that night seems day and day seems night. I must stop there for it is not becoming for a Lady to go on so. I do hope when next we meet I will find you, as I have left you, in good humour and fine spirit. I would like for you to accept this small token of my deepening affection and as a memento of your time here.

Yours with fluttering heart
Beth

I opened the paper bag to find a silver chain with a tiny silver pendant attached.

The pendant was a quill inside a pot of ink. I am still wearing it today.

Chapter 18

I got off the swing and made my way back to the Jeep and felt how one's concept of time differed so dramatically from the days of my childhood compared to now. Then the six-or-so-week summer break seemed to go on forever. In fact, time seemed to amble by then, like some old man shuffling from shop to shop, stopping at each window to take in the individual prices of each item for sale before moving on to the next. Now, and ironically, as one's age increases, it seems that time has become a well-honed athlete sprinting past the shops without pausing for a single glance at anything. I turned the Jeep back on to the main road and decided to take the scenic route to the seaside rather than through town. I headed up the road so I would pass the new graveyard on my right and the old one, with the small church, on the left. It was as I drove by the old graveyard that I suddenly remembered a small adventure we had on one autumnal evening many years ago.

Chapter 19

11 YEARS OLD
GHOSTS

I have always regarded religion as the biggest perpetual con since some hairy missing link decided to stand upright and wonder what kind of animal takes a massive bite out of the moon. Then, another hairy missing link discusses it with the first, and they agree that it must be something infinitely powerful, have large teeth and if they don't hack up several sabre-toothed ducks and bleed them over a flat stone, then something seriously bad could happen to the rest of the missing link clan while nut gathering on a Sunday afternoon – thus organised religion begins – and I really, really hate organised religion. Don't misunderstand me, I have no problem with people believing in any supreme being and take comfort in the notion of heaven for the good believer; in fact, I am extremely jealous of the fact that they have that ability of faith. I remember going to Sunday school once. The vicar and his assistant organised for us kids a series of stories about God, Jesus and his disciples and then we had to sit around a table with paper and poster paints and paint one of God's creatures. I refused to paint any animals because at the time I could only paint robots. Although the vicar never articulated the fact that I was going to burn in the furnaces of hell for ever, I got the distinct impression he was none too happy with my Barry the robot and his death ray eyes. I guess he felt my soul could not be saved because I never went again. I have always believed, somewhat naively, that I reached my conclusions about God and religion independently from my parents. My mother was agnostic but my father generally reserved his loathing for the Roman Catholic Church. He grew up in Belgium sporting the rosette of the Protestant faith although I don't think my Grandparents were particularly religious. They moved home and consequently my father had to move to a new school which happened to be Roman Catholic. He had the shit beaten out of him every day by the other kids because they found out he was Protestant. He had no idea what a Protestant or a Roman Catholic was and so promptly changed his religion to stop the beatings. I say all this because as a child, like every child, I believed in ghosts and thoroughly enjoyed being scared out of my wits. I really never saw the connection between the spirits and the God thing.

Chip, Fluff, Stomp, Piggy and Bongo believed in ghosts and we had several old churches around our way to go ghost hunting – incidentally we never caught one, honest. There was one particular church which saw both my brother and my sister get married. It was old and the graveyard offered dark corners and a real general spookiness which helped build the tension required. Other places offered up myths and legends of headless this and moaning that but required a car to get to so those were out of the question. Chip had informed us at school that he had seen a panel missing in one of the large stone tombs in the old cemetery in my road. It was a Friday night and so we decided to meet up as soon as it got dark for a spot of ghost hunting and general spookiness. To our utter delight, the coming of darkness also brought with it a thick blanket of fog, and as we all know, ghosts and demons in general only come out when it's dark, foggy or stormy and a combination of all three is generally regarded as a cast iron guarantee for one of the buggers to make an appearance. Hammer House films did wonders to create the circumstances where demons walked the earth and those images became the benchmark for all things spooky. We agreed to meet at the swings and roundabout at six thirty and were to be dressed in dark clothing and armed with a good torch. Chip called at my house exactly at six thirty and we headed across the fog-bound field to meet the others. Fifteen minutes later we were all there looking like some bizarre hobbit SAS troupe. We sat around for a while telling each other macabre urban myth ghost stories just to get the blood truly chilled and one in particular was requested. This story I have heard repeated many times in films both here and abroad. It was the one where the young couple break down in the car on a country lane miles from anywhere. It was of course foggy or stormy, take your pick. The man instructs the woman to stay in the car while he goes off in search of help. He seems to be gone ages when several car headlights appear and stop short, facing the car. The woman looks through the windscreen but cannot make out who it is. Then she hears a man's voice call her name. It is a policeman who asks her to slowly get out of the car but not to look back. She opens the door and steps out of the car. She realises there are several policemen and they are beckoning her to move towards them slowly but on no account must she turn round. As she takes the first few steps she hears a dull, *thud, thud, thud* from behind. She turns slowly and discovers a man dressed as a monk holding a short timber stake on which her husband's head is skewered and he is banging it against the roof of the car. When I had told the story, Bongo seemed a little uneasy but he usually did on these occasions. The old cemetery was surrounded by an ornate six-foot metal railing with spikes on the top and two huge metal gates in a similar style. At the end of the railings, on the road side, there stood a red-brick house where the caretaker lived. His lounge window looked directly across the gates and we could see the side of his head and the light from his TV flickering in patterns across the glass. The gates had a simple slide-bar latch mechanism which wasn't secured. Chip slid the bar back and the gates opened without a creak, which was disappointing really but necessary for stealth reasons. We decided to take a general look around the churchyard before looking at the tomb. There were some seriously old gravestones that dated back to the latter half of the 17th century, their inscriptions barely visible from the years of erosion. Bongo spotted a black cat that disappeared through the slots in the railing and we argued whether it was good luck or bad but agreed, in the end, it was a positive sign that the ghosts would be out and about tonight. After half an hour of unconsciously augmenting the sensation of fear we decided to go and take a look at the tomb and its contents. The tomb was constructed of white stone with carved pillars at the corners and bevelled edges to the lid. We found the missing panel then Chip and I shone our torches into the tomb to discover a crypt underneath. In the centre, about seven feet down, was another tomb in white stone. Sitting on the top of the lid at the head of the tomb was an upturned glass bowl over a stone carving depicting a cluster of flowers. There seemed to be a shaft running down from the missing panel with a series of metal foot plates imbedded into the concrete similar to those found in deep man holes. We could only see two sides of the crypt because the shaft blocked our view of the left-hand side but we could ascertain that the room itself extended beyond our vision. We scanned the graveyard again to make sure the coast was clear. The fog had got worse and we could see for only about fifty yards; bloody fantastic!

"I'll stay up here and keep watch," said Bongo, his face taut with nerves. Bongo always volunteered to keep watch.

"Actually, I'll stay and keep watch," said Fluff holding up a bandaged wrist, the result of him falling off Algebra Tony again.

"But I always keep watch," he said looking to me for some kind of official adjudication.

"I can't climb down there with my wrist," said Fluff.

"Well, we can both keep watch," said Bongo nodding as if the matter was now closed.

"It's your turn to go down with us," said Chip checking that the head of his torch was screwed on properly.

"Yes," Stomp interjected. "You've not come with us on any hunts yet." Bongo's face clearly showed an edge of panic.

"We'll just pop down, have a quick look and then come straight back up," I said trying to offer him some reassurance.

"You're not scared are you?" said Stomp.

"No," said Bongo clearly lying.

"Well, that's that," said Chip. "I'll go first, and then Don, then Bongo, then Piggy and Fluff can keep a look out."

"Wait!" said Bongo.

"What?" said Chip.

"How do we get down?"

"There are some foot plates in the wall, it's easy." He began to step through the opening.

"Wait!" said Bongo.

"What?" said Chip.

"What if someone comes?"

"I'll give you a shout," said Fluff. Bongo shrugged his shoulders, clearly resigned to the fact that he would have to join us or completely lose face. Chip swung through the opening and began to descend. As soon as he was at the bottom I swung my legs through and followed him with the others close behind me. The crypt smelled damp, the walls were concrete and a thick layer of dust covered the floor and the lid of the tomb. We could see a bricked-up arch in the wall that had been hidden from view and towards the top there were a couple of bricks missing. Piggy stood on tip toes and shone his torch through.

"I think there is another crypt through there," he said, his voice reverberating off the stark walls. Chip gave the lid of the tomb a push to see if it would slide.

"Don't you fucking dare take that lid off!" said Bongo sharply.

"Relax," said Chip. "I just want to move it a bit, just for a quick peek inside."

"No!" said Bongo.

"Give me a leg up, Bongo," said Piggy. "I can't quite see into the next room." Bongo refused to move away from Chip. Stomp bent down and cupped his hands to make a foot hold. Piggy jumped up and shone the torch through the gap again.

"Bloody hell!" he said. "There is a really big room through there and I can see at least three tombs."

"Let's have a look," said Stomp. They changed positions and Stomp confirmed what Piggy had seen. We all wanted a look, all except Bongo. The room was at least twenty feet across and Piggy was correct: there were three other tombs all in a line similar in design to the one next to us.

"Come on, give me a hand," said Chip, his attention now back to shifting the lid of the tomb.

"Chip, no way," said Bongo again.

"I think Bongo's right," I said. "I think we should leave it."

"But we might find treasure," said Chip, his face very pale in the white of the torchlight. "I heard that sometimes people are buried with gold and stuff." The mention of gold seemed to gel our thoughts.

"Please, Chip," said Bongo. "We should not disturb the grave." Suddenly we all heard it – a deep moaning sound coming from the other room.

"What the fuck was that!" said Bongo. Piggy, who was nearest, turned his torch on the hole in the wall and slowly stood on tip toes and peered inside and, as he did, we heard the sound again, louder and more clear – it was more of a groan than a moan.

"Shit, there's a fucking nun in the corner!" shouted Piggy who dropped his torch. Then sheer, blind terror and panic gripped the lot of us and we all tried to get out at the same time; five of us all fighting to be up the shaft first. Chip was out in a blink of an eye, his monkey boots gripping air, Piggy was next, Stomp and I were scrabbling for third place and poor

Bongo was last. As we cleared the opening we were all laughing hysterically especially when we saw Bongo's ashen face appear.

"What the fuck's going on?" said Fluff.

"There's another crypt down there behind a brick wall," said Piggy catching his breath between giggles. "Then we heard this moaning from behind the wall. I looked through the hole in the wall and the moaning happened again and, I shit you not, there was a fucking nun standing in the corner of the room."

"A nun my arse," said Fluff.

"There bloody well was," said Piggy indignantly.

"We all heard the moaning," said Chip. We all nodded in agreement.

"What sort of moaning?" asked Fluff

"Well, it was more of a groan really."

"What like this…" said Fluff and then walked over to a green metal pipe sticking out of the ground with a wire cover on the top. He put his mouth to the wire and let out a deep moan.

"You complete fucking git!" said Bongo. Fluff just burst out laughing. Suddenly we heard a noise, like a *thump,* coming from the tomb. We all stopped, looked at each other for a split second, and then ran like lunatics out of the gate, across the road, through the fog and headed for the swings.

"What the fuck was that?" said Chip between gasps.

"I told you I saw a nun," said Piggy. We all looked back as if a nun would slowly emerge from the fog and take us all to Hell.

"What the fuck is that smell?" said Stomp and followed his nose to Bongo, who was looking very sheepish, and then noticed that the arse of his jeans looked wet.

"Bongo's shit himself!"

"I've got an upset stomach; I wasn't going to come out tonight…" We all held our noses in mock disgust and stepped away moaning about the stink.

"I'm going home," said Bongo. We all decided that it was getting late and said our goodbyes. Chip suggested we all go back the next night but he did not get a favourable response. I think we all liked to believe that there really was a ghost of a nun in that crypt, guarding the bones of the dead, but somehow we knew it was Piggy's imagination, fuelled by the foggy atmosphere and general spookiness that made the whole experience seem more than real. I bet I wasn't the only one that night who checked under the bed and in the cupboards before trying to go to sleep.

Chapter 20

After the Norfolk fair we continued to see each other. Every two weeks Beth would come and stay with me for a weekend and the alternate weeks I would stay with her. It took a month before we finally succumbed to each other and became intimate. I had often thought about what it would be like when we first made love and each scenario I had painted was different; my bedroom, her bedroom, my lounge floor, her lounge floor, the shower, the kitchen and so on until I thought I had exhausted all the possibilities. Along with my scenarios came the complicated emotions that swept before me, helping me to decide if this was the person I would want to spend the rest of my life with. Since my first real sexual encounter I realised that the actual act of sex changed one's perceptions, not just of one's self but the other person as well. That act of intimacy gave birth to a sudden realisation of depth and intensity of the feeling of love. It has often been said that in the early years of sexual discovery that love can be mistaken for lust but I think that is just an easy attempt to separate the two – maybe a legacy or hangover of religious dogma designed to make sex into something sinful so that sex, in itself, is sinful, unless it is carried out in accordance to an ever-changing social idea. Yet is it possible to separate the sexual act from love so that the physicality of sex has no adhesion to any deep emotion for the person involved?

One of the most complex mixtures of emotion and sexual desire to come to terms with is when there has been a betrayal or breakdown in a relationship. I remember I had been seeing a woman for just over two years. I certainly loved Trudy and she loved me. Eventually she felt that she could not commit to a lifelong relationship and so we split. She told me that eventually she would want to settle down and that she had met me too soon and that it was her and not me and that she still loved me and that she did not want be with anyone and maybe I was the person for her and she was making a terrible mistake and perhaps, in the future and… and… and. Because of certain circumstances and mutual friends we could not avoid seeing each other regularly and so it was difficult to purge my feelings for her. After a year I found out she had been seeing someone and the thought of her giving herself to someone sexually, other than me, turned my stomach into painful knots every time that image flicked into my mind. Yet, I could see myself having sexual encounters with someone other than Trudy without any difficulty. How can that be? How can I feel so deeply hurt by the concept of her with someone else and yet have no difficulty separating my sexual desire for another woman other than Trudy?

I remember my Granddad getting a fishing hook stuck in his back. The barb snapped off and it wasn't until a few years later that his body just pushed it back out again. Maybe that is what happens to love when combined with sexual intimacy. The hook may have left but the barb stays in until one's body eventually pushes it out and then, and only then, is one really free to go fishing again.

The barb from Trudy had long gone when I met Beth, however, the scar would always be there, a constant reminder of how emotionally dangerous it is to venture into a relationship and allow one's self to cast out into the sea without the fear of leaving a barb under the skin. I struggle here to share openly that moment with Beth but I feel somehow that it's necessary to help uncover the emotional foundations which I hope will help me come to terms with what I must do. When we finally made love, it was not like any of the scenarios I had painted in anticipation.

Because of work commitments I could not travel up on the Friday night as I would have done which meant that I would only get to spend one night with Beth. As the villages and fields passed by to the rhythm of the train my mood should have been light, easy and filled with the excitement of seeing Beth. However, I felt an unease of frustration and slight annoyance at the prospect of such a shortened visit but it was mainly due to the fact that not only would I be meeting her parents for the first time, but that we would both be staying in the family home and, of course, in separate bedrooms. I had got used to sharing with Beth even though we had not yet been intimate. She would wear her pyjamas and I would wear thin tracksuit bottoms; we would cuddle and kiss but not go any further. Staying at her parents was partly due to the fact that Jane, her house mate, was having her own parents over and so Beth had said that she could use her room. I tried to inject a feeling of positivity about the night ahead in an attempt to lift my mood. I was keen to meet her parents as it was an indication that I was becoming more than just an at-arm's-length boyfriend and so it was important to make the right impression. My malaise lifted instantly when I saw Beth's beaming smile waiting for me at the station's entrance.

"Are you ready for this?" she asked when we were in the car and on our way to her parents.

"As ready as I will ever be I guess. Any topic of conversation you would like me to avoid?"

"It might be a good idea not to talk about you or me smoking joints or reference to drugs of any recreational purpose."

"No drugs – got it."

"And you might not mention that we share my bed or your bed at weekends."

"OK, no talk of bed-sharing – got it."

"And don't offer me a cigarette because they don't know I smoke and you have to go outside if you want one."

"Smoke outside and don't offer you one – check. So can I mention that we run around naked, dressed as Klingons, prodding each other with pain sticks?"

"Oh yes, that's fine, they do that all the time."

"Good."

We pulled onto a large sweeping gravel drive in front of a fairly substantial clay-tiled cottage. I was removing my bag from the back seat as the front door opened. It has been my experience that whenever I have been introduced to a girlfriend's parents it is always, "Don, this is my Mum and Dad," and so I never know how to address them for the rest of the night; fortunately Beth did not. Her parents stood side by side outside the front door. Beth gave them a hug and a kiss.

"This is Don, Don, my mother, Julie, and my father, Tom." I extended my hand and they each shook it with a warm smile and a simple, "pleased to meet you, Don." I was told to leave my bag in the hall and was given a quick tour of the house. The lounge was large but comfortably decorated and within keeping with the age of the cottage. It had an open brick inglenook fireplace and the walls were painted in an off-white emulsion with a hint of peach. Several watercolours depicting rural scenes were scattered about interspersed with photographs of Beth and other members of the family. I had been told that Tom was a retired cabinetmaker/joiner and I guessed that most of the furniture had been made by him. The dining room was occupied by a long central table surrounded by ten chairs and the walls held the same mixture of paintings and photographs. The kitchen had a slate tiled floor and an old-fashioned but new-looking stove surrounded by solid pine cupboards and wooden work surface. The rear of the kitchen opened into a substantial, double-glazed PVC conservatory filled with an assortment of plants and a four-piece wicker suite. The conservatory looked onto a large brick patio and mature garden with a designed array of shrubs and plants and, at the bottom, a long shed which I suspected was Tom's workshop. I was quickly shown the toilet under the stairs and then we headed to the first floor and shown the bathroom and bedrooms including the one allocated for me. I said how beautiful the cottage was, dumped my bag on the bed and then we all made our way back downstairs. To my delight and surprise, Julie suggested we all go for a quick drink down the pub before supper.

I tried to buy the first drink but Tom refused. We sat either side of a worn rectangular table, its surface stained by years of spilled drink and abuse, which was nestled in the alcove of a large diamond-latticed window. The conversation began on the subject of my work as a construction project manager. It seemed to me that Julie was the most animated of the two and was at ease with the ebb and flow of the conversation. Tom, on the other hand, offered the odd comment and nod where appropriate but never seemed to initiate anything. Any questions I put directly to him were answered articulately and in full but rarely seemed to produce a question of his own. He was at his most animated when we were on the subject of woodwork or the building trade in general and it was only Julie who seemed genuinely interested when I told her I really wanted to write for a living. The conversation was broken when I insisted I would get the next round of drinks. Tom had Abbot Ale, Julie, a small glass of chardonnay, Beth had her usual bottle of Becks and I stuck to my Guinness. I had not smoked since Beth had picked me up and I could feel the nicotine devil clawing at my consciousness. I was wondering how long I could hold out for when about half an hour later Julie announced that she and Tom were going to head back and start the supper and that we should be back at the house for about seven – of course I offered them a hand, and of course, they declined. As they left the pub both Beth and I dived for our cigarettes.

"You don't have to not smoke because of me," she said sucking in a lung full of smoke and exhaling as if morphine had just kicked in.

"I know, but I feel awkward."

"Well, don't."

"How do you cope when you're round there?"

"I either wait until they go to bed or I sneak to the bottom of the garden but I haven't had to do that for a long while. I know it's daft but that's the way it is." She smiled and gave me a protracted kiss on the lips. "So," she said, "they're not too bad are they?"

"No, they are very nice. Your Mum seems a little more at ease than your Dad though."

"Dad's just shy; don't worry, if he doesn't like you he won't hold back, believe me." We had another drink and then headed to the house. We arrived about seven, as instructed, and soon after we were seated in the dining room tucking into a delicious roast chicken with all the usual trimmings. I had brought with me a couple of bottles of good red wine and two of white which they thanked me for and the conversation continued, a little easier now the booze was working. By the time we had finished the chocolate cake and cream, and were on to the cheese and biscuits, the topic had moved towards politics and religion – nothing too controversial but enough for Tom to start being more vocal and animated. Reading between the lines, I guessed that they leaned towards Conservatism rather than anywhere far left and it seemed they did not follow any particular Christian faith rigorously but believed in a God of sorts. I felt the need for a cigarette and then plucked up the courage.

"May I have a brief wander in your garden, as I am afraid I am one of the unclean and require a cigarette?"

"Of course you can," said Julie.

"Come on," said Tom, "I'll show you my workshop." Tom and I went into the garden while Julie and Beth began to clear the plates. We walked directly to the shed. It was timber-framed and about twenty feet long by about ten feet wide. He unlocked the door and switched on the light. The interior was decked out in a way that was so similar to my own father's shed that it gave a peculiar feeling, something uncanny and displaced. The walls were lined with peg board and had every imaginable tool displayed on grip clips and nails. A workbench ran the whole length of one side and in the centre was a pull saw. The workbench continued along the far wall where a drill and a router were mounted. Draws and cupboards filled every available space and lengths of different timber rested on struts in the roof void. I held the cigarette packet and lighter in my hand to display my need to smoke but was not going to light up in his shed. I started asking about certain tools I did not recognise and then waxed lyrical about the importance of buying quality rather than quantity.

"You can have a fag in here, boy," he said as if I should have already known that smoking was permissible in his shed. I took no second bidding and lit up. He pulled an old baked bean tin from one of the shelves and removed a small packet of cigars. "Give us a light, lad?" he said and offered a sly wink. "Don't tell the Misses or Beth, they would kill me."

"Mum's the word," I said and held the flame for him.

"Bit daft me creeping about for a smoke at my age but what can you do?"

"I take it Julie doesn't come in here much?" He shook his head.

"Man's gotta have a place to call his own."

"She has never smoked?" He shook his head again.

"I think she tried a bit of the funny stuff in her college days but, no." He produced another tin for us to use as an ashtray. There was a long silence that followed as we smoked and the longer it went on the more difficult it was to break it without it sounding obvious and contrived. Eventually he broke the silence by farting. "That's better," he said.

"Better out than in." I said the obvious cliché with a smile.

"You serious then about this writing stuff?" he asked with a very subtle hint of disapproval.

"I still have to earn a living but it's something I want to pursue. I may never get published but I think it's important to strive for the things we want. We only get one shot in this life so why not go for it?" He nodded.

"I've always loved what I do. Look at this." He walked towards the end of the shed and pulled a sheet back to show the beginnings of a doll's house. "I'm making it for my grand-niece for Christmas." Three of the sides had been constructed and the first and second floors were installed. "It's gonna be Georgian."

"I can understand the pleasure in this," I said genuinely. "I used to make the odd jewellery box; French polished and I lined it in black felt. Are you going to make the furniture as well?" He shook his head.

"No, would take me far too long. There's a toy and model shop in Norwich that sells all the bits and bobs; I got the scale from them so it would be spot on." I lit another cigarette. "I made one for Beth when she was seven." He talked me through how he was going to hinge the front and decorate the insides.

I stubbed my cigarette out which seemed to indicate it was time to go back inside.

As I entered the kitchen I could smell fresh coffee and Julie suggested we go into the lounge. Tom poured me a large brandy and put some Ella Fitzgerald on in the background. It seemed all too familiar as my parents loved Ella, Bing, Frank, Armstrong and Nat – I even knew most of the words. Trivial Pursuit came out and Julie and I took on Beth and Tom – we won by one segment. After that, Julie announced they were going to bed and that she had put the green towels in the bathroom for me. I thanked them for a wonderful evening and wished them good night. Beth suggested we went into the conservatory, poured us both another brandy, took a small radio in with us and we snuggled up on the large four-seat wicker sofa. She asked me what Tom and I had talked about in his shed. I told her about the doll's house and the tools and how it reminded me of my father's shed but I didn't tell her about her father being a secret smoker; if he trusted me enough to share his secret then I wasn't going to betray that. Even to this day I have never told Beth. Maybe both Beth and Julie knew all along and there was some unwritten rule that kept the pretence alive. Tom seemed to have been more at ease in his shed than in his house; it was as if it was his own personal domain, a place that he didn't have to be anyone but himself and I wondered what other secrets lurked in tins and behind cupboards. After a while Beth disappeared for a while and returned wearing a dressing gown, switching off the lounge and kitchen lights on the way. She pulled the double doors closed behind her and then poured another couple of drinks. I put my arms around her, she lay back in my lap and we sat just listening to the music. The sofa was surrounded by plants and the whole place was illuminated by one soft, yellow outside light fixed to the right of the building. She shifted her position so that she was lying on her back with her head on my lap and she was looking directly up at me. She tugged at the ties to her gown and gently opened the garment to reveal her nakedness.

"Oh my God!" She smiled up at me. I ran the tips of my fingers through her hair, down her neck, over the large swelling of her breast, over her nipple and then down along the flat of her stomach, over her thighs and then back up. "What about your parents?" I said looking over my shoulder.

"I don't think they would want to watch," she said.

"What if they come down?"

"They won't."

"Are you sure? I'd feel a little odd if we were caught, especially after that lovely chicken and…" She took my hand and placed it between her legs and all thoughts of her parents vanished from my thoughts. So there, surrounded by mother-in-law's-tongues, spider plants, cheese plants, rubber plants and Radio 1, we made love for the first time. There was no shyness between us, no awkward sense of our nakedness – and in that moment I realised the hook was in – I was lost to her, and although we did not say it, I knew she felt the same.

The next morning we ate a light breakfast in the conservatory and Beth and I exchanged a brief smile when Tom and Julie sat on the sofa. I thanked her parents for a lovely time and they said that they hoped to see me again soon. We drove to Beth's house to discover the place empty. We went straight upstairs and made love again, free from the worry of discovery. Afterwards we just lay together, limbs entwined and talked of our affection for each other, how spinach can really complement a curry, the first time we lost our virginity and the pros and cons of being a vampire.

"Maybe this is just the honeymoon period," she said. "Maybe we won't feel the same way a few months down the line?"

"I know what you mean but somehow this feels different."

When we said our goodbyes at the station I realised that my feelings for her ran very deep – "parting is such sweet sorrow" – the bloke was a genius.

Chapter 21

I decided to take the back road to the seafront that wound through several fields and passed an old building that was reputedly haunted. I remember Bongo flatly refusing to participate in another ghost hunt following his earlier experience. Eventually I entered the coast road and parked in the Pay & Display car park on the greensward which was never there when I was a boy. Nothing much had changed along that particular stretch and I was hopeful that my Grandparents' beach hut would still be there. I walked across the greensward and found the slope that led to the lower promenade and the rows of painted beach huts with their green felt roofs. The tide was on the way out and the beach was dotted with a few families and the odd fisherman. I found the hut immediately. It had the original shiplap but stained brown instead of painted white and had four large iron angle brackets on each corner. I remember my Dad installing them just after a severe storm that had caused considerable damage all along the coast. They were well rusted now and I doubted they would last many more years. The roof must have been felted many times since I was a child and it looked like it could do with some repair. The only main difference I could see was the door. It had a metal grid plate screwed over the timber and painted brown to match the stain of the wood. Gulls cried above me and the smell of the salt air seemed to open the floodgates of my memories. I walked up to the same café at the end of the row and bought a coffee and a sandwich and then sat on the step, my back against the hut and let the past flick into my mind like the blinking from an old cine film.

Chapter 22

10 YEARS OLD

THE BEACH HUT
EMMA BARTHOLOMEW- SMITH
MY BIG TOENAIL

My Nan and Granddad's beach hut was similar to the rest along the stretch of coast. It was off-white like most of the others because the council had strict rules on colour, size and shape. The only difference was that my Nan could, and often would, cook a full Sunday roast in that little hut for about nine people – including pudding. However, this being a Saturday it would be salad and cold meats with ham, chicken, corned beef and tongue. The latter I have never been totally comfortable with. The other essential ingredient for my Nan's fare was parsley. It had to go on every damn thing she produced and I think if she had her way I would have found it chopped on my custard and floating on my glass of milk. I am not kidding about the parsley. If it had been ten years later she would have been sectioned under the Mental Health Act. I think the fact that she was from Belgium had something to do with it.

On this day my Nan, Granddad, Mum and Dad, two cousins who were six and eight years older than me, sister, brother-in-law and their one-year-old son had arranged deck chairs, towels and a small table and chairs out the front of the hut. The suncream that my mother so liberally applied made me look like a channel swimmer covered in goose fat as I walked across the sand and then limped over the stones to the sea. The day was blisteringly hot but the gentle, cool, on-shore wind helped take the edge from the sun's anger. In contrast, the first step into the sea made your balls want to leap over to France and your scrotum shrink like a slug in a salt hat, but after a while you would be too numb to feel anything much. My brother-in-law and cousins would charge down the beach armed with footballs, Frisbees and a large inflated tractor inner tube and then explode into the water. Anyone under the age of five who happened to be in their way would have been killed instantly or, at best, maimed for life. The beach was packed full of people sporting skin colours from pure white to blistering red and envious golden brown. Flip-flops flipped to and from the shop carrying handfuls of 99s with two chocolate flakes, rockets, choc ices, strawberry mivvies, feasts and chewy toffees. Women and girls were constantly pulling at their swimming costumes to free them from the cracks of their arse and men and boys walked past like they hadn't noticed. Dogs and kids were yelled at, arm bands adjusted while others built uniformed sandcastles moulded from the only two bucket shapes sold in the shop. The smell of the sea was blended with the aroma of fried onions, hotdogs and Ambre Solaire. The tide was out, but on the turn and so in another few hours everybody would be fighting for space on a much-reduced beach. Beer bellies bounced along like bull seals returning to mate and striped windbreaks were erected even if they were not required.

Being only ten years old, my skill at heading balls or catching Frisbees in the sea thrown by men whose arms were the size of my chest was limited. However, shouts of "nice throw, Donny" or "superb catch" made me feel gratefully accepted within the adults' playtime. The beach hut itself was like a summertime shrine for hot sunny days and never a cloudless day would pass by where at least three members of the family would pay homage. The floor of the hut was covered in blue fleck linoleum with always a dusting of sand. Nails protruded from the wall on the right from which hung a host of beach accessories including flippers, masks, snorkels, deflated arm bands and rubber rings, windbreaks and large umbrellas. The right-hand wall contained cooking pots, pans, a shelf with twenty plates, cups, saucers and just about everything else. Along the rear wall was a twin ring butane gas hob and single oven with a rack of spices to the left. To the left of the split door was a hatch that opened up and formed a sort of working surface and allowed a view of the sea when preparing food. There was a large canvas bag hanging up that contained a host of odd flip-flops and sandals (a superb find for one-legged beach bums), a cobbled-together first aid kit, and an out-of-date fire extinguisher. The hut did not have a name. It was simply Number Forty-Three.

After my first salty dip, I returned to the hut for a large towel, cup of tea and a piece of cake. We tended to eat a lot of cake as both my mother and my Nan baked continuously. Nan's fruit cake was a close second to my Mum's but I think Nan had the edge on sponges provided she restrained herself from the parsley thing. The blue hue had faded from my body and gradually the prune fingers returned to normal. I decided to take a stroll along the beach and see if I could find anyone I knew. Access to the beach was via a series of concrete steps that differed in numbers depending on the terrain and they stretched for practically the whole length of coastline for about four miles. The beach itself was divided up in sections by concrete posts and slats that started at the concrete steps and ended just short of low water. They were designed to stop the sand from shifting and were covered in sharp barnacles and other ocean hangers-on. I would like a penny for each time they bloodied a knee or shin. In some places the sand had built up enough to enable one to climb over them without having to use the steps and without too much risk from losing the skin off one's feet. I hugged the water's edge and let the gentle waves wash over my feet as I walked. I passed two younger boys prodding a small washed-up jelly fish with a stick and a toddler who was hooting wildly as he filled up the sea with sand using a tea spoon. A young girl was smacked because she would not stop crying (I could never get my head around that concept) and a really fat woman had got her arse stuck in a deck chair. I threw a ball back to a family cricket team whose wicketkeeper looked like he was about to have a heart attack and I found a fifty pence piece – result! I could stand no more excitement so I made my way back via the path in front of the huts. As I approached our Shangri-La, I noticed that the hut two away from ours was now occupied and my Nan was busy feeding the new neighbours with cake and tea.

"Here's Don," she said as I drew close. "This is Mr and Mrs Bartholomew-Smith and this is their daughter, Emma."

"Hello, pleased to meet you." Emma was about my age and wore a striped blue bikini top and plain blue shorts. Her jet-black hair was shoulder-length with a soft wave and her eyes were dark brown and full of life. She gave me a wide smile and a shy little wave with her fingers. Her skin looked soft with a near-perfect tan – today just got a whole lot more interesting. According to my Nan, they had just bought the beach hut and Emma was at one of the other schools on the other side of town and she was nearly eleven but in the same year as me and has a pony and three rabbits and Mr Bartholomew-Smith sold cars and Mrs Bartholomew-Smith worked part-time in the garden centre and loves lilies but not chrysanthemums.

"You want some cake, Don?" asked Nan.

"No thanks, Nan. I'm going to walk up to the pier."

"Oh perhaps Emma would like to go?"

"Yes, if you want to," said Mrs Bartholomew-Smith. Emma nodded and her father gave her some money just in case she wanted an ice cream on the way back. I said we would not be too long and then, with a small wave, we were on our way but not without a sly grin from my brother-in-law.

"Sorry about my Nan," I said when we were out of ear shot.

"She seems very nice."

"No, she is, but she can talk for England."

"Is she from South Africa?"

"No. She and my Dad were born in Belgium."

"I've never been to Belgium, what's it like?"

"It's full of cakes." She laughed out loud. Her voice was soft and her manner easy and comfortable.

"No really, what's it like?"

"Seriously, it's full of cakes and waffles, ice cream, chips with mayonnaise. The country is much like here I think but the houses are different."

"Do you speak Belgian?"

"Well, where my dad and nan come from, they speak Flemish but in Brussels they speak French. I only know a few words in Flemish but that's all." Emma was maybe an inch shorter and she walked like she knew how to stroll. I have never really been good at strolling; if I have somewhere to get then I get there post haste. We chatted about her horse and I admitted that I did not like the idea of riding the giant beasts but she invited me to try one day. She was horrified when I said that I'd eaten horse in Belgium and laughed when I said I had to stop when I got to the saddle. We did not walk as far as the pier but stopped at a small café and I bought her an ice cream with the money I'd found. We sat on the concrete steps and watched the world at play. There was something quite fascinating about her; the way she wrinkled her nose when she laughed and the tilt of her head when listening to something I was explaining. Her hair curled into the nape of her neck and her eyes seemed full of life and wonder at everything she saw. By the time we were walking back, Cupid had managed to inflict more than a couple of flesh wounds on me. With an hour left before lunch we decided to go swimming. She stripped off her shorts revealing matching bikini bottoms and we made our way to the incoming tide. To my relief, she was just as useless at getting into the water as I was but after a while we both managed the plunge. My brother-in-law and cousins joined us in their usual heroic charge down the beach and for the next thirty minutes we enjoyed being hurled into the air and attempted the football thing again. Then we were called in for lunch.

Emma disappeared to her beach hut for whatever fare was awaiting her and I was handed a plate of salad and cold meats. To my great delight I managed to avoid the tongue and the parsley and then finished the whole thing off with the inevitable cup of tea and piece of cake. I lounged around for an hour having being told what millions of children had been told throughout history that you should not go swimming before an hour after you have eaten.

"You fancy walking up the other way?" said the now-familiar voice. I looked up to see Emma's broad smile beaming down at me and so required no second bidding. I pulled on a T-shirt and headed north. Between the huts and the promenade, at the top, were a series of paths that cut into the slopes and wound their way through coarse grass and shrubs. We climbed up the bank and then headed towards where the land jutted farther out to sea which had stone steps leading around the peninsula that had been formed over a series of giant rocks that led down to the water. When we arrived the tide had already covered the bottom rocks and the waves were breaking against them sending various amounts of spray into the air. We climbed under the hand rail and sat on a large flat rock above the spray line and looked out at the small sail boats criss-crossing their way across the bouncing blue-green water. We sat in silence for a while. I was trying to find a subject we had not covered yet but it was she who broke the deadlock.

"Are you here tomorrow?"

"Yes, all day again. You?"

"Only in the morning. We're going to my Aunt's for Sunday roast."

"Nan cooks the roast down here so we will probably head home late afternoon. What are you doing Monday?" She shook her head.

"Nothing planned. Dad will be at work but Mum doesn't start work until Tuesday so I will have to go to Granny's for the morning." My mind raced with possibilities.

"Do you fancy going to the pictures on Monday?" I asked, having eventually come up with a plan. She looked up and gave me a shy smile.

"What's on?"

"No idea, but there is bound to be something showing."

"I'll ask Mum, but that sounds nice." She turned again to face me.

"You don't know where I live?"

"OK, where do you live?" She told me. I knew the road but she said she would write it down when we got back. We looked at each other and then I had the distinct impression she wanted to kiss. Over the years I have often got these subtle signals wrong but not on this occasion. Her head tilted ever-so-slightly to the side and she made a tiny movement towards me. I did the same. She looked at my lips. I did the same. I guess there is a kind of event horizon that exists between people's lips, a quantum distance, that when reached, there is no going back, drawn in by an invisible and infinite force. Our lips touched. I remembered from my last experience that one's head had to make a kind of circular motion and your mouth was supposed to open and close like a fish out of water. I also remembered that I held my breath until my lungs felt like walnuts. Since then I paid more attention to the TV and the mirror in the bathroom and so concluded that breathing through the nose was the way to go and perhaps a less frantic movement of the head was better. Emma was definitely more experienced in the kissing department. She kept the whole process down to subtle movements of the head and the mouth. At first we got into a slow rhythm, matching each other for pace and firmness. I held her left hand in my right and the other was used to stop myself from falling over. She then pulled away slightly and began to gently kiss my bottom lip only, then did the same with the top. The whole process felt like some complicated dance routine. We pulled apart after about five minutes and she adjusted her position so that she could lean into me and then we began again. I found that I could also breathe through my mouth as well as my nose and this seemed to allow for a greater sense of freedom of movement and subtle adjustments. Each session seemed to last a few minutes and then we would take a break.

"You kiss well," she said and crinkled her nose up.

"So do you." Conversation over, we began again until the skin around my lips started to feel a little sore. We eventually decided to vacate the rocks and climbed back over the railing and continued down the other side of the small peninsula. I stopped the ice-cream man pushing his trolley and bought two bottles of coke. The bubbles enhanced the stinging on my marathon-ran lips. We walked on for a while hand in hand and I felt taller somehow, straighter, more confident. On the way back we took to the high paths above the huts and stopped just outside spotting distance and kissed again. This time her arms went up behind my head and mine wrapped round her waist and pulled her close. I had to cut the kiss short because I felt a distinct and awkward movement in my swimming shorts but was still unable to make any real connection with the whole process. We stopped holding hands and kept an acceptable distance apart as we approached the huts. Her mother asked what we had been doing for the last two hours and she explained that we had been exploring and had a couple of cokes. Her mother seemed satisfied with the explanation and then declared that it was time for them to go home.

"See you tomorrow?" asked Emma innocently as if we had not discussed the possibility of meeting up again.

"Yes, not sure what time in the morning though." She waved and I walked two huts farther on to the awaiting cup of tea and piece of cake. My brother-in-law offered me another sly grin.

Packing up was the usual routine of shaking sand off towels and taking care not to cover passers-by. Deck chairs were folded, cups, plates and feet were washed under the communal standpipe and balls and Frisbees returned to their appropriate designated area in the hut. Finally the hatch was shut, the door locked and with bags and towels in hand, we took the slow walk up the path to the awaiting furnace of the car. I had to sit on the towel for fear of blistering my legs from the imitation leather seats. The intense heat from the sun was lost as we began the short drive home. The smell of salt in the air, the sand on the car's carpet and in the grooves of the seat will always be a part of my childhood memories. I knew the journey home so well I could close my eyes and know exactly where we were at any given moment. However, when I closed my eyes this time it wasn't the journey home that held my focus, but that of a different journey taken in the company of a Miss Emma Bartholomew-Smith.

Supper that night was salmon sandwiches in front of the TV. With the first offering being *It's a Knockout* followed by *The Morecambe and Wise Show* and then, thereafter, kissing with Emma Bartholomew-Smith in the morning and then perhaps the pictures the following day, life was just bloody good thank-you-for-asking. Before I went to bed I checked what was showing at the pictures and was satisfied it would be OK. By the time I had fallen asleep I had gone through a million and one scenarios concerning the next day's events and when the morning burst into my bedroom demanding my attention, I remembered every single one of them. Shame about what would happen.

The same family crew arrived at the beach hut at about half-past nine and already people were busy setting up their own personal space on the sand. When we had fortified our own space outside the hut with deck chairs and towels, Nan and my mother were already peeling carrots and potatoes ready for the Sunday roast. I sat in one of the stripy chairs with a cup of tea in eager anticipation of Emma's arrival. My mind was racing with possibilities for the morning, knowing she would be leaving for her Auntie's roast in the afternoon. Maybe we would begin with a swim or perhaps go for a stroll. I thought about the places we could go in order to kiss without being spotted. The peninsula seemed the most obvious but I did not want to suggest that in case she felt I was taking her there purely for kissing purposes. At the top, along the promenade, there were roofed timber buildings that had open fronts on four sides with slatted wooden seating. They were certainly a possibility except that the majority of the time they were occupied by the elderly eating hard-boiled eggs, but I guess I could check it out. The Bartholomew-Smiths didn't arrive until an hour later. Collectively we said our good mornings and all agreed it was going to be another very nice day. I was watching Emma intently for a signal to come over: a secret knowing smile, a wink of the eye or for her to find an excuse to walk to the standpipe so I could follow. No sign was forthcoming; she didn't even look in my direction. I began to worry that she may have regretted yesterday and that she was now embarrassed by the whole thing. Maybe she just wanted to pretend that nothing had happened and the best course of action was to ignore me completely? Then I began to consider that she was feeling exactly the same way I was feeling; that it was I who felt embarrassed and just wanted to forget yesterday ever happened. With every passing minute my previous new confidence was slowly shifting backwards like the pebbles on the beach. Just when I had lost all hope, she removed her T-shirt and shorts and started down the concrete steps to the beach. She wore a different bikini to the striped one yesterday; this one was just plain dark blue. She reached the water's edge without looking back and began to paddle in the shallows, looking down at her feet and occasionally pushing her hair back behind her ear. I decided to run down the beach and dive into the water just like my thunderous brother-in-law and cousins. This may sound like not-such-a-big-thing, but my fear of entering the water like that stems from something deeper. I can't remember when I heard about it but apparently a young boy (not too sure how old) was working in a greenhouse bedding tomato plants and decided to cool off by jumping into a swimming pool. The sudden drop in his body temperature had caused him to have a heart attack and die. Even to this day I am still reluctant to just dive straight in. I removed my T-shirt and headed down the steps. The water's edge was a little closer than yesterday but it was still a reasonable distance out so I decided only to run when I was about halfway. I kept my eyes firmly fixed on Emma. If she looked up at me before I started running then she would have saved me from the terror I was feeling now. I could just wave and gently walk up to her. I got just beyond halfway but she hadn't looked back and after another few paces I was committed. I picked up speed and then charged at full pelt. I ignored the pebbles biting at the soles of my feet and entered the shallows with full and unabridged gusto. I passed her about ten feet to the right and suddenly realised that I would have to run through the water quite a way before I found it deep enough to dive. My speed slowed dramatically as the water fought against my legs and soon I was completely out of control. I felt myself falling forwards as the top half of my body was now travelling faster than my bottom half and I was only in about a foot and a half of water which was nowhere near enough to dive. The general law of physics took over and I was beyond any possibility of turning this into something cool. I put my arms out and managed to twist my body and my left shoulder struck the water and the sandy bottom first. I kind of performed a half-roll, my trailing legs shot up with the pivoting motion of my body and were flapping about in mid-air before they came crashing down over my left shoulder. Salt water shot up my nose as my body juddered from the cold and when my head found the surface I was coughing, spluttering and gasping for air. I put my hands up to my face as my nose leaked with a sudden rush of snot, sand and sea water. When I finally managed to get things under control I looked up and realised I was facing Emma. There was a moment of silence between us before she spoke.

"Nice dive," she said and then we both burst out laughing. She then waded past me to the deeper water and gracefully dived forward as if to deliberately demonstrate the correct procedure for entering the sea. We splashed and pushed each other playfully as before, I guess as a way of reintroducing ourselves to each other's company. After a while we raced back up the beach, towelled dry and then sat on the sand picking at tiny shells and stones.

"Let's bury ourselves," she suggested enthusiastically. We began by forming a long trench next to each other and then lay down in them and started to push sand over ourselves like turtles hiding their eggs. I enjoyed the feel of the sand's weight over my chest and legs. When we had finished we just lay back looking out to sea.

"Did you ask your Mum and Dad about the pictures tomorrow?" I put the question in a way that made it sound like it was no big deal if she could not go.

"No I haven't yet. Did you find out what was on?"

"Yes, *Herbie Rides Again*. I think it starts at four-fifteen although it says four o'clock but you have all the other stuff before. We could walk from your place and I'll get my Dad to pick us up."

"Sounds OK, I'll ask them later." It was the way she said *later* that sounded strange. It had an edge to it as though she was perhaps afraid to ask them or maybe she was not quite comfortable with the idea of going. I'm not exactly sure that is entirely accurate but I know it threw me a little bit. Perhaps I was just being a little oversensitive. We got bored of just being buried so we had a quick swim to wash the sand off and then I suggested we went to get an ice cream. We were about to wander off when my brother-in-law looked at me from his deck chair in that sly way again and I knew I was heading for a wind-up.

"Going anywhere nice?"

"We're going to get an ice cream," I said cautiously.

"Oh, you couldn't bring me one back could you?"

"Oh... erm... OK, what do you want?" The absolute git! He knew damn well I didn't want to come straight back and his eyes sparkled with the delight of seeing me squirm.

"I don't know quite what I want. What are you having?" His smile broadened into the beginnings of a laugh.

"I don't know until I get there."

"Maybe I'll come with you." I could tell he was going to milk this for all it's worth.

"OK then, let's go," I said and made a motion that suggested I was going to start walking. He started to sit up but then stopped and slumped back down again.

"On second thoughts perhaps I'll wait. You go ahead." What an absolute sod.

"If you're sure?" I said finishing off the illusion.

"No, you go ahead, I'll get one later."

"See you soon then." We walked away with his smug grin burning a hole in my back.

We sat on the concrete steps just a bit farther on from the shop to eat our ice creams and then I realised we had come the wrong way. We were towards the pier and I wanted to head towards the peninsula. There was not a single spot along this stretch of beach where we could kiss without everyone and his dog seeing us. We sat close enough so that our shoulders were touching and I felt a little tingle in my stomach. We finished the ice creams and I brushed sand off her knee that wasn't there then she leaned her head on my shoulder.

"I wish I could stay for the whole day," she said with a gentle sigh.

"Maybe you could ask? My Dad could run you home on our way back?" She shook her head.

"No, I'll have to go. In fact, I should head back soon; we'll be leaving in about an hour." I just nodded. She took her head off my shoulder and gave me a sympathetic smile.

"Sorry," she said and then kissed me. The kiss had all the elements and resonance of yesterday's marathon session but it lasted no more than about ten seconds.

"We had better go," she said pulling away. We could not hold hands on the way back because we were far too close. When we arrived back she walked straight up to her mother.

"Don wants to know if I can go to the pictures with him tomorrow, is that OK?" Both her parents looked up from their respective books. Her mother looked at her father but I could not see any sign of communication between them. Her mother then looked at Emma.

"I guess that would be OK," she said and then focused her attention on me. "What's showing and what time?" I had not expected Emma to ask her parents there and then. I also realised that I hadn't asked my parents if I could go. I didn't doubt for a minute that they would say yes but suddenly I was aware that I would have to engage in a kind of three-way conversation.

"It's *Herbie Rides Again* and it starts at quarter-past four. I thought we could walk from Emma's to the pictures and my Dad could pick us up." Dad heard his call sign and looked up from his cake.

"Well, if it's all right with your parents then I think it will be OK," she said. I then had to bring Mum and Dad into it. I took a couple of steps towards Dad.

"Dad, I thought me and Emma might go to the pictures tomorrow to see *Herbie Rides Again* and if that's OK, could you pick us up?"

"What time?" he said slightly muffled from a mouthful of cake.

"We kind of worked out that if the film started at four-fifteen then six o'clock sounded about right."

"Yes OK," he said and then looked at Mr Bartholomew-Smith for his opinion.

"Sounds fine to us," he said. "Very kind of you to pick them up."

"Not at all," said Dad.

"So what time will you call on Emma?" said Mrs Bartholomew-Smith. I took a couple of steps back towards her.

"I thought at about quarter-to-four?"

"That sounds fine?" she now indicated back towards my father. Dad looked at her then at me.

"What time?" said Dad. I took two steps towards him.

"I said I would go round at about quarter-to-four?"

"You want me to take you as well?"

"No, I'll walk. Emma only lives just round the corner from the cinema."

"So you only want me to pick you up?"

"Yes."

"I just said I'll pick you up."

"I know."

"So you are going to walk to ours?" said Mr Bartholomew-Smith. I took a couple of steps towards him.

"Yes, if that's OK?"

"What, it's OK if you walk?"

"I don't mind walking."

"It's just that I shall be at work and my wife does not drive so I can't pick you up."

"No, it's fine, I can walk."

"I can take you as well," said Dad. I took a couple of steps back.

"No need, Dad, I can walk. I want to walk. It's not far."

"Then that's settled," said Mrs Bartholomew-Smith at last. Emma smiled, I smiled, Mrs Bartholomew-Smith smiled, Mr Bartholomew-Smith smiled and went back to his book and my Dad was already engaged with his cake. A short while later Nan, Mum and my sister were undertaking the roast and Emma began packing up to leave.

"See you tomorrow then," I said to Emma as we all said goodbye.

"See you tomorrow." She smiled and gave me a little wave and I watched her all the way up the hill path until she disappeared from view.

I waited the obligatory hour after the roast chicken, roast potatoes, roast turnips, carrots, peas, gravy and sodding parsley before going for a swim. This time all the family went in except my Nan, Granddad, sister and her baby son. After about twenty minutes Mum and Dad went back to the hut and so I was left with my brother-in-law and cousins with the football. I was standing in about two feet of water when my cousin threw me the ball. It started to curl away from me so I attempted to take a step to the side and sort of dive for it. As I did, my big toe connected with a submerged stone and I collapsed in agony. I pulled myself backwards out of the water holding my foot. When I looked down I could see with horror that my big toenail had split halfway across itself and as far down as the cuticle and was standing up at ninety degrees. Blood was generously flowing from the wound and I began to feel a little nauseous. My brother-in-law was first to the action and he agreed with my cousins that it looked particularly nasty. I managed to get to a standing position and then began to hobble back to the hut. Mum looked up and could see I was in trouble. She helped me into a deck chair and examined the injury with a slight intake of breath. Nan came out of the hut and saw the blood and started towards me. Now I must stop and tell you a little something about my Nan.

My Nan was born in Belgium in 1900 and married my Granddad who was English in 1920. They moved to Birmingham just before the occupation and were, in fact, on the last boat to leave Belgium. My parents were reasonably strict with me and from the stories Dad had told me about his upbringing, they [my Grandparents] were very strict with him. Therefore, as night follows day, my great Grandparents must have been fairly brutal in bringing up my Nan and Granddad. My Dad had some very medieval ways when it came to home remedies. I remember he once thought the best way to tackle a particularly nasty boil on my leg was to avoid the antibiotics I would get from the Doctor and use his own sure-fire method. He told me the best way was to get an empty milk bottle and put it in boiling water. Then he would apply a layer of protective jelly around my boil, place the boiling milk bottle's neck over it and then pour ice cold water over the lot. This apparently would make the boil explode into the bottle and then it was simply a matter of dressing the gaping hole that was left with antiseptic cream and a bandage. I told him if he came anywhere near me with a boiling milk bottle I would call the police.

Another time I had a bastard of a cold which resulted in my sinuses becoming blocked and infected. From time to time my Dad also suffered from blocked and infected sinuses and he said that the best way to get rid of it was to avoid taking the antibiotics I would get from the Doctor and use his own sure-fire method. This method was simply to use No57 medicated snuff that he kept in a small metal box in the bathroom cabinet, which I'd seen him use on many occasions. I was very sceptical about the whole thing but decided to throw caution to the wind and give it a go. I took one large sniff of the brown powder up each nostril as instructed and waited. At first there was a gentle tingling at the top of my nose and my eyes began to water a little – not totally unpleasant. The sensation moved away from tingling to a raging inferno in a matter of a few seconds. Tears poured down my face, my head began to pound and then I began to beg death for a kind release. I endured about ten minutes of abject agony when suddenly Hell began to fall out of my nose. The bathroom sink soon looked like I had been mashing frogs in it and I felt the top of my head caving in. After about an hour I was lying semi-conscious on the bathroom floor when Dad came to see how I was getting on. He looked into the sink and then at me.

"I know it burns a bit but it does the trick." Then he left. I tell you all this because if those were my Dad's remedies for things, you can imagine what he suffered at the hands of my Nan's cure for general domestic ailments. Nan probably made the Spanish Inquisition seem a bit pansy. So, there was I, sitting in the deckchair with my big toenail half-sticking up at ninety degrees, blood dripping over the floor and my Nan coming over just to "have a look".

"What have you done?" said Nan peering over my mother's shoulder.

"I stubbed it on a rock," I said. "Don't touch it."

"I'm not going to touch it; I'm just having a look." She began to move around my mother.

"Looks nasty," said my Mum.

"Oh it's not so bad," said Nan now alongside my mother.

"Don't touch it," I said firmly.

"I'm not," said Nan. "I'm just looking."

"Mum, don't let Nan touch it."

"She won't," said Mum. "She's just having a look." Nan's hand moved slowly to my foot.

"I said don't touch it!"

"I just want to hold your foot still so I can get a better look."

"You can see perfectly OK from there. Mum, she's going to touch it!"

"No she won't."

"Yes, she will!"

"Nan, I beg you, please don't touch it." She placed her hand under my heel and lifted my foot up gently and then raised her glasses to her head.

"It's just the nail," she said.

"I know, I just need a plaster. Please just leave it alone, I'll be OK." She began to move her other hand.

"You said you won't touch it!"

"I won't, sit still."

"Why should I sit still if you're not going to touch it?"

"Because I want to see what can be done." Suddenly with one hand she grabbed my ankle with a force that would strangle a yak and then, with the other, ripped my toenail off completely. It was the only time as a child I got away with the phrase "fucking Hell" and on this occasion they would have heard it all the way across the sea to Belgium.

My toe was quickly bandaged and after a while I stopped crying. My foot was up on a stool and my toe was throbbing in perfect syncopation with my heartbeat; however, there were only two things on my mind – how was I going to kill my Nan and what on earth was I going to do about the pictures tomorrow?

The next morning I was feeling much better for two reasons. The first was that Nan had compensated me for her physical abuse by giving me enough money to pay for both myself and Emma at the pictures and second, my toe did not feel too bad.

Nan giving me the money meant that I would not have to ask Dad for my pocket money, which was slightly less traumatic than having one's toenail ripped off – I will tackle the subject of pocket money in a later chapter. I spent most of the morning watching TV with my foot up. Champion the Wonder horse had helped foil a bank robbery with the aid of Rebel the dog and Sandy the boy. Marine Boy had managed to fend off some underwater baddies with his boomerang and it turned out to be the theme park's owner who had been the monster in *Scooby Doo*. Mum had kept me supplied with tea and toast with marmalade and I was blissfully happy counting down the hours until my date. After lunch I began to work out what to wear and decided on jeans, black T-shirt and my denim jacket. I put them neatly on the bed and then went for a long soak in the bath. I worked out it should take me about forty minutes to get to Emma's house and then allow another ten for my toe and so I left the house at five-to-three exactly. It was a warm afternoon but decided not to take off my jacket because I thought I looked cool – by the time I reached the bottom of my road I realised I was decidedly hot. I threw my jacket over my shoulders and took every opportunity to observe myself in shop windows to see that my jacket over my shoulder was just as cool off as it was on. My toe was slightly throbbing when I got to the top of Emma's road but not enough to make me limp. I could see the number of the first house on the right was one, and so her house being sixty-one, was on the same side and quite a way down. I put my jacket on when I got to number forty-nine and adjusted the collar so it stood slightly up at the back. All the houses were similar. They were set back from the road about twenty feet with a garage on the left and a small gate in the middle of a waist-high picket fence. When I got to sixty-one the gate was slightly open and as I looked up the path to the front doorway I could see Emma sitting on the threshold. She was wearing shorts, a T-shirt and a pair of worn flip-flops. Her forearms and hands were clasped together and she was resting them along her thighs so her clenched hands were just over her knees. She looked up briefly and then looked back down to the path. She was most definitely not dressed to go out and my heart sank. I walked up the path and stood awkwardly in front of her.

"Hello," I said making it clear I understood there was something wrong.

"Hi," she replied in a flat and distant tone.

"What's up?" She shook her head slightly and shrugged her shoulders.

"Aren't you coming out?" She shook her head again but stayed silent. I didn't quite know what to say.

"You want to do something else?" She shook her head again and uttered an almost inaudible "no". I stood in front of her not knowing what to do.

"Have I done something wrong?" She just shrugged her shoulders again. My mind began to try and find a handle on the moment and to attempt turn things around.

"My Nan ripped my toenail off yesterday after you left," I said thinking a change of subject might work. Eventually she slowly lifted her head and looked at me, her face flushed with an incomprehensible expression.

"I think you better go home now," she said without expression. No remorse, no guilt, just flat and emotionless. I looked at her for a few seconds and then she slowly lowered her head and looked down at the path again. I stood there for a while until the silence became unbearable.

"OK," I said and turned back up the path. I closed the gate behind me, took one last look at her, and then when I realised she was not going to look back up again, I walked away. I remember that image so clearly, her sitting on the step looking down at the path: it was the last vision I had because I never saw her again. Many times I have wondered what happened to her since that little wave goodbye on the beach the day before to that moment on the step of her house and could never fathom the mystery. Maybe she had done something bad and her parents told her she could not go out as a way of a punishment but then I'm sure she would have given that as the reason. What gives the whole experience a greater sense of gravity is the fact that the Bartholomew-Smiths never returned to the beach hut – not that summer or any others.

I have had some long walks home since that day but that one was by far the longest.

Chapter 23

I went up to the melamine counter and ordered another mug of coffee from the teenage girl serving who had clearly read the rules on "How To Keep That Pissed Off Look On Your Face All Day". She was chewing gum like a professional football manager and had contrived to look at her mobile phone five times between taking my order and placing the hot coffee in front of me. The sound of her fingernails tapping the keys on her mobile sounded like a death-watch beetle. Her glamorous, designer, spray-painted false fingernails were in direct contrast to the sad-looking hairnet that Health and Safety had forced her to wear. She handed me my change as if I was a condemned man and then her whole body seemed to sag when the man next to me ordered four hot dogs with onions, two burgers and chips and six teas to go. As well as a café, it stocked the usual beach merchandise: buckets and spades, suncream, Frisbees, footballs, flip-flops, post cards, sunglasses, rubber rings, arm bands and outside, hanging up on the wall, inflatable boats ranging from small to large. The sight of them, as I resumed my seat outside, got me thinking about gifts.

Chapter 24

THE WATCH

When you add up all the Christmas days, birthdays and special events, it comes to a lot of gifts, but out of all of them, only a few stand out. However, it's our memories of occasions and times spent with our family and friends that create the history of our lives and our most defined memories. I have often wondered how many children will remember every computer game they have received over the years compared to the treasured memories of time spent with those they have loved and cared for – even those we have disliked or events that have left scars have their rightful place in our memory banks. My brother's wife took me, not to this café, but the one further along, and bought me an ice cream and then suddenly, and without prompting, bought me the largest of all the inflatable boats. I was staggered. This boat, the plastic gun that my brother bought me that day in the toy shop, my first racing bike, my first proper skateboard with kryptonic wheels, goldwing trucks and a fibre-flex deck and a few others I could mention, were all great in their way but what was important was not the gifts in themselves, but the memories of me and my friends using them. Speaking about Christmas and birthdays, I remember a great many of my early birthdays for one particular reason. My birthday fell so close to Christmas that I would usually get a combined Christmas and birthday gift and then on my actual birthday, I would receive a bit of money stuffed in a card. This was not the reason why my birthdays stood out – it was what I did with the money. My father, being brought up in Belgium before the war, believed that if you couldn't make something yourself and had to buy it, then you made damn well sure the thing you bought had to be well-built, practical and should last you all your life and hopefully the lives of your grandchildren as well. Anything that did not conform to the 1930s', 1940s' or 1950s' idea of durability and fashion was neither fashionable nor durable. And considering I was born when consumerism had taken hold, anything at all that was manufactured outside Belgium or sold in a shop that did not have a salesman in a starched three-piece suit with masses of hair growing out of his ears and who smelled of Brylcreem, would simply never last. Because I was young and had a childhood which did not involve me working down a pit or eating coal to earn my money, I had no say (sort of) in what clothes were bought for me. Therefore, my clothes tended towards the well-built and stayed at least an arm's length away from fashion. However, my birthday money was something, by the laws of physics and every other law in the universe, that should have been mine to spend how I wanted – technically that was correct but my father was from Belgium. Every birthday my father would ask me what I was going to buy. "Have you thought what you want to buy?" he would say. Not unreasonable.

The first real birthday I could remember was having thoughts towards a set of matchbox cars and clip-together track.

"I quite like matchbox cars and clip-together track," I said. Not unreasonable. "Right then," he would say, "I'll come with you." We would drive into town with both of us feeling reasonable. On my return my mother would ask:

"What did you get?"

"A set of watercolour paints and brushes," I said trying to sound as excited as someone who had got matchbox cars and clip-together track. The following year I was leaning towards the space rocket from the TV series UFO.

"Have you thought what you want to buy?" said my father.

"The rocket from UFO," I said.

"Right then, I'll come with you."

"So what did you get?" said my Mum on our return.

"A set of watercolour paints and brushes," I said trying to sound as excited as someone who had got a rocket from UFO. This continued every damn year. On my tenth birthday I knew I had got him. There was a particular fashion for a particular type of watch. It had two small dials that rotated past each other so that when they met in the middle it would display the time. They were practical, well-built and sported the reliable name of "Timex".

"Have you thought what you want to buy?"

"Yes, a Timex watch."

"Excellent idea, I'll come with you." Town supported several jewellery shops and my father pointed to a few watches that he thought were good. Now I had to be subtle. I nodded but indicated they were not *quite* my cup of tea. I pointed to a few (not the one I wanted) and my father would nod in a way that was not *quite* approving. We were being so reasonable that "reasonable" could have walked to town and gone shopping on its own. We did the same in the next shop and then the next. I suddenly pointed to the one I really wanted and declared with such conviction that "conviction" could have married "reasonable" and lived happily ever after. "That's the one!" We entered the shop.

"So what did you get?" said Mum.

"A watercolour set and brushes." I have no idea how he did it. He was a bloody genius my father.

Chapter 25

I looked out to sea at a few of those inflatable boats and then I noticed a small fibreglass fishing boat and suddenly remembered something that I had not thought about in years. My father owned one of those boats. It had a small, two-bench cabin at the bow and was painted blue. Moulded seats were down each side and you could always smell the mixture of sea water and oil sloshing somewhere under the ply decking. The boat was powered by a 25hp Johnson outboard motor that was mounted on a black metal retractable hinge. Along the coast, following south, was another coastal town and about a mile out to sea there was a small island that later became a bird sanctuary. I can remember going there and spending the day on two separate occasions but it was the second time that really stands out.

Chapter 26

THE ISLAND, THE GRASS AND THE HIPPIES

My very first friend lived in the same road as my sister. She was, as I said, much older than me. I first met David Lund when I was three-and-a-half and we stayed friends right through our school years. His mother, Tammy, was tall, blonde and sported large breasts and a broad smile. Her voice, however, was soft and shy and it was as though it should have belonged to someone else. Frank, David's father, was the complete opposite. He was short with cropped dark hair, slim, tattoos and had a voice that could skin buffalo. David was their only child and we both shared the same sense of humour. On this occasion my brother-in-law, sister, mother and father, David and his parents all jumped in the boat on a scorching summer's day and planed along the water to the island. It had originally belonged to my Dad who then sold it to my uncle but had now borrowed it for the trip. The island was about half a mile in diameter and was thick with soft white sand which formed undulating dunes towards the middle from which sprang thick reed grass. The boat was loaded with hampers, cooking stoves, gas cylinders, towels, windbreaks, a football and a Frisbee. The wind was non-existent and the glass-like water reflected the sky and the baking sun giving the whole day a Mediterranean feel. (The latter description is post-reflective as I had never been to the Mediterranean until I was in my twenties.) We communally unloaded the boat and walked about in circles like cats trying to decide the best place to settle. We made camp and then David and I were given the responsibility to go and collect driftwood for a fire. Once our chores were complete we were free to explore the island.

I was keen to see if the swimming pool was there. Walking anti-clockwise, the beach flattened out so that, at full tide, the water washed up and filled a natural bowl surrounded by high dunes. It was maybe thirty feet in diameter and about two-foot deep at the far end. The sun would very quickly heat up the water and it would trap all kinds of marine creatures. To my great delight it was still there but would take maybe another couple of hours for the water to warm up properly so we decided to make a complete exploration of the rest of the island. David was tall, had a muscular but slim frame with skin that tanned and a head full of curly brown hair. He also knew how to stroll, unlike me, and so I would often find myself having to stop and wait for him to catch up. We climbed a dune and were heading down the other side when, at the bottom, I realised he had stopped again. I looked back and noticed his interest in something buried in the sand. As I approached he stood and showed me what he had found. It was a bullet. I'd seen similar ones in shops which had been manufactured into belts that were predominantly worn by bikers or heavy metal drummers. This one was rusty. I wanted to hit it with a rock. David thought that was probably not a good idea. Strange that I knew about percussion-sensitive explosives but not what my willy was really all about – go figure. We searched but found no more. On the other side of the island we found a few remnants of previous camp fires and some empty beer cans but nothing to get excited about. A slight breeze began which helped to take the edge off the sun. We headed back towards the centre again and over the sand dune. In a dip we found a dead seagull, a small shiny packet with an odd-shaped smelly balloon inside, and a tin that contained a long hand-rolled cigarette with the end pinched in. We decided we would somehow try and get a light and come back later and give it a go. We hid the tin using the dead seagull as a marker and then headed back to camp.

David presented the bullet to his Dad who then said the best thing to do was throw it in the sea. David wanted to take it back but all the adults shook their heads and agreed with Frank. David went into a strop, started crying and then stormed off only to return ten minutes later as if nothing had happened – he did that from time to time. We had a cup of tea and a piece of cake and then suddenly David said we should go and have another look around and walked off at a pace that was definitely not a stroll.

"What's the rush?" I said when I eventually caught him up. He opened his hand to show me a box of matches.

"Where did you get that?"

"Dad had a couple of boxes in the bag so I pinched one." We dug up the tin and found a place where we would be less likely to be discovered and pulled out the cigarette. On closer examination we discovered that the other end had a rolled-up bit of card and not a filter as my Mum would normally use when hand rolling her cigarettes. David lit it first and tried to take the smoke into his lungs. He coughed for about fifteen seconds and then tried again. He coughed again and handed it to me. I took a draw and joined him in coughing. I gave it another go and handed it back. We had another draw each but then decided that as we were coughing so much and turning red that we had better stop.

"The swimming… *cough, cough*… pool should be… *cough, cough, cough* warmer now, let's… *cough*… go and… *cough*… try it," I said, coughing. "… *cough… cough… cough… cough… cough… cough… cough*… OK." We began to walk clockwise round the island. I suddenly started to feel a little odd – sort of light-headed and a bit wobbly.

"I don't feel too good," I said.

"I don't either," said David. His face had gone from coughing-red to white with a hint of green. "I need to sit down." We slumped onto the sand and the world began to spin. It was not the sort of spin you got from stepping off the Waltzers but it was like the world was starting to spin then it would change its mind, go back, and then spin again and then start all over again. I also felt that the top of my head was quite a way away from my ears, and my toes seemed longer somehow and did not really belong to me.

"My hair itches," said David. Three seconds later we both saw my Mum's cup of tea and fruit cake for the second time. After that we felt a little better.

"What the hell was that?" I said feeling delighted that I was still alive.

"Maybe it was off," said David.

"How do you mean, off?"

"You know… sort of stale." I knew that Mum had said that her tobacco had gone a bit dry from time to time but I never saw her throw up afterwards and I had my doubts that her head flew away from her ears and her toes probably stayed the same length. We could not figure it out but decided we felt OK to visit the pool. After an hour of splashing around we were back to normal but then felt ridiculously hungry.

"You two have worked up a good appetite," said my mother as we had gone through three rounds of sandwiches and two bags of crisps. We both turned down cake – a first in the history of my family. We were told about the hour-thing and swimming so we just lay back and felt the sun on our faces. Later the men took to the swimming pool and we played a kind of cross between water polo and football. The rules were made up and I can't remember who won. Frank told David not to do something and so David cried and stormed off but came back ten minutes later and carried on with the game. Back at camp I declined the cake for the second time that day and I am sure there were Belgian cake-making ancestors of mine flipping in their graves at my actions. (Incidentally there is a traditional Belgian dish called *zura vis* – sour fish. It is usually skate covered in a clear jelly. What it actually looks like is that hand-shaped creature in "Alien", covered in snot and please, trust me on this, it tastes worse than it looks. So if you ever find yourself at a restaurant in Belgium and the waiter suggests it – have him arrested.)

Towards early evening, David and I were on the other side of the island when we noticed a couple in a Canadian-type kayak paddling towards us. They pulled the boat up the beach, unloaded a few items, including a guitar, and set about building their own fire. He had long dark hair and a wispy beard and wore a long-sleeved orange shirt open all the way with a kind of leather pendant hanging round his neck. She was slim with long blonde hair and wore a flowery cotton skirt; a light blue cotton shirt that was unbuttoned halfway so every time she bent down, her boobs fell out, which was fantastic entertainment for us until we were discovered. They gave us a pleasant wave and a kind smile so we waved back. David wanted to go and say hello but at that moment we were called back. Mum and my sister had made sausages and mashed potato with onion gravy, which is still one of my favourites today. After we had eaten we noticed the couple walking towards us; the man was carrying his guitar.

"Hi all, what a beautiful day," said the man waving.

"Hello," we all said.

"You've been here all day?"

"Yes," said Dad, "just finished eating."

"Cool," said the man. They both kept nodding. "Mind if we pull up some sand?"

"No, please sit," said my Dad; he was always keen to meet new people.

"Cool." They both sat cross-legged. "My name's Jet," said the man, "and this is Pin." They continued to nod. My Dad introduced all of us. Frank looked concerned. He was a West Ham supporter and he drove diggers for a living – I don't think he had met anyone call Jet and Pin before. Jet told us they had planned to stay the night.

"So what do you do?" asked Dad.

"I write poetry," said Jet "and Pin makes candles." Frank was looking even more worried. I don't think he was a big poetry fan except perhaps for "I'm Forever Blowing Bubbles" of course.

"Are you published?" said Dad.

"Got a couple of books out – keeps the butter in the fridge. Are you from South Africa?"

"No, Belgium."

"Cool." More nodding. "I love Belgium, cool place, man. The people are really… earthy."

"Would you like some cake?" said Mum.

"Cool," said Jet nodding harder. Jet explained to Dad about some of the places they had been in Belgium and every so often would interject with "nice cake". A few crumbs were resting in his beard. A little pause in conversation lasted for about ten seconds. "Can I play you good people some music?" Everyone nodded except for Frank. "This song I wrote for my beautiful Pin here," he said kissing her head. "It's called 'Like My Woman's Hair'." He closed his eyes for a few seconds and then began. "Shit, man, sorry, wrong key." He moved his finger further up the neck, closed his eyes again and then began. When he had finished we gave him a polite round of applause. "Thanks very much. This next one's called 'If I Could Only Go'." Frank was about to say something but a stern look from his wife stayed his tongue. Eyes closed, he started – Pin swayed – song ended – another polite applause.

"More cake?" said Mum. They nodded but said no.

"I wrote this next one when I was in India; it's called 'I Still Love You Even Though You're Black'." We all exchanged glances. Pin whispered something in his ear. "Did I say black? Sorry, man." They both nodded and laughed. "I meant, 'back', 'I Still Love You Even Though You're Back'." We laughed but Frank looked disappointed. "It's about my first wife. We loved each other but couldn't live together."

"Is Pin your second wife?" asked Mum.

"No, we're not married." I could tell Mum was about to ask another question but Jet closed his eyes again. There were a few more, "and this one I wrote," when Dad said that it was getting late and we needed to get back before it got dark.

"Cool, man," said Jet. "Thanks for your company, you're really cool." Pin gave a little wave and then they walked away arm in arm until they disappeared over the sand dunes.

"Well, they seemed nice," said David's Mum. Frank just gave her a look. We all communally helped load the boat and then motored our way back to the mainland. I wondered if Jet ever managed to write a song about Belgium: I've tried but it's very difficult.

Chapter 27

The chirping from my mobile disturbed my thoughts. The screen showed "withheld number" and my mind painted "hospital" in its place.

"Hello?" My voice seemed weak and shallow as if from lack of exercise.

"Mr England?" I immediately recognised the voice and my chest and stomach constricted.

"Dr Joyce." My mind raced in a million directions all at once.

"Hello, Don. I'm not disturbing you am I?"

"No, no, not at all, just having a coffee."

"OK, good. I've called you because I have just looked at the results of the latest scan and…"

"Good news I hope?" I could picture him behind his desk full of folders and shelves stacked with files and journals, the computer screen casting a green hue over his white coat.

"Well, not much change I'm afraid. There is a small increase in activity around the damaged area but it's nominal and not really significant enough for me to conclude anything but the status quo. I'm sorry not to be able to be more positive but I don't want to give you any false hope, Don."

"There's no change then?"

"Sorry, no."

"OK."

"We will switch her ventilation off again temporarily, but I think Beth will respond in the same way, and if so, well, I think you will have to…"

"Yes, yes I know. I will be at the hospital tomorrow but I can't make that decision tonight. I want…" I fought for control of my voice. "… I want time to sit down with Charlie and explain as best I can to her. I know what needs to be done but… you know."

"Yes, of course. I will be here until about ten tonight so if you need to talk I will be here."

"I know what needs to be done but it's finding the strength. I may call you later."

"OK, until later then."

"Yes OK, and thanks for the call."

"No problem."

I digested the information for a few seconds and then searched the phone for Julie's number and was about to call when I thought better of it. No point in calling with no-change-there news. The world around me soaked back into my consciousness as a man rang his bicycle bell as he sped past a young couple.

"Get off and push, you wanker!" shouted the young man without removing his hand from his girlfriend's behind. The man on the bike turned and offered a middle finger.

"Fuck you 'n all!" They stopped a few steps later and the girl leaned back against the sea wall. She was probably in her late teens and wore a very short white skirt and crop top. She was eating an apple and offered her boyfriend a bite as she drew him towards her. He lifted her onto the sea wall and she wrapped her legs about his bare slim torso. His shoulder sported a large and complicated tattoo that extended down his arm and terminated at the elbow. He took a bite of the apple and reached up under her top and squeezed her breast as she kissed his masticating mouth. An older couple shook their heads with obvious disdain as they strolled by; the fumbling youngsters were oblivious to all but themselves and continued for a while then walked away, his hand back firmly against the cheek of her youthful behind.

"No, I ain't touching 'em wiv a wossaname pole, Tracy, I told 'im already." The café waitress with the long expensive clicking nails was back. In one hand she held a cloth and was absently wiping the table, the other held her mobile tight to her ear. "Cos ees bloody nicked 'em from 'is job." I waved my hand to attract her attention, I wanted another coffee. "No, I ain't getting too pissed cos I got college late morning and anyway, if that tosser's there I'm walking right out I'm telling ya. He is so full of shit that bloke he does m'ed in."

"Sorry, can I get another coffee?" I hoped.

"No, I, do, not, fancy, 'im, Tracy! Bollocks! He's wrong in the ed I'm telling ya."

"Sorry, can I…"

"E smashed that geezer from the kebab shop remember? I ain't into all that shit."

"Can I possibly get another coffee?"

"Hang on, Trace." She pulled the phone away from her ear and looked at me with raised eyebrows. "What was that?"

"Can I get another coffee please?"

"Coffee?"

"Yes, a large one, black, no sugar."

"Yes, I'll bring it over in a minute." She turned her attention to the phone and began to walk back inside the café. "No some bloke wants another coffee – anyway, Trace, I'll call you later."

A few moments later she returned with my coffee and put it in front of me as though it was a final demand. All this would normally have me spitting blood but now I just felt flat – someone had stuck a nail in my emotional tyre.

Chapter 28

The weather had been similar to today. Beth and I were enjoying a lunch of cheese, grapes, honey roast ham, pickles and a chilled bottle of Chablis. I was beginning to regard her home as my own because I spent more time in Norfolk than she did with me in my poky one-bedroom flat in London. We had just come back from a week on the Costa Blanca and life felt pretty fine except that in another three hours I would have to say goodbye and take the two-hour train journey back to London. I felt oddly displaced – it was as if I was not quite whole and the world was out of kilter; even Beth seemed oddly changed. Maybe I was coming down with a delayed Spanish tummy or something. Beth leaned back in her chair, closed her eyes and let the sun wash over her soft, and now deliciously tanned face. We had hired a two-bedroom villa with its own kidney-shaped pool and a short walk to the beach. The main resort contained the usual Brits in their England strips and fortunately our villa was just outside the main drag. On the second day we found a small beach occupied by mostly Spanish and so avoided the world cup replay of '66 re-enacted by overweight lobsters carrying cans of beer, hooting wildly with their calls for "offside" and "fuck off, it came off his leg!" It didn't take us long either to find the back-street restaurants and bars frequented by the locals and thus avoided the short-skirted, tottering nightingales singing "I fucking love you,

Gary" and the dawn chorus from their mating equivalents of "In-ger-land, In-ger-land, In-ger-land", "oo are ya, oo are ya, oo are ya?" and of course that classic, "you're gonna get your fucking ed kicked in".

We made love as if we were attempting a new world record – we sat on the beach at night and let the Mediterranean gently lap our feet – we swam naked in the pool and danced drunkenly to a Dire Straits CD we found in a kitchen drawer. We were told that we made a "lovely couple" by Dawn, Chardonnay and her sister Anne-Marie from Lewisham over several "Depth Charges". Beth was told on several occasions that she looked Spanish and a man called Jeff wanted to arm wrestle me for twenty euros – he lost. We bought a small amount of hash from a local with my winnings and spent an evening laughing like lunatics and then feeling very sick after demolishing a whole box of After Eights and those foreign crisps that you can't quite work out the flavour of. We collapsed into bed that night and let the blanket of emotion and comfortable tiredness wrap themselves around us as we did with each other – replete and sinful.

I cleared the plates from the garden table and emptied the last of the Chablis into our glasses.

"I hate that feeling of going back to work after a holiday," I said.

"It's never good." Her voice was thin and a little shaky.

"I hate even more leaving you." She reached out blindly for my hand and I took it. She gave me a little squeeze as if to say "there, there, never mind" and then removed her hand. She drained her glass in one go and then went into the kitchen. I heard the refrigerator door open and the clink of a bottle. She returned moments later with a bottle of Soave, refilled her glass and then sat down again. I could detect a slight sigh as she resumed her position. "You'll sleep well tonight," I said.

"I dare say."

"I should finish early on Friday so perhaps I could meet you from work, go for a meal perhaps?"

"Sounds good."

"Unless you have other plans of course?"

"No, no plans." There was definitely something not right. I have never seen her less animated. Perhaps she's just tired or maybe it's the universal time-of-the-month. Sometimes when there is a silence, people have a tendency to fill the void with conversation as though they were having to shoe-horn the words into place. This only happens when the silence is uncomfortable. I tried to analyse the absence of conversation in order to fathom whether it was natural or forced and in doing so, the actual act of scrutiny itself had made the silence unnatural. I sat back and tried to ignore the noise – it was like tinnitus, "the sound of silence".

"Don?" She made my name sound like it was loaded with angst and trepidation and it burst into the silence like a drugs bust. My stomach tightened.

"What's up, Doc?" I was attempting to keep it light in order to belay my fears – experience told me it was as futile as swimming up Niagara Falls.

"I need to speak to you about something. I was trying to find the right moment on holiday but… but I guess the moment didn't seem right." *It's over; she doesn't feel that the relationship is for her. It's her, not me. She feels she is not ready to commit to a long-term relationship. Of course she doesn't want to hurt me but better now than let the whole thing drag on. She wants to stay friends – maybe she met someone else – maybe that bloke's back; what's his name? Joe? That's it, Joe! Joe has returned and she had been lying to me about her feelings for him. Maybe she just wants to cool things for the moment.* The thoughts went through in a millisecond.

"It sounds serious." She took another gulp of wine and turned her chair round to face me.

"My company has offered me a job with our parent company." *Shit not again.* "That's the one in Switzerland?"

"Yes."

"OK, tell me." I mirrored her actions and moved my chair.

"They want me to go out there and learn part of the international market system and then come back to head a team to implement that system here."

"How long will you be gone?" There was a pause before she answered.

"Five years."

"Shit!"

"I know." It was my turn to pause.

"Have you made a decision?" I held my breath. She shook her head.

"No, not yet, I have to by the end of the month." I computed a hundred million emotionally imbedded responses in about five seconds but in the end there was only really one thing I could say.

"It sounds a fantastic offer and whatever you decide, I will support you."

"If I take the job, Don, I doubt we could be together."

"I understand. I can't decide for you – *you* have to make that decision on your own."

"Well, you could sound a little more, a little more…"

"What… a little more what?"

"You know… bothered."

"Bothered? Of course I'm bothered, I couldn't be more bothered."

"Well, you sound like, you know… if you must, you must, que sera sera."

"So what do you want me to say?"

"I want you to be honest."

"I am being honest."

"No you are not. What you are being is… is… reasonable."

"OK. Am I happy about you buggering off for five years? No, I am not. Am I happy about the realistic prospect of breaking up? No, I am not. Do I want you to tell them, thanks, but no thanks? Yes I do. Am I going to put you under some sense of emotional press in order for you to stay? No, I will not do that. I will not be held responsible for the decision you have to make. I want you to make it for the right reasons."

"But you are part of me making that decision whether you like it or not." She lit a cigarette and took a deep draw. I did the same.

"It's not a question whether I am part of it or not, love, the decision is yours. You have to look into yourself and find out what it is you really want." We both sat tugging on our cigarettes like they were exclamation marks and let the silence sneak back in. I could see her inner turmoil and it was bitter sweet; sweet because her affection for me and bitter that the affection she felt seemed not enough for her to have dismissed the job offer immediately. She had two weeks to decide what she wanted and part of me wanted her to resolve it now so that I would not have to endure two weeks' uncertainty and self-doubt – ultimately we are all selfish creatures even though what we do seems altruistic – we take what we can best live with or without.

The journey home was one of the worst I've had to endure. We had talked about the possibility that I move out with her and try and find work in the construction industry in Switzerland. It was not impossible but it was unlikely. I did not have any formal qualifications in the industry and so would probably have to take a substantial pay cut and position. When we said goodbye at the station, there was a strain between us that I had never felt before. We kissed, but it was without our usual tender passion; it was as if someone was pulling on an invisible string attached to our backs, trying to draw us away from our embrace and without either of us putting up much of a fight. I sent a text on my mobile to say that I had got home safely but did not get a reply. We spoke briefly the next day and she said it might be a good idea if we didn't see each other the next weekend. She eventually came round to the idea that, although I was indeed part of her life, the decision to take the job offer was hers to make.

The week went by slowly like a weighted, cast-iron second-hand of a clock and with each passing day my heart grew heavier and darker. Saturday she called to see how I was and I tried to inject a sense of lightness in my voice but she knew me too well. She was planning a night out with Jane and some of the girls from work; a meal and then take in a couple of bars and maybe a night club. I said I would probably head to my local for a few beers with the boys. We avoided talking about the "issue" as there was nothing else to add and so we wished each other a good night. That night I sank far too many beers than was probably good for me and staggered home with a kebab that was definitely not good for me. I woke from a recurring dream about a ridiculously large house that had several glass bathrooms. I still get the same dream today and I have never figured out what it means; each time, however, I wake with some distant feeling of dread, like a medieval soldier waiting on a foggy battlefield, he can hear the enemy but cannot see them. I kicked off the duvet and flapped into the kitchen with my headache following me like a cat that needs feeding and making a similar noise in my head. The coffee and the toast were being handled by the automatic pilot while I fumbled in the drawers looking for the ibuprofen. It was while I was fumbling through the vast quantities of un-collectable collectables that I found a small quill fishing float that my Granddad had given me as part of a complete coarse fishing set when I was twelve years old and my thoughts jumped to a two-week holiday I had on the Norfolk Broads with my parents, grandparents and my Belgian relatives.

Chapter 29

FLOATS AND MILESTONES

We pulled up onto the boat yard's loose stone drive outside the felted flat-roofed, timber-framed shed that was the main office. Inside, the room had worn carpet tiles and the timber-clad walls were washed in a once-white emulsion. A melamine-fronted desk ran the full width of the office with a hinged section that was currently in the "up" position. The rear wall held a series of shelves containing snap-ring files, loose paper and, to the right, a large painted ply square that held numbered hooks on which hung keys; each was attached to a cork ball. The man behind the counter wore faded jeans, a plain white shirt that augmented his tan and a matching shock of white hair. My father began the process of booking us all in so I went outside and helped unload the cars. Both boats were blue fibreglass, long and very un-boat-looking, more like elongated caravans. I was horrified to find that I had been allocated a berth in the same room as Nan and Granddad. I have had this experience before only to find that both held world records in snoring, farting and teeth rattling. I was delighted, however, to find my beautiful cousin, Nikki, was to be on the same boat. We were the same age and had never had a single cross word. The last time I had seen her was three years before but now I had noticed she had grown two considerable mounds and thus, physically, could no longer be classed as a little girl. It was as though she was approaching womanhood already running, whereas I, on the other hand, was still very much a young boy plodding to manhood with the reluctant gait of a teenager having been asked to do the washing up. In some ways she reminds me of Beth with her long dark chestnut brown hair, hazel eyes, olive skin and a laugh and smile that would soften the hardest of hearts. As well as my Mum and Dad, Nikki's aunt and uncle were on board. Yossy, the uncle, a slightly built man, did not possess the notion of manners when it came to mealtimes; he would attack his soup like he was doing the hundred-metres butterfly, confront the main course like he was digging trenches in the First World War, and as for jelly and ice cream, well it's certainly not for the faint-hearted. He spoke with his mouth full and thus would share its contents around equally among those sitting in close proximity. All this was punctuated with belches and farts like anti-aircraft fire – when he ate porridge I had to leave the room. Except for mealtimes he was never without a huge cigar in his mouth and as he talked his cigar bobbed up and down like a fishing rod indicating a hooked eel. Having said all this, his heart was generous and kind and we all loved him dearly. His wife, Lou, was almost the complete opposite. She was a large woman but moved with a light step, her manners were impeccable and her cooking sublime; she too was kind and generous both with money and her time, of which, between cooking, cleaning, baking, ironing, and a million other *duties*, she had precious little.

Once on board and our luggage stowed away, the adults sat around the river map and nodded in different languages to various points of mooring – where to stop for lunch and then the overnight berth. The boats were freed of their moorings and then we gently motored upriver. Granddad insisted on taking the wheel only to be relieved of duty when he fell asleep ten minutes later and crashed into a reed bank. He had a nap for half an hour, sank a few strong coffees and then said he was fine and took up the helm once again. Ten minutes later he had fallen asleep and crashed into the opposite bank. With a less narcoleptic relative at the wheel we all relaxed into the trip. Granddad and my father were tackling up the fishing rods while Lou, my Nan and mother were chopping vegetables and peeling spuds for dinner. It was a hot day so Nikki and I donned our swimming costumes and sat on the roof soaking up the sun watching the wildlife and other boaters pass us by. I could not take my eyes off Nikki's breasts. They were fantastic. She took from a small canvas bag a book which she began to read. I wasn't into reading books then and even if I was those breasts would have pulled my eyes from every word. When I had last seen her she had been a child, like me, full of innocence and wonder at the world – now she was a woman, or at least in body, full of sophistication, curves and dips and tanned undulations all bonded together in a simple black bikini. I, on the other hand, was a squat, pale-skinned ginger nut with an expanding waistline and peeling nose. Suddenly our friendship had changed, or at least it had for me. The wolf whistles from passing men with flat stomachs and wafting hair did not bother me; it was the tilt of her head, the peering over her sunglasses and the only-just-a-little-smile she offered in response which twisted the broken bottle in my stomach. She oozed sex like it was corporeal and seemed to be possessed of a separate intelligence that mocked me, challenged me, tantalised me and yet held my hand like a lost child in a vast supermarket of coloured bottles and confused perfume. It would have been an extremely difficult two weeks if I had not discovered two things – fishing and wanking.

Pre-lunch cake and two cups of tea were placed on the roof of the boat, the fishing rods were ready for action and soon we would tie up for a salad lunch with hard-boiled eggs and tinned salmon – soup to start which occurred with every meal, apart from breakfast. The Belgians were soup-makers par-excellence and my Nan was not called Nanny Soup for nothing. A bowl of soup was placed in front of Yossy and he presented himself to the edge of the bowl, not bothering to wait for the starter gun, dived straight in using his bread roll like a surf board. With the butterfly action in full swing it wasn't long before most of those sitting closest were covered in bits of noodle, chicken and soggy bread. The subject of conversation was mainly fishing. Granddad said he had a small rod and reel he could lend me and would show me how to tackle-up, put the bait on the hook and then how to recognise a bite. The tinned salmon salad arrived along with the hard-boiled eggs, corned beef, tongue, ham and buttered bread. Yossy grabbed a hard-boiled egg and I had to look away. The carnage over, the women began to clear away lunch and started to prep for dinner – what a holiday for the women folk, eh?

The rod Granddad had given me was one of those all-in-one affairs, complete with three pre-weighted floats and a few hooks. He showed me how to thread the line through the eyes (not forgetting to insert the end through the lifted bail arm first) and then slide the float on using tiny rubber bands, tie the hook and then finally how to squeeze a lump of cheese on the end. Three attempts at casting later, the float sat perfectly in the lea at the front of the boat. Mum lashed thick white sun block over me and stuck a hat on my head. The occasional wolf whistle aimed at the roof-lounging goddess piped over the noise of the passing boats but my eyes did not move from the bright yellow tip of the float. After a while the float suddenly bobbed, and then bobbed again. The glass bottle in my stomach was now a series of butterflies all wanting to get out at once. Then the float sank until I could see it no more. I yanked hard on the rod and then suddenly felt the vibrations of a struggling fish.

"I've got one, Granddad!" I shouted.

He calmly placed down his coffee and said in a voice with a billion years of experience, "Nice and steady now, start to reel it in. Keep the line taut."

I saw a sudden flash of silvery light and a splash as the fish came to the surface. My Granddad reached for the landing net and then carefully scooped up my first-ever fish – a bream, half a pound. Even Nikki's breasts peering over the edge at the unfolding scene below could not distract me from my first-ever bream! Nikki scrambled down off the roof to take a look. I carefully took the hook out of the fish and then gently put it back in the water and watched it dart away into the darkness below.

"Well done!" said Nikki and kissed me on the cheek, her breast pushed gently on my arm. Then she took herself and those breasts back up on the roof while I tried to squeeze another bit of cheese on the hook. The only time my line was not in the water at the front of the boat was when we were either motoring or I was having supper. When the sun had finally set and I could no longer see the float I went inside. The adults were gathered on one boat playing cards. Gesticulating arms indicated their disapproval of badly dealt hands while Flemish and English swear words duelled in the smoke-filled air like tiger moths and Nikki was sitting on her bunk writing in her diary. She had donned a pair of denim shorts and a thin white cotton shirt. She patted the bed next to her and as I sat down I was suddenly aware that I smelled of fish.

"I'm gonna have a shower in a minute," I said sniffing my hands. "I stink."

"How many did you catch in the end?"

"Six. I think one was well over a pound," I said like a veteran. We sat side by side with our backs against the wall, her knees drawn up to her chest. I could smell freshness of a shower on her and the ends of her hair were wet.

"You want to play cards?"

"Yes, but I need a shower first." She nodded. The rules for showering were strict due to a limited water tank; enough water to wet you and then enough to rinse off the soap. After my brief shower I donned a pair of clean boxers and my dressing gown and made my way to Nikki's bunk and found her asleep. She was lying on her back, her long brown legs stretched out and her face turned to the wall. Her thin cotton shirt was buttoned just over halfway and one perfect breast was exposed to the naked light. For a moment I was transfixed and then I realised what I must do. I switched off the light, said my goodnights to the adults and went to my own bunk. The pressure to relieve the pressure in my loins was almost unbearable but I had no idea what to do. After much experimenting I realised that a simple up-and-down motion seemed to be doing something. Thirty seconds later I felt a sudden and wonderfully frightening surge begin somewhere deep inside. Ten seconds later the surge was released. I thought I was going to have a heart attack. I thought I was going to pass out. I thought I was going to be sick. I couldn't let go. When it was finally over, I lay still, sweaty, panting and then I realised one immutable fact – I would be doing this as often as I could. I got up, put on my dressing gown and went to the bathroom and cleaned myself up. I took a handful of tissues and stuffed them in my pocket and got back into bed. The swearing and shouting from the adults continued and it seemed an oddity that I could have discovered something so fantastically euphoric amidst such banality. A slight tapping sounded on the door.

"Hello?" I said. The door creaked open and Nikki switched on the light.

"Hi," she said and stepped into the room. She sat on the edge of my bed. "Sorry, I fell asleep. I thought we were going to have a game of cards." The cotton shirt remained as it was.

"I know. You were asleep so I thought I would go to bed. I'm a bit tired myself."

"OK then, sleep well." She leaned down and kissed me on the side of my face and I could feel some bare flesh of her breasts against my chest.

"See you tomorrow," I said. She stood, switched off the light and closed the door behind her. Three seconds later my shorts were down and my hand was working like an Irish labourer on a "job 'n knock".

I woke to the boat in motion and it wasn't long before we had moored up at one of the towns along route. I had missed breakfast but Mum made me some toast and a cup of tea. Granddad said there was a big fishing tackle shop in town and he needed some new things and would I like to go with him. I quickly got dressed and walked over the small bridge and into the high street. About fifty yards on the right was a large shop that seemed to be solely dedicated to fishing tackle and associated goods. Granddad took a trolley and began to make his way down the aisle towards the fishing rods. He examined a few and asked my opinion on them all like I was some sort of expert consultant. He eventually settled on a rod and then we moved on to the reel section. My eye was caught by a particularly expensive-looking reel and Granddad examined it closely.

"You have a good eye, Don," he said. "I like the look of this. It's smooth and has a long ratchet and automatic free runner; that's good for carp as well as pike." I nodded. He placed it in the trolley and we moved on again. We stopped at the float section. There were thousands of them all standing to attention in racks and in tubes, their hats were a mixture of glowing red, orange, yellow and green. Granddad looked at a glossy wooden box which held a series of drawers. The top two contained a selection of floats of different sizes and colours. The next one contained small compartments with clear plastic sliding lids. He explained they were for hooks and ledger weights, shot weights, traces, trebles, swim-feeders, flies, bail arms, swing tips, swivels, depth weights, lures, feathers and rubbers. The large box underneath was for bait box, reels, spare line, de-gorgers, pliers, knives and anything that would not fit in the other drawers.

"This is just what I need," he said. By the time we got to the checkout he had added many bits and pieces from the list mentioned including a new landing net and keep net. As we queued we talked about what one could use as bait and how to spot a swim, the best time to catch fish feeding and how to play big fish. Outside the sun felt warm on my back. The attendant said we could push the trolley to the boat as long as we returned it and so we made our way over the bridge. The front of the boat had a large waterproof storage hatch that was empty and Granddad suggested it would be a good place to stow the new equipment.

"Might want to take the tackle box to the bedroom and start to put all the hooks and weights away in their compartments."

"You will have to show me what goes where," I said.

"Why?"

"Because I don't know where you want them."

"It's not up to me. It's your stuff now." I stopped and looked up at his smiling face.

"Mine?"

"Of course it's yours. You have to start somewhere." I still have some of those floats today and my heart aches and smiles every time I see them.

For two weeks I fished until I dropped and wanked until I dropped – what a holiday!

Chapter 30

I cannot leave this age of my life without mentioning the tree house. In our garden between the two sheds was a large tree and for years, it seems, I begged my father to help me build a tree house. It was a Saturday and my sister and her husband were over for the day. We happened to be in the garden when I was asking my brother-in-law how he would go about building one in the tree. We banded a few ideas about when my father piped up that he had some timber left over from a project he had finished which he thought would be enough to do the job. Were my ears deceiving me? Did my Dad just give the "OK" for the tree house?

"Can we build a tree house then?" I asked.

"Sure, why not?" My brother-in-law said he would lend a hand and before he managed to finish the sentence I was off getting hammers, nails, rope and anything else I thought important for the construction of my dream. My Dad and Mike then set about talking. They talked about how to construct the base. They talked about how to construct the walls and which end to have the door. They chatted about the roof design and whether it should be made from ply and felt or the corrugated fibreglass sheets which were stacked at the bottom of the shed. They mused over the best way to gain access to the house once it was complete and then they were considering the base again because the tree would grow and so they would have to allow for arboreal expansion. Then my mother declared that lunch was ready so we all trooped inside for food leaving the nails, hammers and saws untouched. I had finished eating even before the others had barely got going and rushed outside to see if there was anything I could do to push things on a bit. Time ticked by and there were no signs of emerging adults. At last I could stand the wait no more so I went back inside to see what was causing the delay. The adults were still seated at the table and were chatting. Why was my family so keen to talk? Most of my friends' families hardly spoke a word to each other between Christmases so why oh why when an important construction was due to start did they choose to begin verbal discourse? I then realised that my dream of having a tree house was fading like the green from leaves when autumn touched the shoulder of summer: slowly but inevitably. Eventually when the conversation drew to a close and my sister thanked my mother and father for a "wonderful lunch" it was time for them to leave. Lots of goodbyes and kisses and "see-you-soons" later they left. My father looked at me sitting on the settee, arms crossed, bottom lip protruding and eyebrows nearly reaching down to my chin when he must have realised I was not happy.

"You didn't think we would be starting it today did you, Don?" he said knowing full bloody well I did.

"Yes," I said.

"Well, Mike had lots to do today and so have I; we'll do it soon."

"How soon?"

"Soon." Why do parents do that? I asked a perfectly straightforward question and got that age-old ridiculous answer when it is perfectly clear I needed a project start date. "You understood how we are going to build it don't you?"

"Yes," I said hesitantly.

"Well..." I knew something was coming. It was going to be something that was supposed to placate me or distract me from my clear annoyance and disappointment. "Well," he continued, "you could always draw up some plans to show in detail how you want things to be and when we're ready we can take those plans and build from them. What do you think?" Yes, I thought, I could get the bloody watercolour paints out and the brushes and do it all from a finished artist's impression. I was being palmed off, sleight-of-handed. He knew it and I knew he knew it, and he knew I knew he knew it.

"OK," I said

"OK," he replied, "can you put the tools away then?"

"OK." I sighed and like a floppy, stroppy, rug-pulled, deflated fourteen-year-old, I did as he asked. I was putting the tools away in the shed when I decided to look for a suitable door handle for the tree house that would happen *soon*. On the top shelf there were several boxes and old biscuit tins that Dad used for storage of all sorts of stuff that would "come in handy one day". I started to pull down the tins and boxes when I noticed a box at the very back of the shelf I had not noticed before. I grabbed a stepladder as it was just out of reach, brought it down and laid it on the bench. If someone had asked me to guess what was inside, it would have taken me about three years of growing-up knowledge and about a billion guesses before I got it. I opened it up and I am sure my eyes popped out of my head. There must have been at least thirty soft-porn magazines. I quickly checked that nobody was about and lifted one out. It was a *Mayfair* and the front cover sported a big-breasted woman in a skimpy pair of knickers leaning forward with her hand over her nipples. I opened the magazine to find an array of women in different poses showing off their bits and bobs. Then three emotions hit me at once: excitement, sexual desire and utter disgusted shock. The latter was due to the realisation that these must have belonged to my father. Sexual desire won the day and so I took out four magazines and put the rest back carefully. I managed to smuggle the stolen booty into my room and hid them where I knew my mother would never find them. That night I planned the wanking equivalent of climbing Everest.

That night in bed I decided I would take my time. I flicked through some of the pictures then began to read some of the stories. At first I knew I wanted to be a plumber. After the second story window cleaning had the edge – pool cleaner, gardener, mechanic and commercial airline pilot all had something going for it. I grabbed my willy and about fifteen seconds later it was all done. It was a very, very, very long night.

The next morning I woke a bit thirsty and limped to the kitchen for some orange juice. I noticed Mike's car outside in the drive and then heard him talking to my Dad in the garden. When I got there I noticed lots of timber stacked in order of size next to the shed and a ladder leaning against the tree. My Dad saw me.

"Well, go and get dressed then if you want this tree house built." I raced inside (amazing the recovery power of youth) and threw on some clothes and so began the construction of my tree house. I carried timber and held bits of wood in place while Mike or my Dad hammered and cut. By lunchtime we had the base already done and I realised we would certainly not finish that day. Over the years I have learned patience but it took a long time. Back in those early years the idea that patience was a virtue meant absolutely nothing; I wanted it now, five minutes ago or at least within a time frame that I could reach out and touch. Mum brought out mid-morning cake and tea with her usual phrase "Refreshments for the workers". Some discussion was had after cake about the framework to form the walls and I was included in the decision-making process – this was becoming *my* tree house. My Mum inviting Mike and my sister for roast dinner in the evening meant production could carry on into the afternoon. When eventually it became obvious that we had reached the end of the working day, I picked up the tools and put them back into the shed, gathered the timber and stopped to admire what we had achieved. The framework for all the walls was complete and the fibreglass roof was on. The base had extended beyond the profile of the cabin which would form a small balcony that would give access to the entrance. Dad told me he would build a ladder during the week to give me access but "the rest is up to you". This last statement may seem innocuous but it had a profound effect on me. It was the first time I was given full responsibility to realise my dream. My Dad and Mike had given me the opportunity to go beyond my normal experience and take a step into a different world. I cannot remember how long it took before it was finished but I do remember working on it nearly every day; a few hours after school and at the weekend and then eventually it was done. I took advice when I came to a problem I could not resolve and help when I knew something was beyond me. I remember my father and me standing in the garden, Dad smoking a cigarette and looking with a critical eye over the completed works. "Good job, Don, very good job." Pride swelled in me as I am sure it did in him and there we stood, father and son, side by side, his arm on my shoulder and I could have never conceived of a day that he would not be there: he was invincible and wise, he was my father and he would live forever.

Chapter 31

I felt the bulge of the package I carried inside the pocket of my jacket. I was sure by the time I got to the airport exit of the M11 a plan would have surfaced in my dulled brain, but of course, it hadn't. Beth sat in silent contemplation looking out of the side window as the rainwater formed small tributaries across the slightly steamed glass. Some voice from the radio was recounting their adventure down the Amazon and how much they had made for charity. "*Well, good for you,*" I thought sarcastically. I wasn't feeling very charitable; I was feeling angry and desperate. Apparently a Customs and Excise official had confiscated this bloke's blow pipe he had got from some tribe along route and only public outcry had caused them to relinquish it. This had suddenly given rise to a plan and as I drove up to the shortstay car park I knew it was my only real hope.

Two weeks earlier I had been nursing a hangover. I had gone out the night before to my local and got involved in a particularly long game of poker. The game had gone my way and I had netted two hundred pounds so I decided to blow the majority on a few rounds at the bar plus whisky chasers. I had just finished eating a cottage pie meal for one when the doorbell sounded. I opened the door and saw Beth, her face in a smile but behind it I could see fear; I knew she had made the decision to leave. I offered coffee but she held up a bottle and so we sat in the lounge like strangers, drinking familiar wine.

"So when are you going to leave?" I asked eventually breaking the silence.

"Two weeks." I nodded – silence – "This isn't easy, Don."

"I know." More silence.

"I wish..." She stopped; her eyes focused on the inside of her wine glass. Silence.

"I don't suppose there is any point in trying to change your mind?" I said taking the bottle and refilling her glass.

"No. I have thought about this long and hard and it's been so difficult. I love you so much, Don, but at the same time there is this feeling that if I don't take this job then I will be always looking back and thinking – what if? I don't think that's healthy."

"I know and I do understand. It's just so difficult to say goodbye to everything we've become." She nodded. She agreed to stay the night and so I ordered Chinese. By the end of the evening we were both a little drunk sitting on the floor surrounded by half-eaten foil cartons of food. Eventually we went to bed. She, for the first time since we made love, wore a shirt to bed and I kept my pants on. She nestled in my arms, her head on my chest and I looked up at the ceiling and felt utterly lost. There was an emotional barrier between us now that felt it would eventually become permanent. It was as though scaffolding had just been erected in readiness for the bricklayers to arrive and begin building their wall. Eventually we turned our backs on each other and tried to find sleep.

Breakfast was hurried toast and coffee. At first she refused my offer to drive her to the airport but after much persistence she capitulated and agreed that I could drive her when the time came. We hugged at the door after she said she would call to let me know about the flight and then I watched as she disappeared from view as she walked to the tube station. I closed the door.

There is something strange about mourning the death of a relationship. A death of a loved one is final; there is no hope hanging around to scratch at the certainty of it all. With life there is always hope, or at least, the illusion of it. Something nagged at me from the inside. For two weeks I drank, pondered, wept, drank, painted scenarios and then finally I got fed up with feeling like crap and made a tenuous plan.

I parked in the short-term car park and we entered the airport through the glass doors. Armed police strolled about the concourse and between bustling passengers checking in, saying hello or goodbye or simply looking lost. We found the correct queue for her flight which she joined while I made my way to W.H. Smith. I bought a small brown padded envelope, Sellotape, pen and a blank pad of writing paper. Outside, I checked to see Beth was still in the queue and found a seat out of sight and began to write:

Dear Beth,

I want you to promise me something – Only open this envelope when you are in an emotional emergency. Not before, promise me.

Me. X

I quickly wrote another note and placed it in the envelope along with the contents of the package I carried. After sealing the envelope, I taped the letter onto the envelope and placed it back in my pocket and went to join Beth in the check-in line. After her bag disappeared along the conveyor belt she agreed to have a quick coffee with me before entering the departures lounge. We found a table and she insisted on buying the drinks and while she queued I slipped the package in the bottom of her hand luggage. We had agreed that we would only contact each other via email for the first few weeks as it would be better for us both not to hear each other's voice for a while. She would text me to let me know she had landed safely. Coffee finished. We stood and slowly walked to the entrance of the departures gate. She placed her bag on the floor and we hugged in silence, kissed in silence. Our eyes filled with tears and then she walked away – there were no words to say – she was gone.

Chapter 32

"...And the heliphant did a big poo and then it took a banana out of my hand and ate it."

"Did it, sweetheart?" I said to Charlie.

"Yeah, and then we went to see the donkeys and I sat on him and we went round the field with the nice man."

"Wow! Did you see anything else?"

"Yeah, I saw the penguins and giraffes and lots of fish and we saw some owls but they were asleep cos it was their bed time. And I had a chocolate milkshake."

"Sounds to me like you are having a great time."

"Yeah, and... and a farmer did... did... bite Gramps on the bottom."

"A farmer?" I heard Julie in the background howl with laughter and then said something to Charlie.

"Oh it wasn't a farmer, Daddy, it was a llama."

"Oh, I see," I said laughing. "A llama bit Gramps on the bottom; that must have been funny."

"Yes it was but Gramps said a rude word and I told him off."

"I wish I had seen that, sweetheart. So what is Nanna doing for supper tonight?"

"I am having sausages and mash and then jelly and ice cream."

"Sounds fantastic, you're making me hungry."

"Are you coming to supper too, Daddy?" My heart began to ache to be with my daughter.

"No, Charlie, Daddy has some things to do but I will see you tomorrow."

"Are you going to see Mummy?" I could feel my stomach twist and my eyes begin to water.

"Yes sweetheart. I will give Mummy a kiss from you and tell her you had a lovely day but I will speak to you later when you get back to Nanna's and Grampa's."

"Will she wake up today?"

"I don't know, Charlie – maybe." I heard Julie again in the background.

"Nanna wants to speak now," said Charlie.

"OK, sweetie, I'm glad you are having a good day. I will call you later to say goodnight OK?"

"OK." I heard the phone change hands.

"Why don't you and Gramps go and look at the rabbits," said Julie. I heard a cry of delight from Charlie and a brief silence. "Hello, Don," she said and I could hear the tiredness in her voice.

"Sounds like you're having a full-on day."

"Oh yes, but it's fun. I can hear music in the background, where are you?"

"I'm in one of the pubs I used to hang out in about a million years ago. I thought I would have a swift half before heading back; can't believe how much it's changed." There was a brief pause.

"Any news?"

"The Doctor said they would run another test later but..." My chest felt tight as I fought to get the rest out. "...but he says not to hold out any hope. I think we have to face it, Julie, she isn't going to get better." The back of my throat ached trying to hold back the tears.

"Oh my God, Don, what are we going to do?" Her voice was now a laboured whisper as she desperately tried to hold it together. I let out a loud sigh. The barman with blue spiky hair and what looked like a curtain hoop through his eyebrow looked up from his duties but then cast his eyes back to the task in hand.

"I'll come over in the morning and have some breakfast with you, we can talk then. How's Tom doing?"

"OK outwardly, but you know him, he's a stubborn sod. It's eating him up inside and he won't let me in."

"We all have to deal with this in our own way, Julie; we just have to make sure we are there for each other and, of course, Charlie. I don't know if I have the courage to tell her, when the time comes."

"You will, Don, we all love you very much. I have to go now, a few things left to see and then we will head home – call us later?"

"Of course."

I wiped my eyes and blew my nose and then took in the surroundings of the pub I had spent many evenings and many pounds in during my late teens and early twenties. The pub was not very busy but the majority of the punters were young, like the barman; they were equally gelled, dyed, glued and stapled and I wanted them all to fuck off.

Outside the air smelled of the sea, fish and chips and the arcades were discordantly awash with the chinking of falling coins, electronic laser gun fire and simulated Formula One engines that were interspersed with the announcements from a bored bingo caller. I slowly walked along the avenue of demented amusements as the shell suits fed the machines with coin after coin of their dole money – disability pay and child allowance spent on cigarettes, burgers and cheap half bottles of chardonnay bought by Chardonnay for Chardonnay and consumed by Chardonnay – or was it Sharon – who the fuck cares? I walked on, the rabid sounds diminishing and now the High Street loomed. The right-hand side of the street began with Mr Ronald McDonald like some neon plastic figurehead on the good ship *Bargain Stores.* Cheap seaside merchandise filled the shelves as gum-chewing cashiers sat behind their tills tapping their painted talons upon pay-as-you-go pink glittered mobiles; dulled and with no horizon, their eyes were drawn up occasionally from their dreams into the ribcage of the store and its fibrillating heart whose grey customers shuffled around in search of something to purchase for under a fiver. Had it been like this when I was a boy? Was it as depressed, or was I bringing my state of mind aboard ship? Back then the town sported a Butlins Holiday Camp and it seemed more alive, even in the winter months. The Germans may say the town for me was *un heimlich* but it felt like home: there was the familiar but also the unfamiliar, something foreign or alien invaded the peripheral vision making the whole seem out of sorts with my memory. A break in the rows of shops gave way to a small arcade which cut through to a parallel road. This had not changed much; a few of the shops were the same and there was still a flight of steps which used to lead to a small café. I climbed the stairs. It was still a café although the decor had changed. I ordered a coffee and made my way to a window seat – many years earlier I had been sitting at this window drinking coffee with members of a rock band I was in when I saw the girl who would lead me from boyhood to manhood. I was seventeen.

Chapter 33

AGE 17

In spite of the hot weather the three of us had our black biker leather jackets, although we had them, for the moment, hung on the back of the chairs in the café above the shopping arcade. We sat at the window nursing our mugs of tea and were deliberating if we were going to have a band practice tonight or tomorrow, Sunday, during the day. We had got wind of a possible impromptu beach party at the usual place along the coast tonight but so far no confirmation had come via the normal channels. Drunk Dave was the normal channel of communication but he had gone on Thursday to see Dumpy's Rusty Nuts play and had not been seen since. We took our potential rock stardom seriously and only a beach party would prevent us from our practice. That's not strictly true – any party would take precedent as long as there would be a sufficient number of girls going. Dean, our guitarist, was a year-and-a-half older than us and had already lost his virginity and had a regular girlfriend. Pod had lost his virginity last year and had slept with more women than was thought feasible. Pod's proclivity was towards the larger woman – the bigger the better. In fact he had slept with a few whose gender was questionable if it wasn't for the obvious gigantic breasts, which were a must in his book. I remember him a few years later at his twenty-first birthday. He was playing in a different band that night and had just completed a sound check. We were at the bar when something squeezed through the double doors at the end. Not only was gender in question but species as well. She was clad in a leather jacket that must have taken the hide of at least four cows to complete. Her hair was shoulder-length and glistened with grease and her neck was completely hidden by the fat hanging down from her chin. She waddled towards the bar and even from a distance of thirty feet it was obvious that she had some large growth on the side of her head and I wondered if Frankenstein's monster was missing a bride. Pod's face lit up when she docked at the bar and ordered a pint of snake bite. She looked up at us and offered a brief nod.

"It's my birthday," said Pod.

"Happy fucking birthday," she replied.

"I'm drumming tonight with the band."

"I know, I've seen you before." Her voice sounded like a metal drum filled with phlegm being rolled over gravel. I moved away a little and pretended to focus on anything else but them. The barman handed her the pint of snake bite, she took a long draw and plonked it back on the bar with a resounding thud.

"Cos it's my birthday, if I buy you a few pints of snake bite, will you let me shag you later?" She gave him a brief look up and down.

"Yeah if you want." What a poet. I left Romeo and Juliet and joined the other members of the band. Two pints of snake bite later I noticed the two love birds disappear. The next day Pod had given a full account of his encounter with the space hopper. Pod had suggested the back of the guitarist's Transit – and so, on the guitarist's dog's blanket slung over a set of speakers and flight cases, they had done the deed. Pod then admitted a few days later that his dick was red, inflamed, hurt like hell when he had a piss and was leaking a discharge so foul that he gagged when he smelled it.

We agreed that Sunday would be best for band practice and if the beach party didn't happen then we would just go into town and hang about. Dean said he would call me later and left us to the last sips of our tea. Pod was talking about getting a new drum kit and was waxing lyrical about Tama when I noticed a girl walk in. She had long straight blonde hair that shone like she had just been to the salon. Her light cotton blue dress was cut about six inches above the knee and pleated out like something from the fifties. She ordered tea and moved to the table just over Pod's right shoulder which meant I could observe her as he talked. She had a soft tan and her eyes were blue and her full lips puckered as she blew her tea. The top three buttons of her dress were undone and exposed ample cleavage. Pod was now on the benefits of a twenty-inch *Paste* ride and a couple of crashes, maybe a set of *Roto* toms and a double kick peddle just in case he was to get another bass drum. It all washed over me as I was totally besotted with this girl. I guessed she was my age but then I was never any good at estimating the age of the opposite sex. She looked up and saw that I was looking at her and I offered a brief smile and then back to Pod and his wish list of percussion extras without waiting for a response. I was trying to be nonchalant and mature. I took another glance at her but her attention was drawn through the window. We finished our teas and decided it was time to go.

The impromptu beach parties contained the usual suspects but sometimes strangers would show up with their Party Sevens or bottle of Thunderbird. We were a fairly incestuous bunch in as much that Bob would be seeing Jane for a couple of weeks and then split up and then Jane would be seeing Paul when Bob started to date Sandra, Jane's best mate, until of course she was no longer Jane's best mate when she started seeing Bob. Sue, on the other hand, had been seeing Drunk Dave for over a year while Drunk Dave had been seeing everyone he could get his hands on for over two years. Tony Toes, so named because he had webbed feet, had been seeing Jackie until he discovered Jackie had slept with Drunk Dave on the anniversary of their first date three months before. Shaggy, named after the character in *Scooby Doo,* was generally stoned most of the time and could never remember whom he had slept with until he was reminded by a sudden slap on the face the following day. I had had my eye on a girl called Pauline for some time but so far I hadn't stolen so much as a kiss. I arrived, just after the sun had dropped behind a calm sea, with Pod and Dean armed with cans of beer and a bottle of cheap brandy. A large camp fire was already underway and I could see several of the usual crowd sitting on blankets. The girls were wearing jeans and over-sized jumpers; the boys were in their leather jackets, jeans and white baseball boots. Someone had brought a huge ghetto blaster and a bag full of batteries and the sounds of Thin Lizzy rocked through the salty, sultry air. We pulled up a rug and exchanged gossip. Shaggy was already off his face and had fallen asleep with a girl using his stomach as a pillow. His arm was across her with his hand firmly on the mound of her breast. I had seen the girl many times but never learned her name; she was one of the peripherals but clearly did not mind an unconscious grope. Pauline was there, opposite me, and her raven hair shone in the light of the fire. She was sharing a rug with Sue, Debbie and a boy called Tim. Tim was not part of the core group but had designs on joining the family and it was clear he was interested in Pauline and her body language, the playing with the hair, the leaning in towards him, the shy laughing, the acceptance of a swig from a bottle of Thunderbird without wiping the top first and her tongue exploring the inside of his mouth, all led me to believe she was interested in him too. Everything about Tim was 'quiffy'. His shock of straw-blond hair had a quiff at the front and his jumper was sort of vogue-baggy and fluffy in a sort of non-effeminate but feminine way. His leather jacket had tassels and his jeans were naturally faded and slightly torn; he looked like a fucking quiffy, fluffy rock star from some European semi rock group whose lead singer had an impossibly high voice. I hated the git. In my heartbroken angst I accepted a magic mushroom cake, smoked a joint, drank some beer and had a few swigs of brandy. Half an hour later, the sparks from the fire were actually mini dragons leaving their molten womb for the first and last time to begin their hazardous journey across the dark waters to Middle earth. We were nomads, homeless warriors on a long journey to fight against the darkness spreading across the world. *She* would learn the nature of his treacherous heart and *she* would learn of my true lineage, my unbroken line to the Kings of old. And we will fight until the very back of earth is broken and the last of us passes across the great sea to the home of the victorious dead – we will pay the ferryman – and let them weep for none like us shall walk this earth again. Shaggy sat up and announced he needed a shit – I laughed until my lungs were the size of walnuts. The music was changed and *The Dark Side of the Moon* came on. I lay back, closed my eyes and now I was on stage at a festival playing in a Pink Floyd tribute band. We had the lights and the lasers and Pauline was at the front looking up at me, her face filled with love and wonder, while I made my guitar sing. I was halfway through a blistering guitar solo and Pauline was getting a tad moist with desire, when I heard voices approaching. I sat up and noticed a few people walking towards us. They were on the opposite side of the fire but I heard one of them, a girl, ask if it was OK to join us. A general murmur of approval ensued and the newcomers sat down. It was only when she put another log on the fire that I noticed it was the girl from the café earlier. My heartfelt desire for Pauline left via the front door without stopping to put on a coat. She was in the company of three other girls with different grades of *shagability* and two boys, who from my intense observations, seemed not to belong to any of the girls. She wore jeans and a long cream fluffy jumper which seemed all the rage and her fine, long blonde hair lifted gently in the slight off-shore breeze. She sat in close proximity to Pauline so I could observe them both at the same time. There was no doubt that Pauline was attractive but this girl was just off the planet, which incidentally, describes my state of mind at the time. If I could have focused my eyes long enough I am sure they would have been permanently fixed and dilated on every nuance of her glorious being. I decided I would at least try and clear my head a little and perhaps go for a short walk along the beach. I got to my feet determined not to display that ridiculous wobbling effect drunk people have when they are determined not to appear pissed. My ascent to the horizontal was near perfect.

"You off?" said Dean.

"No, just woing for a galk," I said confidently.

"OK, you wo for a galk," he replied and I staggered off knowing that this beautiful nymph, this goddess from the land where the shores are golden and where, at the dawning of each new day, the sun shines forth its wossaname and fills the land with the light of the heavens. Well, she was certainly going to think I was some dung-head druggy git now. It is difficult, at the best of times, to walk on deep sand with a cool and matter-of-fact gait. It is totally impossible when the sand you're walking on is moving away from you so that you think you are moving backwards even though you know you are walking forwards. It also doesn't help when small blue creatures with high-pitched squeaks keep running over your feet which seem an awful lot longer than normal and seem to be flapping at the ends. I think I made it about twenty yards before I fell over and just drifted into a deep sleep.

I woke to the gentle sound of the waves lapping at my feet. I jumped up and staggered back a few paces. The beach was deserted save for the remains of the fire, which was about to be claimed by the sea. I had no idea what the time was but it felt early and I was ravenous. There is only one café on the waterfront which is open early on a Sunday and I put on my marching feet and headed for it. The café served, in the height of season, the early risers; the anglers from the end of the pier, old folk out for an early morning walk and the sobering-up brigade from the night clubs. All found their way to *Jenny's Café* for a full English or just a cup of tea. Apart from the hunger, I felt very refreshed and it did not seem long before *Jenny's* loomed up close. On entering, I saw that the café was very busy and on closer inspection could see that some of the revellers from the beach party were there including the goddess who was sitting with two of the three other girls she was with and one of the boys. Next to her table sat Pod and Drunk Dave. I ordered a full English and joined them.

"What happened to you?" asked Pod.

"I went for a walk and fell asleep on the beach."

"We thought you'd gone home." Drunk Dave picked at a plate of chips and filled me in on the events during my absence. Tim had apparently gone off with Pauline and had done the deed and Shaggy had eventually left with the girl whose name I can never remember but apart from that there was little I missed. I felt a faint pang at the news that Pauline had had sex with quiff boy but not with the intensity I would have expected. Suddenly the object of my new obsession looked up at me with her blue eyes.

"How are you feeling?" she said in a voice that was light and airy but with no real accent I could determine.

"Surprisingly good," I said. "Considering the state I was in and for spending a night on the beach."

"You did look a bit wobbly."

"When did you all leave?" I said wanting to get away from analysing my poor performance.

"About an hour ago. We haven't been here long." She introduced me to her friends she had met through Tanya, the other girl from last night. Finally she told me her name – Yule. I discovered that she lived in my road only further up the hill. She knew where I lived because she had seen me there a few times when they had driven past. *They* consisted of her mother who was from Sweden and her father who was born in Hertfordshire; she had no siblings. After breakfast was over she asked me to walk back with her. We didn't walk as much as ambled with a good dollop of strolling thrown in. I discovered that as a family they lived in Chelmsford where her father worked in a factory making precision tools. He was laid off at the beginning of the previous year but had managed to secure a position at a tool firm located on the industrial estate at the top of my road. They had decided to rent out the property they owned in Chelmsford and rent a house here in the hope that they could return if work picked up again. Yule went to a private school in Chelmsford and lived with her Grandparents during term time and this was her first summer break with her parents. She was seventeen and had planned to go to university to study law straight after her exams next year. I told her about the band and that we had a couple of gigs this summer and she promised to come and see us. Although we were the same age she was far more mature and sophisticated than me. She was relaxed and confident and walked with a grace that was neither forced nor pretentious. She laughed openly and without caution and by the time we reached my house I wished we were starting the journey again.

Chapter 34

I was very excited. I was excited on two major fronts. The first was that we had a gig that night in the Old Church hall and second, Yule would be there. We had seen each other on a few occasions during the last two weeks leading up to the gig and I had the distinct feeling that she really liked me, the evidence of which presented itself in the following way: she constantly leaned into me when we walked; she kept hitting me when I playfully insulted her; she rested her back against mine at another beach gathering; and her friend Tanya said "she really likes you". The latter was told to me the day before the gig. Indications were that about thirty people had promised to come and so we were hopeful that a few more would show on the night. After much consideration I chose to wear faded blue jeans and a plain white shirt with a granddad collar. We arrived at the hall about two hours before the gig and began to set up the equipment. We had borrowed two lights from a friend who owned a disco: a red filter was added to one and a green to the other. We also had two car headlights which were wired to a car battery via a simple on/off switch which one of our friends would operate. We placed them behind the drummer, shut all the curtains, turned off all the hall's lights and tested out our simple effects. We agreed it looked good but could do with some smoke to enable it to reach its wow potential. Kipper, an unofficial roadie, claimed he might be able to sort out the smoke as he knew someone in the trade and without another word he left. Nobody could remember how Kipper came into our lives, he seemed to just gradually morph into existence. He could not play any instrument; however, he was a fantastic air guitarist, air bass player or air drummer, or on occasions, an air penny whistle player. He was named "Kipper" because of his unusual feet position when he walked. He was a frenzied Black Sabbath fan and slept in a coffin much to the dismay of his long-suffering parents. He had a tattoo on his arm of a human skull that was so badly done that when he bent his arm it had the same expression people have when they fart and then follow through; not in the least bit scary. He was a lad of few words and at first we thought him deep and mysterious; it was only later we realised his silence was due to the fact that he was basically shy and had a limited vocabulary. We ran through a few numbers and the sound, although a bit bouncy, seemed good enough. We opened a few cans and made some subtle adjustments to things that didn't need adjusting and tweaked things that should have been left well alone. Kipper returned with a big grin on his face carrying a large black case. He placed it on the stage and we gathered round. He theatrically flipped open the lid and we all peered in. The case contained six mini spotlights of various colours, a series of black interconnecting poles which turned out to be the light stands and four black metal boxes with electrical wires protruding from the base, containing what looked like blocks of toilet disinfectant. Kipper's mate, who also owned a disco, agreed to loan us the lights and had given us four electrically operated smoke generators.

"All you do is wire them up to the battery and when you want them to smoke you just touch the two ends together," said Kipper with the confidence of a bomb disposal expert on his first day on the job. Fantastic! There followed much debate to determine the correct placement of said lights and smoke thingy but in the end we decided that two should go at the front and two behind Pod, the drummer. We were to use them at the beginning of our opening number and then again towards the end. We rigged a tape deck to the PA and put on some music. People started to wander in. Cans were shared among the growing crowd along with a bottle of vodka and the inevitable bottle of Thunderbird. Yule showed as promised and the butterflies in my stomach seemed to go from a passive fluttering to an all-out punch-up. She wore a pair of faded tight jeans and a black lacy top and my heart and groin ached for her. At nine o'clock there were approximately sixty people and so we decided to get to the stage and make music history. Yule gave me an extended kiss on the cheek and her eyes glistened. Kipper switched off the main hall lights plunging everyone into total blackness until he found his zippo and made enough illumination to find his way to the side of the stage and switch on a small stage light. (It was my mother's knitting light with the shade taken off.) We switched the amps off standby and Dean's guitar started a controlled screech of feedback. We were ready. The opening song was "Don't Believe a Word" by Thin Lizzy. I nodded to Kipper who nodded back, poised with a bare electrical wire in each hand. The crowd clapped and whistled wildly and turned our butterflies into raw adrenalin. Pod clicked his sticks together for a four-count and on the fourth the lighting man switched on the car headlights behind

Pod and Kipper touched the wires together and Dean struck the first chord. The gig at the Old Church hall is still remembered to this day. You see, what Kipper had omitted to tell us (due no doubt to his lack of vocabulary) was that his mate who lent us the lights was also a member of the Territorial Army and the smoke things were in fact adapted army standard issue thunder flashes. On the count of four, two small thermo-nuclear devices went off. Sixty members of the audience, four band members, one lighting man, Kipper and a bloke who just happened to pop his head round the door to see what was going on all experienced the same consuming thought: "I am about to die". We didn't. We gained and we lost. We gained the smoke that we wanted (albeit a tad more than we intended), we lost our hearing for a few seconds, Dean's white training shoes turned black, we gained a few white spots in front of our eyes, we lost the fire exit sign and we gained a shared insight into our own mortality. Directly after the explosion there was absolute silence, no doubt due to our brains working out whether or not we were still alive. Dean broke the silence.

"Kipper, you wanker!"

The next night I lost my virginity.

Chapter 35

After the gig we loaded Pod's father's van with the equipment and arranged to pick it up the next day. When the shock of the explosion subsided everyone seemed to be in an ebullient mood, no doubt due to the fact that they had survived with no injuries. We started the song again and this time there was no nuclear involvement, Kipper had disconnected the other two devices. The crowd made a lot of noise for just sixty people and we managed two encores.

"I really had a good time tonight, Don," she said grabbing my arm as we walked home alone. "I thought the band was great."

"Thanks," I said trying to act cool.

"Do you fancy coming over to mine tomorrow evening?"

"Yes, absolutely, love to. What time?"

"Maybe after supper, about seven-thirty OK?"

"Yep, I'll be there." We took our time strolling back and I insisted on walking her to her door but just before we got to her gate she stopped under the streetlight and turned to me. Her eyes were bright and the intensity of her stare made me feel as if she could see beyond my own eyes and into my inner self.

"Will you kiss me?" she said. It was a subtle mixture of a question and a command, the butterflies were back and they had brought some mates with them.

"Well, if you insist then, how could I possibly refuse such a…" I never got to finish the sentence. Her slender hands reached behind my neck and pulled me towards her. My hands took her waist and pulled her even closer. The next few minutes were a rush of emotion and physicality I had never experienced before; its intensity was so great that I thought they would overwhelm me. Blood drained from my head and filled my dick and when her thigh pressed against it my body reacted automatically by pressing against her, placing my hands on her hips; I pulled and pushed at the same time. Was I in love, in lust? Absolutely. In that small occupied and orange illuminated part of the universe one human being was experiencing the most intense pastiche of… of … stuff… he had ever had. The torrent thundered through me. It was like a shallow raging river, ankle-deep but fierce and determined to knock me off my feet and carry me away. Love, lust, fear, inadequacy, doubt, certainty, confusion and clarity were all mixed together, boiling under the skin and shouting for my attention and when her moist tongue pushed gently between my lips and into my mouth I grabbed the lamppost for fear of falling.

I eventually got home at about three in the morning. I jumped into bed and then had the quickest and most intense wank of my life – *thrapping* had reached a whole new level.

I woke about midday and the previous experiences flooded back. I grabbed my dick again just as my mother knocked on my door announcing she had a cup of tea for me – I let go. After breakfast my father ran me in the car to pick up my bass and amplifier from Pod's house. I told my Dad about the explosions. "Bloody hell, you could have all been killed!" He was always a bit dramatic. "Don't tell your mother," he said leaving the drama behind and finding his usual pragmatic self. For the rest of the day the anticipation of seeing Yule again was a constant companion. I tried to watch the TV or read but my concentration was so ephemeral that I gave up trying and as a consequence, time seemed to slow. Love had taken on a completely different meaning. It became undefined but somehow sharp at the same time and attached itself to every thought; it became omnipresent and was as disquieting as it was comforting.

Being keen gardeners my parents spent most of the weekend potting, re-potting and watering various plants and vegetables so sometimes the traditional Sunday lunch got demoted to an evening meal and today would be no exception. My father insisted that we eat as a family and tonight my brother and his wife were coming to join us which meant we would not be eating until about seven. My pre-occupied brain calculated that by the time we had finished it would be near eight and I said I would be at Yule's at around seven-thirty. The idea that I would be half an hour late was inconceivable; I have always been one of those people who would rather be an hour early than a minute late. I had no chance to incline my mother towards an earlier meal and even less chance with my father as he was building a second compost enclosure. In the end I decided I would have to call her to say I would be late. I tried on three attempts but the telephone kept ringing. Maybe I would write her a note and put it through her letterbox but just as I began the search for a piece of paper and a pen, my father requested my help. Damn. Turning over compost has a way of focusing the mind and, to a certain degree, the nose, away from the future and placing it firmly in the here and now. By the time I had finished it was the moment to have a bath, decide what to wear, eat my dinner as fast as I could and get out of the door. The bath was a success, choosing what to wear, however, was less so. My brother and sister-in-law arrived and as usual the conversations were jovial and happy and reminded me of an episode of the *Waltons* all be it with a lot more swearing. We sat down to eat about ten minutes before seven and by seven fifteen I had cleared my plate, thanked my mother for a lovely meal, brushed my teeth for the third time, applied more aftershave, told my mother for the second time that I did not want pudding, fended off my brother's enquiries into "so who's this bird then?" and was out the door and heading towards Yule's house with an optimum speed that would get me there as quickly as possible without causing me to get all sweaty and eventually arrived at her house three minutes before the half hour. I knocked on her door and waited – nothing. I knocked again, a bit harder but still no sign of life. I checked my watch and all the evidence pointed towards the correct time on the correct day. I knocked again about as hard as I dared and was about to walk away when I saw movement through the obscured glass. The door opened and a tall blonde woman with striking blue eyes offered an open and friendly smile.

"Ah, you must be Don," she said with a hint of an accent. She offered me her hand and I shook it gently. "I'm Eve, Yule's mother."

"Hello, pleased to meet you."

"Come in, come in." She stepped aside and in the space of a nanosecond I had taken in and processed a great deal of information. She looked just like a slightly bigger version of Yule. She wore a knee-length deep blue, splash-patterned light summer low V-neck dress showing a more than ample bosom and the top of a white lace bra. The image went straight to the top of my best wank list, knocking Pod's Mum of the number one slot. On her feet she wore simple leather flip-flops, toenails were painted blood red and she wore silver rings on two of her toes. Her make-up was subtle and her lips full and void of lipstick. As I passed her I detected a waft of gentle sweet scent that I could not be certain was not natural. "We are out the back," she said. She closed the door and I followed her through the hall, kitchen door and onto a patio. A man next to Yule, whom I took to be her father, was half-reclining in a sun chair. His hair was short and dark and his even tanned face was framed by a close cropped beard. His bright blue Hawaiian shirt was open exposing a hairy chest and his shorts, cream coloured, were knee-length and sported large pockets on the side of each leg. He stood as I approached and offered me a strong handshake. If I thought Yule's eyes were blue, they were nothing compared to this man – maybe his tan accentuated them but they were sapphire blue and seemed to have their own light source.

"Pleased to meet you, Don, I'm Graham," he said smiling, exposing film-star teeth.

"Pleased to meet you too."

"Beer?"

"Yes, please." He reached into a cold box at the side of the sun chair and pulled out a bottle. Grabbing an opener, he popped the lid and handed it to me, raising his own as he did.

"Cheers."

"Cheers," I replied. Yule patted the chair next to her and as I sat she leaned over and kissed me on the side of the cheek.

"Hello, handsome," she said easily and I flushed slightly.

"Hello, yourself."

"So, I hear you tried to kill my daughter along with most of the audience last night," he said, his face beaming with false anger.

"Yes... I mean no... well, it did make us jump a bit." We all laughed.

"Good to know my daughter's dating a pyromaniac."

"Dad!"

"Well, it's more exciting than golf isn't it?" So, I thought, it seems official, I am dating their daughter. For a while we just chatted about music in general; he was a big Dylan fan and loved Pink Floyd. Eve, on the other hand, preferred folk. Eventually Yule grabbed my hand and pulled me towards the house.

"Come on," she said, "let's go to my room and listen to some music." I padded after her and waved to her parents in a way that I hope suggested that in no way, no way at all did I have any thoughts towards playing with their daughter's rude bits: no way ma'am, no way. I had no idea if I was convincing but they waved back and I could see no concern on their faces. Their home was a bungalow with a loft conversion which Eve used as a studio where she painted, made jewellery and, oddly enough, repaired watches. Yule's bedroom was located at the front of the bungalow opposite the lounge. As we entered I was surprised to see a lack of personality but then remembered she was only here during holidays. The walls were plain magnolia which was broken by splashes of colour from the heavy curtains decorated with yellow and green patches. Two paintings hung on the wall which looked original and Yule informed me were by her mother's hand. They were modernistic with lots of heavy texture and bold colours. I had no idea if I liked them. The pine double bed in the corner against the wall was covered with a sun-coloured duvet and adorned with several large cushions. Next to the bed was a pine chest of drawers with a record and tape player resting on the top. Several albums and tapes lay on the floor or were leaning against the wall and on the far side of the room by the window stood a double pine wardrobe. Yule switched on the two shaded wall lights above the bed and turned off the main light, which gave a softer and warmer glow to the room.

"You choose the music," she said as she sat on the bed cross-legged. I began to flick through the albums: Pink Floyd's *The Wall* was the first I spotted and as I flicked through I saw several familiar bands including Japan, Sad Cafe, Roxy Music, Dire Straits, Soft Cell, Human League and several from Led Zeppelin. I chose *The Wall*. I joined her on the bed sitting in the corner propped up by the cushions. She leaned against me and stretched out her legs. My arm moved round her and rested on her waist and there, in the soft glow of the wall lights, sipping beer and listening to Pink Floyd, I found myself looking down her bra-less cleavage. It was like showing a starving man a full roast dinner and telling him to wait until permission to eat was granted. For a while we didn't speak;

her breasts gently rose and fell. The music faded and the sound of a baby crying signalled another track on the album.

It was at this point she sat up, put her beer on the chest of drawers, took mine, placed it next to hers and then sat astride me. She leaned forwards and we began to kiss. My groin began to ache with the swelling as her tongue found mine. She suddenly stopped kissing me and sat upright. She slowly undid the buttons at the front of her dress and then carefully let the straps fall off her shoulders exposing her breasts; she placed her hands on the wall and leaned forwards inviting me to kiss them. I cupped her left breast with my right hand. Her skin was soft and her breast firm. The nipple stood erect like Cleopatra's needle and I moved towards her anticipating the moment when it entered my mouth. The knock on the door sounded like a gun going off.

"Yule," her mother's voice said, "do you want some...?" and the last bit was a word I didn't understand, probably due to the fact that now I was shitting myself.

"Yes, please," said Yule with enthusiasm. She put her straps back over her shoulders and buttoned her dress with the speed of a spitting cobra. Breasts safely away, she jumped off the bed and opened the door. Her mother handed her two bowls.

"Thanks, Mum," she said and handed one to me. It was a special Scandinavian apple dish which had been modified over the years and was served hot with ice cream. I wanted the breasts back but I accepted the pudding with good grace. In fact it tasted delicious. The apples were sweet and there was a crunchy thing going on with a hint of vanilla and cinnamon. To this day I never learned the name of the dish but it was fantastic. When we had finished she took the bowls back and on her return put on the second part of the album. She closed the door and walked towards the bed.

"Right then, where were we?" She undid her buttons again but this time she reached for the hem and lifted the whole dress over her head. "Take your top off," she ordered. I took my top off.

"What about your Mum and Dad?"

"Oh, they won't disturb us."

"Are you sure?"

"Yes. Now take off your jeans." I took off my jeans. She slid one of the drawers open and removed a silver packet and threw it on the bed. I looked down at it as though it was alien technology. My inexperience must have beamed out like a lighthouse because she offered me a smile which contained an understanding and maturity which went beyond her years and mine.

"Lie back." I lay back, grateful for the direction. She sat astride me – and then it began. Most people will tell you that their first time was not what they expected or did not live up to the hype. Of the women I have spoken to since, most said that they had just wanted to get it out of the way like it was some chore that simply needed to be done. The earth did not move; there was neither a choir of angels nor the gentle rain of rose petals. For me, however, I had Pink Floyd instead of angels and a girl whose experience was far greater than mine and she directed the symphony of sex as though every movement was orchestrated with improvised genius. Aren't I the lucky one? Thirty seconds after penetration we lay back with me wondering how on earth blokes in those porn films keep going for hours. Twenty-three minutes later we began the second movement of the symphony with "*adagietto*" as our tempo. The third and concluding movement combined elements of the first and second with the dénouement covering us both with glossy sweat and racing hearts. I had entered the world of men and the world was changed forever.

We dressed each other slowly and deliberately and then it was time for me to leave. Her parents were watching television in the lounge as I entered to say goodbye.

"Are you going now?" said Graham.

"Yes I am and thanks for having me?"

"No problem." He waved a hand.

"Oh and thanks, Eve, for the apple thing," I said. "It was delicious."

"My pleasure, see you soon."

"Goodnight."

"Goodnight," they said in unison. Outside the air was warm and still. We hugged and kissed and promised to see each other the next day. She waved from the front door as I walked away, my step light, my heart full and my willy a little bit sore.

For the rest of that summer we saw each other nearly every day and the sex got better and I got more confident. The time for her to return to school arrived and so it would be back to live with her grandparents and her life there. We said goodbye halfway between her house and mine. She told me that she would not be back at half-term and Christmas would be in Chelmsford with her grandparents.

"So when will I see you next?" I failed to keep the desperation from my voice.

"I don't know," she said flatly.

"Maybe I can visit you?"

"My Grandparents aren't like Mum and Dad, they're very old-fashioned."

"I don't care; I just want to see you."

"We'll see. I'll write."

"Well, OK I suppose."

"Will you write to me?"

"Yes of course."

"Good." We kissed and then I watched her walk away. She turned once and waved and then she was gone. I never saw her again. She wrote eventually telling me that she had met a really nice boy and I would really like him and how she had a really nice time during the summer. She broke my virginity and my heart. Every time I hear *The Wall,* I cannot help feeling a little sad at the last line of the album.

Chapter 36

It had been two weeks since she had arrived in Basel and had sent a text informing me that all was well. All wasn't bloody well actually. We had not spoken on the phone or contacted each other by email. At first it had been difficult. Sleepless nights, too much booze and far too much self-pity were all just bearable when you knew the pain and heartache would ease – it wasn't, it didn't. Then I got an email.

From: beth@btnet.com
To: england@exnet.co.uk

Hi, Don,

Things here are all a bit hectic and strange. The Swiss are odd. They have a unique sense of humour which so far I have failed to understand. Work colleagues are OK and very patient with me. Rula is very nice and she has shown me around the place. Hans I like too although at first I thought he was a bit stand-offish but later I realised he was shy. He invited me out for dinner but I insisted Rula come along; I didn't want to give him the wrong impression. My apartment is small but well-equipped and has a large balcony that looks out across the city. It's very pretty at night. It's also very expensive here but I think I will be able to buy better when I've sussed the place out more. Everyone speaks English to me so how I'm ever

going to learn Swiss-German I have no idea. Anyway, that's enough about me. How are you doing? How's the writing going? By the way, I got your mysterious letter and parcel. I haven't opened it, promise. You are very strange you know. Email me soon and let me know how you are doing.
Love, Beth. X
Ps. It's hard for me too you know.

Hans! Who the fuck is Hans! Bastard! I bet that prick is thinking *"langsam, langsam erwischen die Affe"*. I'll fucking give him slowly, slowly catch a fucking monkey. Prick! Cunt! Wanker! I was a bit cross. I grabbed my coat from the back of the chair and stormed out of the flat and down to my local. I sat at the bar and ordered a pint of Guinness and a large whisky chaser. Fifteen minutes later I ordered another.

"Steady on, Don," said George the landlord. "You on a mission or what?" As all good bar persons he listened to my tale of woe with the occasional nod of the head or "you're fucking right there, mate". As the drinks continued to flow the abyss grew closer and my mood darkened. A man had parked himself next to me at the bar and it did not take me long to realise he was of the type that gradually encroaches not only on your time but on your personal space as well. Anyone who had half a social brain could see that I was not in the mood for idle chat but, like these people all over the world, it simply did not compute. After a few tentative in-roads with comments like "not bad beer this" and "Man U are probably going to do it again", he eventually introduced himself.

"I'm Geoff," he said and offered his hand.

"Don," I replied and shook it weakly. I ordered another drink which he offered to pay for.

"No, thanks, Geoff, I don't want to get into rounds." Geoff was short and stocky and had a nose which indicated he had been a serious drinker most of his life. His grey hair was cut extremely short and his face sported a small neatly trimmed goatee. He wore white and blue shell suit bottoms, Nike trainers and on his wrist was a thick gold chain. A grey plain hoodie covered his blue T-shirt on which was written "God knows I'm good" and a few stains which looked like curry.

"It's no problem; I've got plenty of money." He opened his wallet and flicked through at least thirty twenty-pound notes.

"Good for you, Geoff."

"I'm a consultant," he said. I supped my pint. "I only have to work three days a week." I took a sip of whisky. "I charge five-hundred pounds a day." I checked my phone for messages that I knew were not there. "I'm sorting a problem down in Dartford. They got stuck and couldn't figure it out so they called me." I looked about the bar to see if I could spot a newspaper. "I'm actually semi-retired; I do this for a bit of beer money." He sniffed and then ordered a brandy.

"What one do you want?" said the barman.

"I'll have the better one, the Remy. Can't stand the cheap stuff; I always go for quality."

"On its own?" the barman asked.

"No, with coke and ice." I could see this being a very long night. Some other person came to the bar and so I was let off the hook for a while but the man left shortly after Geoff offered to buy him a drink as well. I downed my whisky and ordered another along with a pint of Guinness.

"You married, Don?"

"No."

"Good lad."

"What?"

"Just fuck 'em and leave 'em. It's for the best. I've been married three times and I swore never again."

"Oh."

"You know what they are?" He stepped closer.

"What?"

"Women, you know what women are?" I did not answer. "I'll tell you. Women are just life-support systems for their twats." He laughed like a truck and looked about the bar to see if anyone else had thought it funny – they hadn't. "I'll tell you a joke."

"No, thanks."

"This one is a belter."

"I just want to sit here quietly and…"

"There was this bloke, right, watching TV late at night and having a few beers when his five-year-old son comes down the stairs rubbing his eyes. 'What's the matter, son?' he says, 'Can't you sleep?' 'No,' says the son. 'Why not?' 'I heard a word at school and I don't know what it means.' 'What's the word?' 'Cunt,' says the son. Well, the bloke thought about it and then says, 'You know that torch you got for Christmas?' The son nods. 'Go and get it.' The son returns with his torch.'

I could feel at this point the whisky was making its presence felt and my patience was leaving fast, but I did not care and so ordered another.

"Anyway," he continued. "The bloke took the kid by the hand and they crept upstairs to the main bedroom where his wife was sleeping. He slowly peeled back the duvet and then opened her legs. 'Now shine your torch up there, son.' The boy clicked on his torch and did as his Dad asked. 'Right,' says the Dad, 'you see that furry black thing there?' The boy nods. 'Good. That's called a vagina.' The boy nods again. 'The rest,' says the Dad, 'is a cunt.'"

Geoff roared with laughter and looked around the bar convinced this time he had an appreciative audience – he didn't. Eventually his roaring faded to a few chuckles and then silence. After the tumbleweed had left he spoke again.

"Sea bass!" said Geoff.

"What?" I said.

"Sea bass."

"It's a fish."

"I know. How do you cook it?" Fair enough, I thought. The man obviously doesn't know how to cook sea bass so I thought I would help him out, besides it would stop him telling shit jokes.

"There are several ways to cook it but…"

"I know all the ways to cook sea bass. What do you reckon is the best way?"

"Grilling."

"No," he said and stuck out his chin.

"Yes," I said.

"No."

"You asked me what I thought was the best way and I think it's grilling."

"Why?"

"Because it is a delicate flavour, as indeed most fish are. So I think grilling or maybe shallow frying is the preferred way, maybe with a hint of dill and then just a squeeze of lemon to taste."

"No."

"OK, what do you think is the best way?"

"Deep fry."

"What! You must be joking. Deep fried!" I was now very drunk and very annoyed.

"Yep, all fish are best deep fried. Take the fish, rub it in flour, drop in beer batter and deep fry it."

"Are you fucking Scottish or something?"

"No, why?"

"Because in Scotland, anything that can be eaten gets covered in batter. You might as well deep fry English asparagus or plunge smoked salmon into hot fat."

"It's been scientifically proven that the intense heat and beer batter brings out all the flavour in fish."

"Scientifically proven, what a load of bollocks! Where the fuck did you read that? In the in-depth science page of the *Sunday Sport* perhaps? I'll bet you're the type who thinks the Americans never landed on the moon or that Bush ordered the twin towers to be blown up so he could have an excuse to go to war."

"Well, he did." Then I lost it.

"No wonder you've been married three times. What I don't understand is how a misogynistic, chauvinistic, depraved, socially deficient arsehole ever persuaded any women to marry you in the first place. What did you do, strike them senseless with your rapier-like wit and intellectual insight into world politics and fine dining? Or maybe you wooed them with your fantastic collection of landfill-rescued clothing? But deep fried sea bass? You must be the only bloke I've met who has deaf taste buds!" It was then he hit me. I flew backwards off the bar stool and hit my head on the jukebox. When the world stopped spinning enough for me to get up, he had gone. I guess he really, really likes his sea bass deep fried.

I woke on my sofa fully dressed and with a headache so large that it probably had its own passport. I eased myself up to a sitting position, my head screaming in opposition and felt the side of my face; it was sore and most definitely swollen. I smelled of sick. Gradually I made my way to the bathroom and just made it before I was sick again. I looked in the mirror and Quasimodo looked back. Fuck! My eye was jet-black with deep purple around the edges and my cheek was red and swollen with a dry blooded cut. I only had snatches of memory and those that were intact weren't good. Oh bollocks! I popped some painkillers and managed to hold down a glass of water and then found my bed, got undressed and pulled the duvet over my head and dived head first into oblivion. When I woke again my headache had been reduced to a dull woolly-type existence but my face still hurt. I managed a light bite of egg on toast, switched on the computer and replied to Beth's email:

From: england@exnet.co.uk
To: beth@btnet.com

Hi, Beth,

Well, it's been an interesting couple of weeks. I've been busy writing and it seems to be flowing well. Work is work, the usual crap but apart from that not much to report. Glad to see that you've made some friends; Hans sounds a right scream. I'm jealous that you've got a balcony. I went to Basel once, pretty in places. There was a bar called LUPO, is it still there? You seem to be settling in OK, bound to be strange at first but knowing you it won't take long before you're part of the furniture. I was going to make a joke then about flat-pack furniture but you're in Switzerland not Sweden. Take care of yourself and drop me a line soon.

Love, Don. X
Ps. I miss you so much my face aches.

I pressed send. It was Sunday night. I called my boss and told him I needed a couple of weeks off; he moaned a bit about short notice but in the end said OK. I grabbed my coat and headed for the pub. I had a pint, apologised to George, went to the off licence, brought three bottles of whisky, a bag full of junk food and headed home. Being in a dark place does not necessarily mean sitting in a room with the light off. I don't believe in God but I do believe in Hell because for the next two weeks I went there; I think I even redecorated. Men, in general, are not good at dealing with emotion and I was crap. We are fixers. If it's broke we will pull it apart, clean all the bits, oil them and then put it all back together. I tried that but it still stayed broke. I am Kafka man, I am the underground man. What's the fucking point of it all? Drunk by day, drunk by night.

...and all the fucking ghosts come out to play. Hold my hand if you can, Mr Spectre, and we will dance a pretty tune – I have sugar on my teeth – let us play air guitar to my favourite tunes and let the neighbours call out the boys in blue to tell me to turn it down – I have a bed full of crumbs – Choose box twelve, you fucking idiot, don't listen to Edmunds he's in league with the banker – Ping! What have we now? Could it be sweet and sour chicken or is it chicken madras? Oh my, you've only a seven-hundred-thousand pound budget to move to the country, you poor, poor bastard – there can't be that many men in the world with dicks that big can there? – go on, over the tits again – Dory you poor demented fish, tell Nemo you love him and go back and do the jelly fish thing again – I'll clear that up tomorrow – if I ruled the world everyday would be the first day of spring – bad... bad... bad...

My eye had only a faint hint of yellow now. I cleaned up the sick and shit but could not work out where the blood had come from. Oh well. I vacuumed and dusted, cleaned the kitchen and did the washing up. I stuck a load of washing in and jumped into the shower and let the hot water sting my skin. I scrubbed clean, put on a fresh pair of jeans and a crisp white shirt and sat down at the computer to write. I made myself a sandwich and a coffee and wrote some more. I answered my voicemail and called the worried people back. I gave my neighbour a nice bottle of wine and said I was sorry. I took a deep breath and opened my emails. Most was the usual crap; round robin jokes, insurance quotes, several online porn responses and one from Beth. I deleted all but Beth's:

From: beth@btnet.com
To: england@exnet.co.uk

Hi, Don,

You really are crap at lying aren't you? I know you feel Hans is a threat but he is not. Anyway, what if he was? Sooner or later we both have to face the fact that we have to get on with our lives. I'm not that fickle. You think that I don't hurt every day? At least you've got your mates around to prop you up. I love you very much, more than you know and that feeling isn't going to go away anytime soon. I got drunk, very drunk, after I read your email and cried for hours. I ate too much chocolate and now I have two very large zits and that's not good when I have to meet clients. I nearly opened your box thing but I didn't. You are so much in my head I have hardly room for anything else. Please don't hate me.

Love, Beth. X

Ps. Email me soon.

From: england@exnet.co.uk
To: beth@btnet.com

Hi, Beth,

You're right, I am crap at lying. I'm finding this very difficult. I've had a bad couple of weeks but am getting the hang of feeling shite. Of course, there have been a few women since you left – nothing serious. In the end I had to switch my phone off. I took a couple of weeks off work but I am back on Monday. I love you too, sweetheart, and I have no idea what the answer is but I guess in time we will both find someone else. Oh, Christ! Just writing that makes me feel sick. Long way to go I guess. Just think, when I'm a rich and famous writer you can say to your mates "I shagged him".

Love you
Don. X
Ps, there is no Ps.

From then on we emailed each other every two weeks or so. It seemed to me she had settled in very nicely and had picked up the odd sentence in Swiss-German. We kept it all light and fluffy and there had been no mention of Hans or anyone else of the dating nature. I went through the motions at work but threw myself into the writing; there's nothing like a bit of angst to bring out the muse. I learned that she had flown over to spend a week with her parents but thought it best not to let me know. It hurt like hell but I knew she was right. I spent a bit more time with Bret, Des, Simon and Kath. Sue, who had a boyfriend called Paul, seemed affable enough and we went out for a few meals. One night we all met up at a night club where a blonde woman chatted me up. It was all very flattering but I was simply not interested.

"You want your head tested," said Kath. "It's been, what, six months now?"

"I know, but when I'm ready..."

"You need to get your end away that's all. Once that happens you will be fully on the road to recovery."

"Why, are you offering?"

"No."

"Why not?"

"You're a mate, that's why." I went on bended knee.

"Oh, please sleep with me and make me feel better. Go on, you'll enjoy it."

"Get up, you idiot!" I raised my voice.

"Kath, please, please, let me hide my willy in your rabbit's hole?"

"Will you please shut up, you crude bastard!" I stood and put my arm around her and gave her a kiss on the cheek.

"I know you want to really but I think it's best we don't so please stop begging me." She hit me across the back of the head.

"Twat." It was good to be among friends.

Chapter 37

Life just ticked on in the way it does and although my thoughts never strayed too far away from Beth I was beginning to get familiar with the feeling of displacement. The emails were less frequent and probably, if I'm honest, less important to me; I even managed a whole two days before I opened one. The last one, however, I got the feeling things were not going as well as they might. Her past news was the usual mix of likes and dislikes when it came to Basel itself and it did seem that Rula and Beth had become pretty good friends. She had, in previous emails, mentioned Rula's brother who happened to be engaged but in this last one mentioned the engagement was off and she had not really gone out anywhere with Rula for a while. It was difficult to pinpoint why I felt things were not right but somewhere, between the lines, it seemed odd. There were perhaps more dislikes than likes and there was hardly a mention of Rula. Beth's description of work had a downward feel and not many positive comments so, taken as a whole, it left me feeling that perhaps she wasn't particularly happy. I felt a flutter of hope and then dismissed it.

Chapter 38

It was a Saturday in early November and it was one of those bright mornings where the sun still had a little strength left and combined with no wind at all, the day felt warm. It was late morning and I decided to nip to the shops to get a paper, bacon, eggs and a couple of fresh crusty rolls. The baker was just around the corner and the smell of fresh bread is always intoxicating. I donned a large woollen jumper, grabbed my keys and headed out the door. Somewhere someone must be having a bonfire because the air had that waft of burning leaves. Today felt good. In the bakers I said hello to Old Tony, a local character who always wore a flat cap, purchased my two crusty rolls and then headed up to the Tesco Local. I was mulling over whether to go for the smoked or unsmoked bacon when I happened to glance down the cooked meat section and saw a woman thumbing through the cured hams. I was immediately struck by her physicality. She was tall, shapely and wore tight faded jeans and a close-fitting woollen jumper which did not hide her ample bosom. Her long blonde hair hung over one shoulder and it had a modern cut-in style. She looked at me briefly and gave a quick smile. For the first time Beth did not enter my head. I was immediately attracted to her; smoked or unsmoked? She moved closer and now the corned beef had got her attention. I put down the double pack of unsmoked bacon and picked up the smoked. Now she was at the sliced beef. I could detect a hint of perfume, subtle and expensive. She dropped a pack of sliced beef into her basket and stepped nearer. She was now at the scotch eggs and coleslaw. I put down the smoked bacon and picked up the unsmoked.

"Sometimes the simple decisions are the hardest," she said. Her voice was soft and clipped.

"I know; the wrong choice and many a ruined breakfast lie in wait." She smiled.

"Yes, I know what you mean. Personally I would go for the smoked, but don't let me influence you." I dropped the smoked into my basket.

"No problem, I simply needed a nudge in the right direction."

"Don't blame me if the breakfast doesn't work."

"No, I won't: my decision, my breakfast but thank you for your concern." She smiled again, walked past me and headed for the tin section. Her arse was very nice. I caught the odd glimpse of her but then I got to the checkout and was heading home. The bacon and egg with crusty rolls, while I perused the newspaper, was a damn good success and gave me the required energy to spend on a fairly domestic day; by the time I'd finished the flat was looking clean and respectable. My local watering hole was host to a birthday party that evening for one of the usual suspects and George had splashed out on a disco. Should be a bit of fun, I thought. As I ran a bath I checked my emails and noticed one from Beth but decided to read it on Sunday. Clean shaven and armed with a new packet of cigs, I headed for the pub. It was still early when I arrived and the disco man was just setting up. I bought a pint and sat with a few of the locals. Morris, the birthday boy, was already well on his way and we didn't think he would last the course. Terry challenged me to a game of pinball and I lost all three rounds. Slowly the place filled up as locals and friends of the birthday boy arrived. The disco started and before I knew it the party was in full swing. I ordered another drink when someone next to me spoke.

"How was the breakfast?" I turned and saw the blonde from Tesco.

"Oh, hi, yes, the breakfast was a raving success."

"Good, I didn't want to carry such a responsibility."

"Are you friends with Morris?" We had to raise our voices as the music was quite loud.

"Well, sort of. Morris is married to Emma who is my sister's friend. She asked me to come along. My sister has just split up with her boyfriend who also knows Morris so, just in case he turns up, she wanted some moral support."

"And what about you?"

"What do you mean?"

"I mean, where is your fella tonight?" The conversation was interrupted when George asked her what she wanted to drink.

"I don't have a fella."

"Oh, OK."

"What about you?" she asked with a hint of a smile which suggested that she knew that I knew we were both on the road to the great "chat up highway".

"No, I don't have a fella either?" She laughed. "What?"

"You're not gay."

"How do you know, I might be."

"I have an extremely good gaydar and you are most definitely not." She paid George for her drink and took a sip. "Catch you later." She walked away to a table where I saw a few people sitting; one I assumed was her sister. How did I feel about all this? To tell you the truth I was struggling. I had not had sex since Beth and that drive in me is a strong one. This woman certainly ticked the boxes and yet I had an enormous feeling of guilt. As far as I was aware Beth could already be in another relationship and had moved on emotionally. I, on the other hand, clearly hadn't. Why? Was I still in love with Beth? Of course I was. Suddenly a fight began in my body. The brain stepped into the ring and flexed its intellectual muscles in a bid to knock out the heart that currently held the title. The bell sounded and the two went at each other with measured punches. The brain led with a few jabs of "time to move on" and then a quick combination of "she's the one who decided to leave" and "you have to live too you know". The heart feigned left and right and the blows were ineffectual; a fancy bit of footwork and then it threw a right with "yes, but deep down you know Beth's the one for you" then it ducked under a haymaker of "but I need a shag" and forced a body blow into the ribs with "you'll regret it". It was going to be an epic battle so I asked for a large scotch and I could hear the heart screaming "foul play!" After a while she indicated that I should join their table and in doing so I thought it was an opportunity to give the heart a fighting chance; after all, if she turned out to be lacking in the personality department I could call it a draw and walk away.

Her name was Sarah and she was fantastic. Bollocks! She was friendly and attentive, a good listener and very sharp-witted. She was also about six months out of a relationship and did not want to get involved in anything serious. Did that mean she just wanted a shag? I could feel the heart already heading for the showers. I was aware that the music had changed. 10cc's "I'm not in love" began and she looked at me. The heart had now finished showering, had got changed and was getting in a cab heading for home, a comfortable duvet, the TV and a box of chocolates.

"Fancy a dance?" she asked.

"Why not," I replied and the next thing I knew we were slowly moving to the music, bodies grinding together like two millstones with a throbbing banana stuck between them. Three slow dances later I had told her my flat was only just around the corner and she had said it would be nice to see it. Her sister had given me a sharp look when she was informed of Sarah's decision to leave, but leave we did. At the off licence I bought a bottle of Pinot Noir and some After Eights and we made our way back to the flat. I poured two glasses and after a whirlwind tour, stopping briefly at the bedroom, I put on some music and we sat on the sofa, sipping wine and waiting for that inevitable moment when lips and tongues got together and clothes came off. We engaged in a bit of small talk for a while then she announced she wanted to freshen up. I took her glass from her and as she left the lounge, heading for the bathroom, she turned and offered up a smile which simply and unequivocally said "we'll get down to it on my return". She shut the lounge door, which to my mind indicated she might fart, and then my mobile rang. It was Beth. It was ten forty-five p.m.

"Beth?"

"Hi, Don, I've been trying to contact you. Have you read my email?" She sounded tense and a little worried.

"I haven't opened it yet, are you OK?"

"I've tried to call as well." I looked at the phone and noticed the voicemail icon in the corner of the phone was flashing.

"Shit, sorry, Beth, I can see a voicemail. What's up?"

"I'm at Luton airport." She sounded pensive. "Can I stay at yours tonight? It's too expensive for a cab to Norfolk and Dad's car is in for a service."

"Yes, sure, I can't pick you up though, I've been drinking."

"No, it's OK I can get a cab; should be there in about an hour-and-a-half or so. Are you sure it's OK? I mean I'm not interrupting anything am I?" My heart was beating fast now and my eyes darted towards the lounge door.

"Beth, it's fine, just get here, no problem." I could hear her let out a sigh of relief.

"Thanks, Don. I'll call when I'm close."

"OK, see you soon." Just hearing her voice was enough. The door opened and Sarah came in and the look on her face told me she had heard the conversation.

"If I head back now I can get a lift with my sister." I nodded.

"I'm sorry about…"

"Oh well, shit happens." She grabbed her bag. I stood. She gave me a prolonged kiss on the cheek and I showed her out, the door gently clicking shut. I leaned against it for a few moments to collect my thoughts and then sprinted around the flat clearing away any evidence of company. I even opened the windows to let in fresh air and let out the perfume. Yellow spring air freshener liberally squirted did the rest. I then opened the windows again because it smelled as though I was trying to cover over a smell. I made some coffee and deliberately burned some toast. That should do it. I then checked the email.

From: beth@btnet.com
To: england@exnet.co.uk

Hi, Don,
Things here are not working out for many reasons and I will be flying in late on Saturday at Luton. I know it's a cheek to ask, but will it be OK if I crash Saturday night? Dad can't pick me up and it will be too expensive for a cab. I have much to tell you. Please let me know if this is OK?
Love, Beth X
Ps. Be really nice to see you.

I checked the voicemail and got more or less the same message except a hint of uncertainty and panic in her voice. The phone rang again. Beth.

"Hi, Don, I am about fifteen minutes away."

"OK. Are you hungry, shall I stick something in the oven?"

"No, but I could do with a drink."

"I've got about half a bottle of wine and a few beers."

"Perfect."

"See you soon." I poured myself another coffee and checked the bathroom again; all was in order. I heard the cab pull up. I helped her with three cases and deposited them in the hall.

"Wine?"

"Beer." I popped the lid and handed her the bottle. She took a sip, looked at me and I could see the tears welling. I simply put my arms around her and hugged her and then the tears and the sobs flowed. When she had settled we sat on the sofa and I put some music on in the background.

"OK. So you want to tell me what's been happening?" She took a tissue from her handbag, blew her nose and then took a swig of beer. She looked at me, smiled and then nodded – then began.

"At first everything seemed good. The work was difficult and challenging but slowly I was getting to grips with it. Rula was great. She helped show me the ropes and after work we would go into town, take in a few bars and the odd restaurant. At weekends I sometimes would go over to her place and she showed me the shops and other useful stuff like how the public transport worked and how much I should pay for a taxi, you know the usual things. That was all positive. The negative was in truth I missed you more than I ever could have imagined. I kept thinking that Don would hate this or Don would really enjoy this place and it never really went away; I just tried to bury it away. Things began to get easier." She finished her beer and I automatically gave her a new one while pouring myself a glass of wine. "I met Rula's brother, Tomas. He was engaged to Anke, a Swiss-German, and I liked them both very much. We all went out together but as time went on I began to become attracted to him." My stomach took a nasty lurch but I did not let it show. "The company had arranged for a bit of a bash to celebrate second quarter figures and we were all meant to meet up at a bar. Anke could not make it so Tomas came alone. Rula and Tomas suggested we move on to a club they knew so a few of us went. Tomas told me he had split up with Anke, called off the engagement and everything. Rula did not know and he begged me not to tell her. When I asked him why he'd broken up, he told me that he realised he did not love her enough because he had fallen in love with me." I took a deep swig of wine and again my stomach lurched in anticipation of where this was leading. "Rula got a bit drunk and left with two of the others and that just left Tomas and me. He told me that as soon as he realised he had fallen for me he finished with Anke. He gave her a load of old-hackneyed bullshit about not being ready and needed some time to think. I told him that I had feelings for him but I wasn't ready to get involved in a relationship. He asked if we could go out for a drink later in the week to talk about it and I said OK. I didn't say anything to Rula at the time and, looking back, maybe I should have done." She excused herself to use the bathroom. It felt like something dramatic was still to come and that she needed time to compose herself. I was dreading hearing that she had slept with this bloke but tried to mentally steel myself for the news. It was a peculiar notion that I was prepared, this very night, to have sex with another woman and yet felt betrayed and jealous of the fact the she may have already done the same. It was a most odd feeling. I heard the toilet flush and then a few moments later she came back. She sat down again, took another swig of beer and continued. "We went out on the Wednesday, to break the week up; anyway Thursday morning I had taken off to get some stuff done at the bank so

Wednesday was better for me. There is a nice, but expensive, restaurant just off the main square and he suggested we meet there. He was already seated when I arrived. He told me that he had felt a strong attraction the moment we had met but did nothing about it because he was engaged, but as time went on he realised that his feelings for Anke were not as strong as he had thought. Maybe he was just used to being with her; after all, they had been engaged for the last two years and been dating two years before that. I didn't know what to say really except I wasn't ready for another relationship. I was nervous and drank too much too soon and I was getting a little drunk. We finished the meal and he paid the bill and insisted on walking me home. I did ask him in for coffee, only coffee and he said 'fine' but he could not stay too long as he had work the next day." She began to tense and took several small sips of beer. "We sat on the sofa drinking coffee when suddenly he made a play for me. He leaned forward and tried to kiss me and for a second or two, I admit, I let him. But then I had the most powerful surge of guilt. I realised that I was still so very much in love with you. I pushed him away and said that I wasn't ready. He got angry saying that I had encouraged him. I told him that the reason why I was not ready for a relationship was because I was still in love with you." She looked directly at me, her deep brown eyes were pleading with me to believe her and I had no doubt she was telling the truth. I took her hand.

"It's OK, Beth."

"He got really cross and, like some spoiled child, he just flung his coffee cup off the table. It smashed on the floor; coffee went everywhere. I told him to leave and at first he just ranted. He then seemed to see sense and then left, slamming the door behind him so hard it knocked a few of my CDs off the shelf in the hall. I called Rula the next day and she went completely cold on me as if it was my entire fault that her brother had broken off his engagement. From then on she just spoke to me when work demanded it. No warmth, no kindness, nothing. I took a few days off work, claimed I was ill, and just thought about my life and what I really wanted."

"And what do you want?" I asked, keeping my face impassive despite my stomach not knowing if it was filled with butterflies or knives.

"You."

"How do you know?" She looked at me with honest incredulity.

"I needed to do what I did, go out to Switzerland and give the job a go but what I did not bank on was how much of you affected me. On the surface things were good but underneath my life was shallow. I may have held out and eventually met someone else but when you have found your soulmate… well, what can you do."

"What indeed." I poured myself another wine and Beth a beer.

"So what about you; has there been anyone else?"

"It was a close-run thing, but no, there has been no one else."

"How close?"

"Close." She nodded. "So what about work?"

"I called Geoff and he said that it would not be a problem coming back. In fact, they are having a shift around and it looks like I will be promoted."

"Bloody hell, Beth, that's great news!"

"Yes, fell on my feet on that one. What I really want to know is… what about us?"

We woke the next morning having made love like we had never made love before. It was not just about the closeness but the pent-up sexual desire we both felt was let loose like a breached dam. We lay together in relative silence; we were just enjoying the closeness and stillness. Eventually Beth spoke.

"I'm hungry, got any eggs and bacon."

"Yep."

"Is the bacon smoky?"

"Yep."

"Are you going to make it, or shall I?"

"You."

"But it's your place and I'm the guest."

"It's my eggs and bacon and you're the one who is hungry."

"So if I make some you don't want any?"

"That's not what I said. Here's an idea. Let's do it together." I got out of bed. She fluffed up the pillows, turned over and pulled the duvet around her. "Oh, no you don't!" I grabbed her ankle and pulled her off the bed.

"Bastard!"

"I know, but I'm your bastard." The television was on low; Andrew Marr's politics show blinked in the background as we ate bacon and eggs. I had no fresh rolls so I made toast instead and fresh coffee. It felt as though she had never been away. She was almost finished when she dropped her knife and fork on the plate and suddenly looked up at me. "What?" I said startled.

"I've just remembered."

"Remembered what?" I asked as she disappeared into the hall unzipping her cases.

"Where did I put the bloody thing?" Her voice was slightly muffled. After a short while I heard her shout, "Found it!" She walked back into the kitchen carrying the envelope and box I had put in her bag at the airport over six months ago. She sat down but kept them from my reach as though I would suddenly snatch them back. "Shall I open it?"

"What does it say on the envelope?" She didn't have to look.

"Open in case of emergency."

"Well, is it an emergency?"

"Well, it is kind of isn't it?"

"How do you come to that conclusion?"

"Well, I'm going to open it anyway." I sat still, my heart raced. Oh, shit, I thought but did nothing to stop her. She carefully opened the envelope and pulled out the white folded paper, opening it she read aloud.

Dear Beth,

If you are reading this then I guess you must be in a pretty bad state. I am not saying this will be the answer but it is one you can most certainly rely on. Now open the box.

She looked at me, her face etched with curiosity. The box was about four inches square and covered in a naff "happy birthday" wrapping paper. She tore it off. The box itself was coloured a plain dull brown and a single piece of sticky tape held the lid closed. She used her nail to lift an edge and peeled the tape off and opened the lid. Nestled on cotton wool in the centre was a ring and on the underside of the lid it simply read, "Marry Me". She took out the white gold ring which held a single bright diamond. She looked at me. It was not what she was expecting. Her face was unreadable. Shock? Horror? What? She placed the ring on her finger.

"It fits," she said, almost to herself rather than me. I kept silent. Then she took it off, placed it back in the box and handed it back to me. Tears had welled up and were in danger of spilling down her face and in a cracked voice she said, "You... you... you have to do it right."

"What?"

"You have to do it right, on one knee." I took the box, moved the chair and on one knee over the scraps of smoky bacon and eggs I asked Beth to marry me.

"Yes, of course, you bloody fool," she said.

One year later we were married. It was a small and simple affair; no more than forty guests. I accepted that the wedding ceremony take place in the small church in the village where her parents lived and swallowed back my objections to "and in God's name" blah, blah, blah. We did the meal and the speeches and about another forty people showed up for the evening. We had a band, kids slid on the dance floor, small boys tried to look up the women's dresses, bad dancing all around and hardly anyone sober. We honeymooned in Morocco and then two years later Charlie was born and four years after that I was preparing myself for turning off Beth's life-support machine and saying goodbye to her forever – forever.

Chapter 39

I stared into my empty coffee cup and then out of the window. Cars and shoppers passed below; people went about their business and all of them were ignorant to my history, my plight, my agony and I was ignorant and scared of the future; not the long distant future that no one can imagine, I mean the immediate one. My chair scraped the floor as I stood and the waitress looked over and pulled from her apron a small book. I cannot remember how many coffees I had had today but my bladder told me it was many. I indicated I wanted the small room which was located near the entrance. The tiles were blood red and not particularly well installed and the off-white porcelain urinals had seen better days. As my full bladder drained I noticed a bit of graffiti scribbled on the tiles in front of me: "Barry F takes it up the arse". I wondered who had written it and did Barry enjoy anal sex? Was he gay? Was this slander? No, slander is verbal, this is libel. I wondered how many people had thought my thoughts since this poetic gem had been first scribed. I washed my hands in cold water because the hot tap was stuck. How long had it been stuck? I dried them on a drier that sounded as if it were in the throes of death; its death rattle making one last attempt to do what it had done all its short inconsequential life. I paid the waitress and left a generous tip which she thanked me for. Outside felt odd. It was like stepping into a bright room having spent a whole day with the curtains closed; somehow I felt detached from this grainy world. I looked at the back of my hand and discovered that it too seemed unfamiliar to me; too much coffee maybe. By the time I had made it to the car I felt a little better. I started the engine and just sat back and closed my eyes for a few moments, took a deep breath and then both body and mind decided it was time to go home and face the inevitable. As familiar places drifted by I wondered whether I was the same person now as I was way back then in those summer days of my youth. I could hear my friends, the echo of their voices, their laughter and their tears and I could feel them all reaching forward from the past with tiny fingers. I realised with sudden clarity that I was not the same. There were trace elements of my personality still with me, connecting me back to the past like an old telephone line. If the small boy that was me could pick up the phone I doubt I would hear him; his voice would be weak and uncertain, but then so was mine now. In less than twenty-four hours I will have to nod my head to the doctor to switch off the machine that had kept Beth's and my hopes alive for so long. How will I do this? Do I lean over, kiss her tenderly on the lips and whisper "goodbye, my sweet darling, I love you so much but it's time for you to go now" and then nod to the doctor? Maybe I will actually have to say "switch off the machine"; something in law perhaps requires my utterance. I'm sure I will have to sign some papers. What then? Do I sit and wait until the doctor declares her dead and then step out of the room, turn my back on her and walk away? How will it play out in the end? And then there was Charlie. Fortunately she was young enough not to fully understand and so the loss would be confusing but not heart-wrenching. She would grow up with just a distant memory of her mother and would ask me in later years "what was she like?" Then there is Beth's Mum and Dad; no parent should outlive their children. Beth created a life and touched many more and the loss would be terrible. The living carry the greatest weight of death and they cannot detach it like a rucksack; it's for them to heave through life until they, through their own death, pass it on to others. I finally passed my old home, the small stream, the playing fields, the cemetery and then away from the memories as I left that small seaside town behind.

The drive home was an automatic one. Roads passed underneath the car and fields and houses flew by the windows practically unregistered. As I entered my village I pulled over and parked outside the off licence. It was an old-fashioned shop which boasted a large selection of single malt whiskeys. I exchanged brief pleasantries with the shopkeeper and then decided on a bottle of Oban. I would not get pissed and maudlin; after all I had to speak to Charlie later. I decided I would order an Indian takeaway after I had a long soak in the bath.

As I entered, the house felt empty; not just the absence of people, but empty. It also felt cold and I shivered. I built a fire and when it was well under way I ran a bath. I put some bubbles in, went downstairs and poured a large whisky, dropped in a couple of cubes of ice and headed back upstairs. The answering machine was blinking as I passed and so I hit the play button which then informed me I had two new messages. The first was from the hospital and my stomach knotted instantly; it was almost like cramp in its severity. The message from the doctor simply said that there had been no change and so he would see me as planned tomorrow and if I needed more time it wasn't a problem. The second message was from Julie.

"Hi, Don, we are back. Charlie has had a great day and she's managed a little nap on the way home so she will be up for a while yet. Give us a call when you get in."

"There are no more messages," said the machine. I decided not to call yet; I would have a bath first. I let the hot water and bubbles tackle the outside of my body while the whisky massaged the inside. I put on some Mozart, something neutral that did not have any links between me and Beth. I just wanted my mind to stay flat and non-thinking. I no longer wanted a metaphysical relationship with my brain. I had done enough over the last few weeks and I had the feeling it could overload at any time and I would end up painting potato prints from a padded room for the rest of my life. Strange though it may seem, that last thought evoked a feeling of comfort and, in an even stranger way, I wanted to swap places with Beth. I wanted to get drunk. Eventually the bath lost its warmth and with it its appeal so I pulled the plug and lay there feeling the water drain away and me getting slowly heavier and heavier – and I just continued to lay there, not moving, seeing the steam rise off my body and sensing my skin cooling, drying, tightening like an all-over face lift. I didn't want to move – I just wanted to stay like that in a state of mental and physical blankness. Eventually I began to shiver and that broke the bonds that held me there.

"Hello, Daddy," said the little voice.

"Hi, sweetheart, did you have a good day?"

"Yes, I did."

"And what did you see?"

"I saw the penguins and they are funny…and I saw lots and lots of rabbits and I did stroke one of them I did…can I have a rabbit, Daddy?"

"Well I can't see why not. Maybe we will get one next Saturday?"

"Yes. Nanna, Daddy said I can have a rabbit." I heard Julie's voice in the background say "That's fantastic!"

"So what else did you do?"

"I saw…" I heard Julie whisper to Charlie. "I saw a hippo… totus… sum."

"A Hippopotamus?"

"Yes and a baby one as well; Daddy, can we have a hippo… mus… tom?"

"I don't think so, Charlie, they grow so big and we don't have the room. Let's just start off with a rabbit and see how we get on OK?"

"OK. I went on some rides and Nanna said I could have some ice cream and I had some cake."

"Ice cream and cake?"

"Yes and I had lots of milk."

"You'll go pop!"

"No, I won't, Daddy."

"No, OK; but I might have trouble lifting you up if you keep having lots of cake and ice cream."

"I'm only little, Daddy."

"I know you are, sweetheart."

"Are you going to see Mummy tomorrow?" My chest tightened.

"Yes, I am."

"When can I go and see her?"

"Tomorrow maybe, later in the morning. Come down with Nanna and Grandpa."

"OK, Daddy, I have got to go to bed now?"

"OK, Charlie, sweet dreams."

"Night night, Daddy."

"Get Grandpa to take you up to bed, Charlie and I will come and read you a book… Hi, Don."

"Hi, Julie, thank you so much for today, sounds like she had a really good time."

"It's never a chore spending time with our granddaughter." She let out a deep sigh and her voice began to crack. "What time are you meeting up with the doctor?" Julie already knew the answer to this; it was her way of approaching the subject.

"The meeting is set for nine. They will run through the test results again then…" I was struggling now. I did not want to talk about it but I knew it had to be done, to be faced down and dealt with, once and for all. "Then I guess I'll call you. We don't have to rush it, we can take our time to say… goodbye." Julie sniffed. "How's Tom?"

"Not coping well. Charlie's been a great tonic for him but he just refuses to talk to me about it. He doesn't want to face saying goodbye to our daughter and I can't blame him but I hate being shut out; we are all hurting, Don."

"I know. We all have to deal with this the best way we can and I guess Tom just wants to work things through in his own head first."

"And what about you, Don, have you worked it out in your head?" There was a hint of sarcasm but that was just the grief coming out and I ignored it.

"I spent the day trying to come to terms with it but the simple fact is I can't. No matter how logical or philosophical I try to be, it's all too close to be distant, if you understand me. I simply can't stand outside myself and give myself objective advice. I am going to have to tell the doctor tomorrow to end my wife's life, your daughter, my daughter's mother. How do I do that, Julie?" There was a silence and I was aware my voice had been a lot harsher than I had intended.

"I don't know," said Julie, and I knew the tears were falling from her. She sniffed and cleared her throat. "Roger has landed at Heathrow so he will be here in about three hours."

"He's going to be shattered."

"I know." I had not seen Roger since the wedding and had only spoken with him a few times. He's like Tom, quiet and shy. Beth had kept in touch regularly with her brother via webcam, email and telephone but I didn't really know him.

"Listen, kiss Charlie for me, say hi to Tom and I will call you after I have spoken with the doctor OK?"

"OK," she said almost inaudibly and then hung up. It was my turn to sigh. I entered the lounge and switched on the TV and flicked through until I found some easy innocuous film to wash over me. I poured another whisky and then put the bottle back in the cupboard out of sight and ordered an Indian. I was not in the slightest bit hungry but I knew I had to eat. However, when the delivery arrived and I began to unpack it, the smells triggered my hunger and I ate until my stomach ached. The film ended and I flicked through until I found another. I did not want to go to bed. Eventually my eyes began to close and the clock showed it was close to midnight. When I brushed my teeth I took extra care; I even flossed. I set my alarm on my phone for seven-thirty which would give me enough time to have a shower, a coffee and perhaps a bite to eat before I headed for the hospital. It took several attempts at fluffing pillows, turning over and scratching before I found a comfortable position. And then I dreamed.

Beth was sitting on the swing in the garden wearing her long blue dress with the lace hem. The sun was shining and I was seated at the garden table. In her hand she held a mobile phone and occasionally she held it up to her ear and spoke but I could not hear what she said. Charlie was playing on the grass between us and she was making something from old toilet rolls and elastic bands. "The bands keep breaking, Daddy," she kept saying but I couldn't reply. I was immobile and on the table my laptop was open, the cursor blinking on a clean white page. I tried to answer Charlie by tapping it out on the computer but none of the keys matched the letters. She began to cry as the elastic bands broke and snapped against her little fingers. Then Beth put the mobile to her ear and suddenly I heard a distant ringing. Charlie responded and picked up an empty toilet roll to her ear and began to speak to Beth. I could not hear what was being said. Charlie stopped crying and smiled and then laughed. "OK, Mummy, I will see you soon," she said. Then Beth tapped the phone again and this time the ringing was louder. I looked next to the laptop and I could see another empty toilet roll. I put it to my ear and I could hear Beth's voice. It was faint and crackly as though she was calling from the other side of the world.

"I can't move," I said.
"I know," said Beth, "but you will soon."
"Why don't you come over and sit with me."
"Because I have to go now."
"Why? We can just talk?"
"No, I have to go now."
She stood and walked towards the garden gate and as she went through she smiled and offered a little wave.

I woke. The first thing I noticed was the tightness across my chest and then I realised I was drenched in sweat. The duvet and sheets were wet too. The digital clock blinked out the time, 05.32. I switched on the side light and noticed my phone indicated a missed call and voice mail. I went to the bathroom and wiped myself down with a towel. I dialled the number to retrieve my mail and it told me I had one new message. The background seemed noisy, crackled and distorted and I could only just make out the message.

"Message for Mr England; this is Nurse Baily, I am sorry, Mr England, but there has been a development, you had better come in. There is no need to rush." End of message. I knew then that she had died. It was the very same message I had received when my father passed away. I drove my mother to the hospital, we did not rush. At the hospital we were ushered into a small room and then the doctor arrived to tell us he had died a while ago. I was numb.

In the end I would not have to make the decision; fate had made it. I calmly went to the bathroom and switched on the shower. I let the hot water run over me and then slowly, methodically sponged myself down, washing away the sweat and dreams. I dressed in clean jeans and a shirt, applied a little cologne and cleaned my teeth. The coffee machine puffed and gurgled and the fine aroma filled the kitchen as drip by drip it dropped into my cup. I had a cigarette. I was not rushing, they had told me not to. The coffee was both bitter and sweet. I dropped a slice of bread in the toaster and carefully opened the refrigerator and removed the spread and jar of marmalade. The toast was warm and complemented the coffee well. I brushed my teeth again. I found the car keys and grabbed my jacket from the kitchen chair. I locked the front door and then I was in the car. I was driving now. I lit another cigarette and opened the window and let the cool air blast around the car. The drive to the hospital was straightforward and I had done the journey many times. I was on automatic. Buildings flew past, blurred and indistinct, as did cars, streetlamps, fences, junctions and people. The road climbed and on the summit I looked down on the hospital, illuminated by a thousand lights and it seemed quiet, almost dreamlike. It had a haze about it like some special camera effect. I parked and put some money in the meter from the collection of coins I maintained in the side box of the car door. The car bleeped as I locked it and then I walked towards the entrance. The doors automatically opened with a slight swoosh and I was in the reception area. The security guard simply nodded. I turned left and walked towards the lift. I suddenly did not feel too good. The realisation that I was now visiting my wife's corpse instead of my wife overwhelmed me. I pressed the button and the doors opened immediately. It was a large lift and I was thankful that there was no music playing. My heart was thumping so hard I thought it would leap out of my chest. I tried to slow my breathing. I hit the button for the second floor and sat on the floor. "Get a fucking grip!" I shouted and my voice sounded muted and dulled in the carpeted lift. When the doors opened onto the second floor I had gained some control of myself. The ward was busy but not as active as it would be in a couple of hours. I turned right and then right again and was in the long corridor which held Beth's private room. The door was towards the far end and I began to walk. I noticed that the door was open. I stopped a few metres away and leaned my back against the wall and took a few measured deep breaths. Suddenly from the room a nurse appeared pushing the ventilation machine out. She walked away, her back to me. That was it. The moment to say goodbye had arrived and I stood straight to face it. At the door I looked into the room. Her legs were covered by a white sheet but I could not see her face because the doctor, who had his back to me, obscured my line of sight. The only sound in the room was the scratching from the doctor's pen as he wrote on a clipboard. I gently tapped against the door and he looked over his shoulder and then stood to the side. Now I could see her. She was smiling. I did not understand. Then she offered a weak little wave. The doctor was smiling; he walked up to me and rested a hand on my shoulder.

"I don't believe in God either, Don," he said, "but I guess sometimes miracles do happen." I looked at him. "She can't speak too easily because of the ventilation tube being in for so long but I'm pretty sure she will make a full recovery. I'll give you a few minutes." He left. Her face was thinner and her skin paler but her deep brown eyes shone. I have never known anything more beautiful in my life. She beckoned me over with a little movement of her hand. My shaky legs brought me to her bed and I sat on the edge. I gently lifted her into a sitting position and she put her arms around my neck and whispered, "I bet the garden's a mess."

I looked at her; her lovely face beamed back, she lightly touched my cheek. I put my arms carefully around her and then all the emotion I had ever owned finally burst through and I cried like I have never cried before or since.

Chapter 40

Apparently, according to the doctors, the brain can rewire itself although the scans never showed increased activity. They only had educated guesses as to what had happened but I didn't care. I had my wife back, my best friend and my lover – I had my life back. As I looked through the kitchen window at Beth and Charlie sitting at the garden table, Charlie concentrating hard on her drawing, I wasn't thinking about brains and wiring, I was soaking in the scene of the two most precious human beings in this universe enjoying and sharing their simple lives.

I have experienced something profound and yet I find no words of wisdom to put to paper, for in doing so, I fear that the meaning will just evaporate. Words, no matter how clever, are simply not enough: some experiences go beyond even the complexities of language. What I do know and understand as I look upon my wife and child is love. Poets and writers through history have tried to express the true nature of love and in my opinion, they have all failed. My love for Beth and for Charlie are different yet they are both my reason for living and if necessary, my reason for dying. There is a price to pay for that kind of love and I very nearly paid it. Eventually of course we all have to pay but for now I will just enjoy the time that we have and that time is so much sweeter than it has ever been, so much more precious and ever more real.

I am still an atheist. I don't believe in God but I thank him every single day. The coffee smelled good and the garden was tidy.

Epilogue

Two years after Beth came out of hospital she went back inside, this time to give birth to a baby boy, Adam.

Beth eventually left us. We went to bed one cold winter night and I was the only one who woke. Her last words to me were, "Goodnight, my darling, sleep well." That was two years ago and she was eighty-five years old. Those last words both comfort and haunt me. I still say goodnight to her when these old bones lie down on the bed we shared for so many years and I can hear her voice utter those words to me, and then I am able to sleep. The words you have read I put to paper shortly after Beth's recovery from her fall. I don't know why I wrote it, perhaps I just wanted to record the events or maybe it was something cathartic. Now in the year 2050, it all seems a long time ago and if I had not put pen to paper then I just could not have remembered half of it now. As I tap these words into the computer and think back on my long life, I can take great comfort in the fact that I did the best I could. What enjoyment I get in life now is through my children and my grandchildren. Charlie married and had two girls of her own, Julie, after Beth's mother, and Rebecca. Antony, Charlie's husband, is a good egg and we both took to him immediately. He's a great Dad and, according to Charlie, a loving, caring husband – just as well or I'd have to break his legs. Adam's first marriage did not work out and he was divorced within the year. His second, however, worked out fine and produced a boy, Thomas, and a girl, Annie.

They keep me young, or as young as an eighty-nine-year-old can be. I do get very tired now. I don't write much any more, just a few articles for a couple of the broadsheets. My last novel was published when I was eighty and for me it was the best and a good one on which to bow out. I guess, however, if you are reading this then I am already long dead as I never planned to publish this in my lifetime but my children might. So much have changed since those days; I can't get into the music and the young fashion looks ridiculous. Who would have thought the Middle East could have changed so much but I guess the writing was on the wall for America. But as I shuffle towards the horizon on my aching slipper-clad feet I feel so very much alone and as the horizon closes I know there is nothing beyond; no further horizons to aim for. Beth and me, well, we walked together towards the horizon and now my friend is not here to hold my hand and I am frightened. When Beth died, so did I. Yes I am still breathing and my poor heart keeps pumping the blood around but essentially we were not two individuals, we became one. I no longer fear death but life without her, it will come soon enough though and then my children will be sad for a while but then get on with their lives and that is right and proper and as it should be. I'm going to have my tea now and maybe a drop of whisky, which my doctor tells me I shouldn't but fuck him I'm nearly ninety. And if I too fail to wake up then so be it. When I go to bed I will pull the covers up and wish my wife goodnight and hope to meet her in my dreams, where we can hold hands again and amble towards perpetual horizons, my Beth, my beautiful Beth.